HIDDEN PURPOSE

MICHAEL J. LIVOLSI

W & B Publishers
USA

W & B Publishers

For information:
W & B Publishers
Post Office Box 193
Colfax, NC 27235
www.a-argusbooks.com

ISBN: 978-0-6923532-7-1
ISBN: 0-6923532-7-5

Book Cover designed by Dubya

Printed in the United States of America

Destiny

The way one person, in a world with six billion others, can find the only person with the key to unlock their heart.

Happy Wives Club

*F*ate is not the flip of a coin, nor is it the winning number on a roulette wheel when the ball stops. A person who finds a gold nugget in a mountain of rocks and dirt can only lay claim to luck and fortune. Fate has a more profound meaning, as you will discover in "Hidden Purpose."

Dedication

To my wife, Carol, an angel on earth if there ever was one.

Acknowledgement

It takes many people to create a book and I am indebted to quite a few. I would like to express my deep appreciation to all the people who helped me in this process, including:

- ➢ Chuck Humble, friend and colleague, who took time from his busy schedule to provide expertise in the sport of amateur scull racing.
- ➢ Frank Marzano, whose knowledge of medical protocol proved invaluable.
- ➢ Gary Mobereg, who patiently listened as the story began to take on a life of its own.
- ➢ The Hamilton Homes Book Club, for their critique of the story in its raw form, and for their collective encouragement.
- ➢ Finally, a special thanks to Shirley Eckhardt, whose razor-sharp editing made the manuscript come alive, and believing in my talent even more than I did.

The first time he saw her, his future...his life...his world had just come crashing down around him. The next time he saw her, his life had just begun.

As John Henning drifted in and out of the shadows of his uncertain world, he managed to memorize elements of her beauty amid the darkness of the night. He remembered staring straight into eyes which resembled the shallow, clear, blue waters off the shore of some Caribbean island. He remembered gazing at the radiance of her skin as he drifted in and out of consciousness. He felt a compassion in her manner and her voice soothed him when the life within him seemed to be slipping away. Even though he was helpless to pursue her, the hands of fate would somehow bring them together.

Twenty-six years earlier

The police had cordoned off the Broadway Department Store at Los Arcos Mall in Scottsdale, Arizona. The officers had detained everyone for questioning. News crews and reporters gathered around police and fire personnel as they searched every corner of the store and parking lot. Two hours of exhaustive searching turned up no clues or viable information. Too much time had passed after the original 911 call. Lawrence Crawford received a call while in the middle of an important meeting. He dropped everything and rushed to the Scottsdale Police Headquarters.

Lawrence's wife Marion and her daughter Jessica waited in a room off the main hallway. Marion was hysterical. She was being consoled by a uniformed female officer. Jessica sat in a chair beside her mother, still and quiet. Lawrence barged into the station as if he had control over everything and everyone.

"Where is my wife?" he shouted, stomping his way across the tile floor to the front desk. "Who is in charge here?"

One of the sergeants quickly intervened. "Please calm down, sir," he said in a calm, professional voice. I presume you are Mr. Crawford? We have your family in a separate room down the hall with one of our officers, and they are fine."

"Fine, you say?" Lawrence replied, in an angry tone of voice. "You say 'fine,' after what I've been told? What the hell does that mean? I want to see them. Take me to them."

The sergeant escorted Lawrence to the enclosed room, opened the door and signaled for the officer sitting with his family to step outside and wait, allowing them time to process. Through the glass door with the blinds opened, they both watched as Lawrence went on a rampage, yelling and screaming at his wife. In the next moment, he grabbed his seven-year-old daughter by the shoulders and began shaking her violently.

Chapter One

Present day

Saturday
December 31st.

The New Year's Eve party at Carriage Brokers dragged on well past the midnight hour. For the second year in a row, John Henning had been awarded 'Sales Associate of the Year'. John, considered handsome, young, aggressive, and a full-of-piss–and-vinegar kind of guy (which, by the way, are essential credentials of success for a Commercial Real Estate Broker), was making the brokerage lots of money.

The next morning found John alone, stretched out sideways on his bed, the effects of too many beers and Jose Cuervo margaritas, no doubt. He wasn't a heavy drinker but, on special occasions, he had a tendency to lose control. When out with customers, however, it was different. While everyone was chatting it up, pouring down the liquor, John would sneak to the bar and order club soda with a martini olive shoved on a tooth pick dropped into the glass to pretend he was keeping up. This was his way of staying in control around big-money clients.

As if bringing in the New Year at a wild office party wasn't enough, John had another party to look forward to…Gary's annual New Year's party.

***

Normally off on holidays, Ofelia Flores, John's trusted housekeeper three days a week, let herself in at seven-thirty in the morning. She was not surprised to find John still sleeping it off. It was déjà vu...the same thing every January 1st morning. Knowing John was going to be lying there out like a light and softly snoring away, she tried not to bother him and went about her business quietly. John, sometimes cranky in the morning until his motor got running, was no candidate for an early morning wake-up call, especially on New Year's Day.

Ofelia spent the next two hours tidying up, and it was time to head over to Gary's place to help him get ready for his party that evening. She left John the same way she found him. Housekeeping was no longer easy for Ofelia, now in her late fifties and very much overweight. The money was good and she never complained. Even though she was sometimes aggressive in her manner, John liked that about her.

***

John and Gary Mathews had become close friends while working for Carriage Brokers. When the two of them were not drumming up sales or putting in outrageous hours at the office, you could find them at Orange Tree playing golf or at the gym working off the stress of being in the high-end real estate sales and management business. Gary started working for Carriage Brokers two years earlier than John; and although *he* was well-respected, when it came to closing the big deals, no one in the company could compete, client-for-client, with John Henning.

Over the past few years, John led Carriage Brokers to remarkable growth in sales for the commercial property end of their business. The privately-owned real estate and lending company, with its full-service real estate listings, mortgage financing and escrow services, is headquartered in the middle of the vacation oasis of Scottsdale, Arizona. This was John's fifth year with Carriage. By the end of his second year, he was closing multi-million dollar contracts...playing golf and rubbing elbows with major developers and city officials. John was winning away clients from larger, more-specialized firms that sold commercial and industrial-type properties on a regular basis.

Though only in his early thirties, he was already considered one of those so-called "American Success Stories." His flair for words had a way of convincing people to spend money on just about anything he was selling. His coworkers, friends...and some competitors, for that matter...claimed he could sell swamp land in Florida and get the outrageous prices for it if he set his mind to it. Even those who envied him the most referred to him as 'a lucky guy.'

***

Ofelia worked a few hours at Gary's place before catching the bus back to John's, arriving around eleven-thirty. She let herself in again...but, this time, *was* surprised that John was still out like a light. She kept an eye on the time. It was two o'clock in the afternoon... *Ah, se hace tarde. I must wake Mr. John up,* she thought. After returning the vacuum cleaner to its resting place in a closet, she went into the kitchen, took a spaghetti pot out of the cupboard, a wooden spoon from the drawer and started beating on the pot like it was a drum. The noise was loud enough to wake bears from hibernation; but it seemed to have no effect on John's state of unconsciousness. Barging into his bedroom wasn't something Ofelia wanted to do, but after five minutes had passed and he wasn't moving, she decided to do it. *I'll take the chance and he will thank me for waking him...for reminding him of Mr. Gary's party.*

"Mr. John," she called as she cracked the door slightly and peeked in. She waited a moment before swinging the door open the rest of the way. "Mr. John," she called softly. She kept her distance and waited for him to stir. "Mr. John, are you still going to Mr. Gary's party tonight?" The soft tone of her voice wasn't working.

"Mr. John," she called out, elevating her voice a notch. *Is he alive?* Ofelia's nerves were on edge. *Maybe Mr. John is dead. Dios ayuda me! What will I do if he is?*

Suddenly, there was a slight shifting of his body. *Gracias a Dios!* Ofelia made the sign of the cross. After a moment, he moved again; but not enough to convince her that if she left him alone, he would ever get up. *No more waiting,* she thought.

"Mr. John!" she cried out, one hand resting on her hip, still gripping the wooden spoon she'd used to drum the pot. *A few taps to the bottom of his shoe should do it.*

"Ah, ha," she said under her breath, "it worked." She watched his leg jerk as he let out a deep moan. The movement was so slight it reminded her of a snail stretching from its coiled shell. Once again, Ofelia called him...but this time with no cordiality in her voice. "Mr. John!" she said, sending another sharp rap to the bottom of his shoe. John exhaled as he managed to roll himself over. Ofelia made a mad dash to the window and opened the shutters. A direct strike from the sun peeking between gathering clouds pierced John's eyelids. He threw up the palm of one hand towards the window; and, with one squinting eye, scowled down to notice he was still wearing the clothes he had on the night before.

Ofelia replaced the hand holding the wooden spoon to her hip and said waspishly, "Mr. John! You have to get up and get ready, remember...Mr. Gary's party."

Jesus, John thought, *she just won't give up.* "If it's alright with you, Ofelia" he mumbled, "I think I'll just lay here until next year rolls around."

"But, Mr. John... Mr. Gary is expecting you to be there. He made me promise to remind you. He said you had too much to drink last night, and I see he was right...look at you," she went on, shaking her head."

"That's all I need, Ofelia...another party." He shook his head and started massaging his temples. After a moment of indulging in self-pity, he said, "Thank you, Ofelia. It's good that you woke me up. You are always looking out for me, and I appreciate that. You have now officially brought me back from the dead."

"No digas eso, Mr. John!" she huffed, shaking the spoon at him. "You shouldn't say those things. Don't you know that it is bad luck to talk about death in that way?"

"Oh...don't worry, Ofelia," he said, planting both his feet on the carpet and managing a grin. "Someone once told me that having a little bad luck can make you a wiser person."

The metaphor brought a curious look to Ofelia's face but, after a moment, she dismissed it. She offered to cook John one of her Spanish concoctions...claiming it would make him feel better...but just the mention of food made him flinch.

"Whoa...no, please, Ofelia. I'll be just fine. I promise. Don't cook anything for me now. God... no... please don't cook." *I'd probably throw-up.* "Tell you what," he went on, "I *would* like some coffee if you'll make it...and some juice. Yeah...that's it...a glass of orange juice."

"De volada, Mr. John. I'll do it right away."

John vaguely remembered driving home the night before, but knew it was late. *Around two o'clock in the morning might be a good guess, maybe even later*, he thought, rubbing sleep from his eyes. He pushed himself out of bed, hobbled over to the window and glanced down to the street. He could see that his car was askew in the driveway, halfway onto the used-brick walkway. *Whoa*, he thought, dragging a hand through his thick head of hair. *Someone must have been watching over me last night. I can't believe I drank that much and drove home. It was the curse of Jessica that made me do it, I know it.*

It wasn't like John to be completely out of control like that. He wondered how much of a fool he had made of himself at the party. He knew, however, that Gary would tell him straight up when he saw him. He headed for the bathroom and climbed into a hot shower. Although the water running over his body eased the throbbing in his temples, it only washed away some of the cobwebs. The clammy, weak feeling still persisted.

He wrapped himself in a towel and wandered into the kitchen, downed the juice, grabbed the coffee Ofelia had waiting for him on the counter, and made his way back to the bathroom. After setting the cup of coffee on the sink, he leaned in and studied his image in the mirror. He was looking at a man in his early thirties with intelligent, probing, deep-blue eyes which now had a tint of red surrounding the iris. His angular facial features, augmented by a strong chin with a thin vertical crease, was covered by a thin coat of stubble. After his close examination proved he looked like he felt, he backed away and noted that the reflection of his tall, lean and physically-fit body, sculpted by a weekly schedule of jogging and weight training, now looked fatigued and abused. *Damn...* he thought. *I wonder what the other guy looks like.*

John's thick, medium-length, almost-shaggy dark hair, normally resting with grace behind his ears, was now towel-dried and shooting every which way. He reached into the medicine cabinet, popped the lid off the bottle with his thumb and downed two aspirin with the coffee. *Now it's coming back*, he thought, keeping his gaze fixed on a mirror which now seemed to be projecting images of the out-of-control events of the night before. Empty martini glasses stood like wooden soldiers everywhere… accented by dry olives stuck to tooth picks. Beer cans and margarita salt adorned every desk, counter and copy machine, making the office look like the aftermath of a congressional reception. The music was loud, vulgarities over the top, and interaction too loose for coworkers. John remembered that Gary had made a tongue-in-cheek comment that management should repost the company's policy regarding employee relationships in a larger font.

Chapter Two

The effects of having a few too many drinks the night before didn't deter John from spending what was left of the day reviewing contract language in his latest commercial proposal and debating with himself whether or not he was up to attending another party. By eight o'clock, boredom set in. By nine, he got a second wind and decided that listening to Gary's rant the next day about what friends just don't do to friends wasn't something he wanted to endure. *I'll get to Gary's house late, but it's better than not making the party at all*, he thought as he rushed out the door, jumped into his Porsche and headed for Scottsdale Road.

Earlier, a weather disturbance had moved into the Valley from the west that brought with it light showers. By now, most people had already arrived at their destinations and/or settled into their own routine for New Year's Day celebrations with families and friends. Even though traffic was sparse, the rain had spread just enough water on the streets to make night driving a challenge.

As John negotiated the turn onto Twenty-Fourth Street, he thought about the award Carriage Brokers had given him for his sales achievements and how bittersweet it was. Two hours into the party, John couldn't get out of his mind what had happened the night before. He had to talk about it...so he grabbed Gary by the arm, shuttled him into a back office where he closed the door and told him what had happened during his dinner with Jessica. John knew Gary would not betray his confidence and keep tight to the vest what he was about to disclose.

While John talked, Gary listened as he nursed his third crushed-ice margarita of the night.

"He wants me to work for him," John said.

"Who wants you and work for what...?" Gary replied with a confused look on his face.

"The old man...Jessica's father," John replied. "He's using Jessica to recruit me again. He wants me to leave Carriage Brokers high and dry and work for Crawford Investments."

"Well...what do you know," Gary chimed in. "What did you expect? You're dating the daughter of one of Carriage Brokers' fiercest competitors, for God's sake. I told you this would happen a long time ago...didn't I?"

"Yeah, yeah," John replied, scoffing. "I don't need a lecture here. I just need a little advice with a modicum of intelligence behind it."

"Well if you ask me..." Gary said, taking a swig from his drink, "I would tell *her* to tell *him* to fuck off. As a matter of fact, if she were here tonight, I'd tell her just how to approach that old bastard so my 'no' would sink in. How is that for intelligent advice? And...be assured of this," he went on, "so far, everyone here has accepted the fact that you are sleeping with the enemy's daughter. If the boss finds out Jessica is trying to lure you to the competition, awards won't mean anything. Carriage Brokers will say adios to you in a heartbeat."

***

The illumination from the overhead street lights bounced off the damp street like the reflection off a rapper's bling. Headlights from oncoming cars were like starbursts rather than beams shining parallel to the road. John had to search for the yellow lines in the middle to keep from compromising the centerline...still the dinner with Jessica played over and over in his head. The more he thought about it, the more he was convinced that it was because of Jessica's devious attempt to deliver her father's message that the New Year's Eve party and the award he received for the second straight year ended up playing out like a non-event. What should have been a positive milestone in his life and business career with Carriage Brokers was cloaked with the dark cloud of Jessica's father. It was John's personal distraction the entire evening. Details of the dinner kept flashing through his mind as he tried to concentrate on the road. Instead of the casual dinner at Vincitorio's, a glass of wine at his or her place, then unbridled sex until the early hours that he had planned, the evening was cloaked in a business twist.

***

The evening started off with John meeting Jessica at Morton's Steak House for a 'surprise special occasion,' as she had characterized it beforehand. John remembered noticing, as he and Jessica sat in the lounge waiting for a quiet corner table, that two well-dressed guys also waiting to be seated took special note of Jessica's tall, slender frame…from the collar of her Armani Collezioni suit to her Azzaro Ring sandals. He had glanced at them and they politely smiled as if to say...'right on, man.' The overhead lighting in the lounge area accented the honey-blonde highlights in her brown hair, which cascaded stylishly below her shoulders. Her legs were crossed in an elegant straight line which made her look business-like, yet utterly feminine.

Jessica, the thirty-four-year-old daughter of Lawrence C. Crawford, founder and CEO of Crawford Investments Inc., worked for her father's company and had achieved high marks in the Valley for her track record of being on the winning end of several real estate projects.

It was rumored, although never proven in a court of law, that Lawrence Crawford conducted his business with questionable ethics and shady real estate acquisition techniques. John had heard these claims many times but had more or less ignored them. He chalked it up to typical big-business practices and tough competition.

John was smart and, although he knew that Machiavellian games were played in real estate, he always maintained that *his* good fortune was due to his belief in the old cliché that 'honesty was the best policy.' John favored doing business when the playing field was level and preferred a fair fight when competing to win over big clients. In any event, when he heard the claims about Lawrence, he had always given him the benefit of the doubt. John was in love with Lawrence's daughter...at least, he thought he was. Once again, Lawrence was using Jessica's intimate relationship with John...and the vows they were preparing to take...as a vehicle to lure John away from Carriage Brokers and onto the Crawford Investments sales team. Jessica had now become a soft recruiter for her father.

***

The waiter presented the wine list and, as usual, Jessica was quick to demand her favorite Cabernet Franc. She consistently bragged about how she had acquired a taste and knowledge of different wines from her father. She made sure it was well-known at every party or social gathering she attended. Lawrence taught her that most people were easily intimidated by wines and that she never should be. In his eyes, even though he had always wished his only child had been a son, any display of weakness from Jessica, whether it came to choosing fine wine or working business deals for his company, was unacceptable. It was because of his paternal tutelage that Jessica could describe the regions, grapes, vineyards and vintages of an assortment of wines.

The cork from the bottle popped just as Jessica handed John an envelope. Locked on his eyes, she said simply, "It's from my father." A tense moment passed and Jessica began to feel uncomfortable. She turned to the waiter, who was standing there trying to look inconspicuous, shifting from one foot to the other, as he gave the wine time to breathe. She angled her head and frowned at him with narrowed eyes, making him feel like an uninvited guest. The waiter shrugged his shoulders and quickly moved away, leaving their glasses standing empty on the table.

John placed the envelope on the table in front of him. He leaned back in his chair, folded his arms and, for a moment, just stared at it. Glancing up, he said, "Jessica, you know I don't turn thirty-three until March… so am I safe to assume that this isn't a birthday card?"

Jessica leaned in, fluttering her eyelashes in a cutesy manner. "Listen, baby…if it was your birthday, I'd be naked, wrapped in a red ribbon, and we'd be at my place instead of sitting here."

John found no humor in Jessica's self-confident response and she knew it once she saw the steel in his eyes. He had the look of a man who knew he had been set up. John shifted his gaze to the envelope, then back to her.

"You should have been honest, Jessica," he snapped. "You could have told me this was a business meeting. I'm beginning to think that your father's alleged reputation for doing anything to satisfy his wants at the expense of others has some element of truth. But what really surprises me," he went on, staring hard, "is that you set this dinner up under false pretenses…'surprise special occasion'…I should say. What else do you have up your sleeve?"

Jessica wanted to give some ruthless response but instead managed to stay composed. "Come on, baby. Lighten up." She leaned in and reached across the table with both hands, looking for his. John subtly leaned back to avoid contact. *It isn't going to be that easy*, he thought. Jessica frowned.

I could scratch your eyes out! She pulled back, lifted her left hand and dangled her ring finger with the large diamond in the cathedral solitaire setting in front of him. "Daddy thought, John, that if I used my influence…harmlessly, I might add…and since, at some point, this engagement ring will turn into a wedding ring, you would finally change your mind and realize that it's time to work for us *now*, rather than later. So why is that such a bad thing?" She abruptly leaned back in her seat and crossed her arms defiantly.

John contemplated his answer. He recalled what had happened a year earlier when 'old man' Crawford tried to get him to make the move from Carriage and the covert role Jessica played then. The recollection irritated him. He knew then the timing wasn't right. After what was happening now, John wasn't sure if he'd ever make the move. *Let's see how much bait daddy is willing to put on the hook to get his way.* John picked up the envelope, removed the folded note from inside and studied it. He raised an eyebrow, re-folded the note, stuck it back into the envelope and laid it back on the table. "Not bad... Daddy even threw in three weeks in the Bahamas for the two of us…how thoughtful."

"See, honey," Jessica whispered confidently, spreading her arms widely. "My father really wants us to be together on this. He wants what's best for *us.*"

That's a load of shit! He wants what's best for him.

As she inconspicuously extended a foot beneath his side of the table and searched for his leg, she smiled coquettishly. "Tell you what, baby. Let's hurry and order. Afterwards, we can go to my place. Once I get you home and I strip those clothes off you, we can negotiate this whole thing and have fun doing it."

What John really wanted was to debate the issue now... put a stop to the whole idea. *I'd better back off a bit before she goes berserk. She's been acting too damn weird lately,* he thought. *Besides, this too will pass, just like before, if I say no.*

A moment passed...then John reached for the Cabernet and filled their glasses. *I've made my point...now I'll change the mood. Besides, she does look hot!* John slowly moved from across the table and took the seat by her side. He took her diamond-pointed chin lightly in his hand, smiled and, for a moment, softly touched her lips with his.

"Look, Jessica... I appreciate what your father wants, but it has to be on *my* terms. Because of you, it's difficult for me turn him down at this point. I need some support here. I told you last time that I can't just abandon Carriage Brokers and feel good about it... or myself, for that matter. You know our relationship means a whole lot to me. When the time is right, we will get married...and it will be to satisfy *us,* not your father. Please understand."

John reached past the attractive rose-pink cheek to the side of her face and lightly brushed aside the hair, exposing the soft, curved ridge of her ear. He leaned in and whispered, "What's say we sip the wine, skip dinner and head to your place?"

Chapter Three

At nine p.m., Alexandra finished filing her last activity report of the day, climbed into her Toyota and headed for home. It was a day filled with no surprises. Psychologists studying abnormal behavior in humans have proven that anxiety, loneliness and depression are the primary cause for the increase in suicide attempts, car accidents, heart attacks, premature childbirths and gunshot wounds leading up to Christmas and the New Year. While the front line of tragedy might seem exciting for some people, like a street cop looking for the thrill of the chase, people dedicated to emergency response are only interested in one thing—saving lives.

A life dedicated to being an Emergency Medical Technician is never easy. Requiring considerable bending, heavy lifting and hoisting bodies on and off gurneys is a task for the physically fit. Alexandra's five-foot-eight frame is in remarkable physical shape. When *she* looks into a mirror, she sees average-looking, pretty-ish...but what others see when they look at her is physically-fit, strong, outdoorsy... with beautiful features and a profile that would thrill a portrait artist.

The fine, light brown hair which cascaded naturally down the sides of her face and rested on the tops of her nicely-developed deltoids, was often seen in a ponytail hanging out the back of a standard EMT-issue ball cap. Her sculpted body gave her a statuesque appearance. Her deep blue eyes, set wide, blended perfectly with her golden-olive skin. As a kid, Alexandra's passion for water sports earned her a place on the high school swim team.

She finished first place in both the backstroke and free-style in most of her competitive events. On any given weekend, she could be found at the Tempe Town Lake, rowing with her best friend, Susan, or practicing with the women's amateur rowing team.

***

Alexandra Morgan, thirty-five years old, was born in San Diego, California. She was ten months old when her father, Frank Morgan, was killed in a tragic accident. A decorated member of the San Diego Fire and Rescue Department, Frank died the night his unit responded to a fire at the El Cortez Hotel. During what should have been a routine rescue from a room on the ninth floor of the building, Frank handed a woman, who was vacationing in San Diego with her husband, out of the window to the ladder man standing in a rescue bucket. After Frank handed the woman to his partner, a gas line in a maintenance room off the hallway ruptured. Within seconds, the entire floor was engulfed in flames. Their room quickly became an inferno and, in a panic, the woman's husband forced his way around Frank to get out. In the blink of an eye, Frank lost his balance, slipped through the window and hung from the sill outside the building. His partner, the man, and his wife could only watch helplessly as the flames shot out like a giant torch into the night sky and Frank tragically fell to his death in the street below. It was soon after that Ruth, Alexandra's mother, decided to pack their things and move to Arizona.

As Alexandra was growing up, her mother never hung the traditional nets filled with stuffed animals or crayon-colored pictures on the child's bedroom walls. Instead, she hung pictures of Alexandra's father, along with his many medals of commendation, in a museum-like fashion around her room. Ruth wanted Alexandra to know her father...to know what he was and what he did. She wanted his memory to always be present in her life.

Alexandra attended college at Arizona State University where she graduated with honors. She could have easily gone on to be an attorney, or a heart doctor, but genetics or some higher power had taken control of her destiny. Her drive and her passion for human life led her to follow in her father's footsteps. Saving lives was in her blood.

***

Alexandra was anxious to get home and into a warm bath. She eased off the gas pedal and stopped for the red light at Twenty-Fourth and Oak. In the rear view mirror, she noticed a small sports car coming up from behind at what seemed to be warp speed.

***

Lost in thought, John suddenly noticed the red light and slammed on his brakes...barely avoiding a skid right through the intersection...and ended up idling in the lane next to Alexandra. A lonely pole light in the median hung over the street and provided just enough illumination so that, when Alexandra glanced to her left, she saw the shadowy figure of the guy behind the wheel turn and look at her. For that moment, it crossed her mind that, whoever he was, he was probably rushing off to pick up a girlfriend for a night of fun and romance. *I should be so lucky*, she thought. The sad reality of what her New Year's evening was going to be like set in.

Memories of the past flashed through her mind in rapid succession. Time spent in college, working in a profession that commanded most of her time, having no night life... let alone a boyfriend to share anything with. *The best it would get for me tonight is two glasses of Merlot and some cold shrimp,* she thought. *I'll curl up with Chester and watch television. Holidays depress me.*

The guys she worked with had tried to drag Alexandra along with them to some New Year's evening party on Mill Avenue but, after the hectic day she had experienced, she was tired and not in the mood. They were all single and a rowdy bunch. Denise, the only other female member of the team, seldom turned down a good time. It was when the guys outnumbered the girls that Denise was ready to play. Alexandra didn't like the sexual overtones that always seemed to follow an invite to their social gatherings. She wasn't impressed in that way with the guys she worked with. Bob Collins, the off-shift Medical Team Leader, was smart and tolerable, but only to a point. Denise played him hard but got nowhere. Bob made a play for Alexandra several times; but although she thought him good-looking enough, he wasn't her type. The fact that Bob was full of himself turned her off.

***

The light turned green. Before Alexandra could move her foot from the brake to the gas pedal, it happened. The noise from the crash sounded like a gigantic bolt of lightning had hit the ground in front of her. A black Ford Expedition with huge chrome rims was blocking the middle of the intersection in front of her. The front end of the Expedition was mangled, smoke spewing from under the mangled hood. Alexandra could see that the air bag was deployed. She noticed the guy in the driver's seat moving around. The Expedition had come from the right, failed to stop for the red light, and plowed into the passenger side of the Porsche, tossing and spinning it around like a toy car in a crash-match that kids play. The Porsche took the brunt of the impact. Parts of the car and glass were strewn all over the street. The Porsche did a one-eighty and, out of control, headed towards the median across the road and came to an abrupt stop as it slammed against a pole. Steam spewed in all directions.

Alexandra quickly shifted into response mode. She threw the gear shift into *park*, activated her flashers, set the emergency brake, and jumped out of her car. She darted over to the Expedition and shouted at the top of her lungs. "Are you alone? Are you alright?" She looked through the window. The driver slowly raised a hand with a thumb pointing upward. Alexandra quickly glanced in the Expedition's back windows and could see no one else inside the vehicle. She didn't remember hearing skid sounds. The driver of the Expedition never applied the brakes. *Thank God for air bags*, Alexandra thought. In her experience, if the driver had enough warning to slam on his brakes, the impact would fracture the leg as it applied pressure to the brake. *He must have been fooling with a cell phone or the radio*, she thought. *Lucky for him, not having a chance to apply the brakes probably saved him from a likely compound fracture to his femur. And the poor guy in the Porsche...who knows?*

Alexandra sprinted to the Porsche. John appeared to be unconscious. There was no easy way to get into the car. The driver's side door was wedged against a pole and the passenger door was smashed in...with the window completely shattered. She grabbed the door frame and jerked on it with all her strength. It wouldn't budge. Seconds seemed like minutes. Two cars stopped short of the intersection and Alexandra yelled out, "Call 9-1-1! Call 9-1-1!" hoping someone had already made the call.

She ran back to her Toyota, grabbed the tire iron from the compartment in the rear, then rushed back to the Porsche. She wedged one end of the tire iron in between the door and the frame. *It will take a miracle to get this open.* She extended her leg and pried hard, using her foot against the rear panel as leverage. She pulled and groaned and strained until she heard the scraping sound of metal-on-metal. The door opened just enough for her to squeeze in and position her knees on the passenger seat. She leaned in close.

"Hey, buddy, can you hear me? Come on, man, say something." John didn't move or respond. The compartment was totally dark with the exception of a wedge of light slicing through the shattered windshield, casting a golden band across his face. She moved his head slightly and could see blood oozing from just above the ear. *This isn't going to be easy.* Alexandra tried to determine if John was somehow wedged in his seat and would eventually have to be extricated from the driver's side with spreaders or cutters. "I can't get you out until help arrives," she said, praying for any kind of response.

John's body was bent forward as far as his seat belt would allow and pressed against the door, with the left side of his head resting on the frame of the window. She needed to get his pulse. In what little space there was to work, she reached over his torso and placed her index and middle finger to the side of his neck where the artery passes close to the surface. She positioned her watch in the stream of light to count the seconds. John's heart rate was significantly below normal guidelines. At this point, she couldn't tell if it was the result of his body being in shock or if his blood vessels had been damaged in some way.

"Where the hell is the ambulance!" she hollered. *I won't lose this guy on New Year's. Not here in the street.*

It wasn't like Alexandra to panic in these situations, but this time it seemed like she was the victim. She had always been the one everyone waited for...the one whose arrival was heralded by sound of sirens and flashing lights. She was the one with the expertise and the gear and whatever else it took to save a life. This time, she was the one waiting. She was the one who desperately needed to hear the sounds of response units and fire trucks screaming towards her. *Jesus, where are the floodlights and equipment needed to remove this guy from the car? Where the hell are they?* She felt tiny beads of sweat forming on her forehead. She noticed that John's left shoulder was pushed out, possibly dislocated. *That would be the least of this guy's medical problems,* she thought. *But…at least he's still breathing. That's a good thing!*

John's injuries didn't look good, especially the open gash on his forehead, which was bleeding profusely. She ripped a sleeve from her uniform, turned it inside out and carefully wrapped it around John's head. *Typical whipsaw with impact against the window frame,* she concluded. Alexandra had no ability to accurately diagnose John's injuries, and it frustrated her. *What's going on in that head of yours, buddy*? She couldn't tell the extent of the trauma or if the damage was internal involving the skull, the blood vessels within the skull, or the brain. At the same time, she was concerned about spinal damage at the cervical. Given the situation, she couldn't even check him for weakness or paralysis. Everything imaginable was flashing through her mind. *An MRI will sort all this out soon enough,* she thought.

"If I could just get some *goddamn* help here!" she hollered out loud and furiously.

A small crowd began to gather, mostly people going in and out of a convenience store near the corner who were fixed on the drama and not on helping. A few cars had stopped or tried to maneuver through the intersection. Alexandra could hear the sound of sirens in the distance.

She knew from experience that what seemed like an hour was, in reality, only about ten minutes. *Finally!! It's about damn time!* She kept hoping for some sign of consciousness.

Suddenly, John's head slowly turned and their eyes met. The fuzz on her arms and the back of her neck stood up.

What a relief, she thought, and smiled...mostly for his benefit. She wanted to appear positive even though she knew John was not out of the woods and that he could have injuries he wouldn't know about, even fully conscious.

Alexandra said, "Thank God you're awake." She waited for John to respond. *Just blink or something, damn it... anything!* "You've been in an accident and the ambulance is on its way. It won't be long now and you'll have medical attention. Hang in there, buddy... Can you tell me your name? What's your name?"

It was the eerie blank stare. John was non-responsive, staring right at her with no expression... nothing.

"Oh, shit" she muttered under her breath. "Don't even think about dying." Alexandra knew that, in many cases, the last thing that happens is the blank stare. She'd seen many victims die, staring without purpose in the same way. "Stay with me. Please...stay with me."

His eyes closed.

Her heart pushed against her skin so hard she could almost hear it. The best she could tell, his breathing had stopped. *Don't panic. Save this guy. Just save him!* She put an ear close to his face. She listened for a sign or a wisp of warm breath coming from his mouth or nose. She pressed her mouth to his and blew her breath into him. She applied pressure to his chest, in and out. Resuscitation was tricky under these circumstances, but she was used to it.

Suddenly, Bob Collins tapped Alexandra on the shoulder. "Did you do forget that you're off duty? Or is it that you can't get enough of this stuff?"

"Never mind that!" she shot back expressing a sigh of relief. "This guy is hurt bad. His pulse is irregular. He has head trauma and Lord knows what else."

Bob said, "OK, sweetheart, back out of the car. You're now officially off duty. I'll take it from here."

Alexandra turned to Bob. "Just get him the hell out of here, pronto! And stop calling me sweetheart, damn it!" she snapped as she backed out of the wreckage.

"Well…" he replied, rotating himself sideways to get his body through the opening Alexandra had made with the tire iron, "aren't we cranky tonight?"

"I'm riding with him in the ambulance, Bob."

"Oh…? And why is that, Alexandra? Do you know this guy?"

"Well enough!"

"Does he have a name?"

"I'm sure he does," she answered after a moment's pause. "…but I couldn't get it out of him."

"So… you know him but don't know his name, and you want to go along in the ambulance with him. Isn't that a little strange?" Bob said, in a confused tone of voice. "You know that's against procedure, don't you? You're off duty. Besides, blue just got here and they will want to talk to you."

"Listen…Bob," she responded, leaning in. "They can ask all the questions they want…here or at the hospital. Just fix it. Tell them you need me. I *am* in uniform."

"Is it OK if I say 'yes, dear'?" Bob said, grunting as he fidgeted with the latch on John's seat belt.

"No!" she shot back.

As Alexandra gave her eyewitness account of the accident to the police, Bob was still working on John inside the car. Establishing a perimeter around the vehicle were four cops and what seemed like half of Fire Station Twenty-Four, all taking action to secure the area and execute medical and safety procedures. The rest of Bob's team attended to the man in the Expedition.

The fire crews quickly and efficiently moved the Porsche away from the pole to extricate John. In minutes, the crews had John on a gurney and hooked up to oxygen. Alexandra watched Bob attend to John as he was being lifted into the ambulance. It crossed her mind that, even though Bob at times acted like a jerk, he was the off-shift team's primary with extensive experience. *The guy's a jerk, but he knows what he's doing.*

***

Tucker Potts, or "Tuck" as Alexandra referred to him, scurried around the emergency room rationing the limited medical resources available at Scottsdale Memorial Regional Trauma Center. As the Reception and Orientation Physician, Tucker made decisions based on external trauma as well as information provided by the emergency response teams to determine the action required to minimize potential for further injury or even death.

The triage tag Bob's response team had prepared while on their way to the hospital was red, which meant life-saving intervention was necessary upon arrival. Alexandra hurried alongside the gurney as the team wheeled John through the motion-activated doorway. Her eyes swept the crowded ward until she spotted Tucker. He was directing his emergency support staff as if he were conducting the philharmonic orchestra.

"Tuck!" she shouted over the noise and chaos.

Tucker spun around, scanned the room and spotted her. With little hesitation, he handed the clip board to the person he was talking to and hurried over to meet her halfway, shoving his pen in his coat pocket.

***

Potts, an imposing figure in his late forties with cropped blond hair turning gray at the temples, had supervised the emergency ward at Scottsdale Memorial for the past ten years. Doctors, nurses, administrative personnel and emergency response team members from all over Scottsdale respected him for his experience and his interpersonal skills in dealing with patients and their loved ones.

"Alexandra," Tucker said, grasping her shoulders with his massive hands. He peered down at her from his six-foot-five, gangly frame. "Less than an hour ago, you wished me a Happy New Year and said you were headed home for the evening. Now you're back looking as if you lost your best friend. What's up?"

She pointed across the way to where Bob, a couple of interns and the triage support staff were huddled around John's gurney.

"He's got head trauma, Tuck," Alexandra replied, rushing her words. "I was at the scene of the accident. I resuscitated but couldn't do much more than that."

"Maybe that was enough."

"Maybe…" Alexandra said. "But the guy has been lifeless ever since."

"You look a little traumatized over this, Alexandra. What about vitals? And is that a tear I detect in your eye?"

There was no hesitation in Alexandra's response, "No tears…just frustration and tiredness. His vitals are border line."

Tucker studied her hard. Alexandra was never awkward or emotional in these situations. She was always strong, settled and professional.

"Is there something about this guy that's different from the other injured people you've carried in here?" he asked curiously. "Just who is he?"

I wish I knew. Alexandra didn't immediately answer. Staring at nothing in particular, she tried to think of some logical explanation as to why she should be so emotionally attached to this case but she couldn't think of one.

"His name is John Henning," Bob said, stepping up beside them as he glanced at his notes. "He's thirty-two years old; his resting heart rate, at this point, is normal and..."

Alexandra interrupted, "Is he awake?" She anxiously stood on her toes, looking over people in the direction of where the support staff still huddled around the gurney.

"Uh...the answer to that one would be no," Bob replied.

"Is he alive?" Tucker asked.

"Yes."

"OK, then," Tucker said, in his commanding voice, smacking his hands together at the same time. He moved Bob to one side, hooked Alexandra by the arm and guided her across the room. "Unconscious, folks!" he called to his staff. "This patient is priority admission into intensive care. Let's move, everyone...let's move"

Alexandra watched as the triage staff shifted into high gear. Once again, Tucker was conducting his orchestra.

Chapter Four

The hot bath and the lemon-grass-scented candles burning on the rim of the tub were exactly what Alexandra needed to counteract the mayhem of the day. By the time she got home from the hospital, bathed and settled into her usual spot on the divan, it was eleven p.m. Chester, spread out on the floor near Alexandra's feet with his nose between his paws, whimpered for attention. Alexandra couldn't get John out of her mind. Her obsession with this perfect stranger had Bob Collins, Tucker Potts and her other colleagues puzzled. *What is it about this guy that made me act crazy-like? Am I just becoming too sensitive for this line of work?*

She gazed at the untouched wine glass filled with the Bordeaux she had promised herself still resting on the oval coffee table along with the shrimp she'd pulled from the fridge. She was alone again the one night of the year when everyone was finishing up celebrating with friends and family...probably still wearing funny hats and blowing whistles from the New Year's Eve parties the night before...and it really bothered her. There was something else bothering her...an empty feeling in her stomach that brought a strange sense of lost purpose.

Even though Alexandra had lost her father when she was too young to remember him, she had always felt his presence, through grade school, high school and college. She had felt her father's presence when she won the swimming medals and the trophies that rested on the mantel next to the pictures of him. It seemed he was always near, watching over her, guiding her every action. Then her thoughts went to those agonizing ten days in the hospital praying, and the painful task of burying her mother. She thought about how she tried to will the cancer away and how exhausting it was. When the doctor told her that her mother was semi-comatose and warned that death could come at any moment, reality set in. She would then be all alone. She fought to stay awake as she relived those memories, but her eyelids were losing the battle. The Bordeaux went untouched as she fell fast asleep.

***

Alexandra sat beside the hospital bed, holding her mother's hand. With the exception of a light from the patient-monitoring equipment, the room was dark and dreary. Suddenly, inexplicably, something changed. She no longer needed the wool blanket the nurse had given her to wrap herself in when the cool air from the vent seemed to penetrate deep into her being. An aura of warmth and comfort flooded the room…and her father appeared out of nowhere. She reached out, but her hand clutched empty air. Her father looked young…young and strong. He stood there in his red, yellow, and black helmet, his firefighter uniform and bunker boots. He looked the way he did in the pictures that decorated the walls of her bedroom when she was young. He looked down into her misty eyes and rested his hand on her shoulder

"Alexandra, it's time for your mother to be with me…she's suffered too much, my child," he continued in a calm and consoling voice. "I promise you that your mother's pain will be gone forever. It's time to let go."

Alexandra loved her father and trusted him…but she knew that losing both of them would be unbearable. *I want to be selfish, but I can't be.* She forced herself to let go of her mother's hand. She tried to speak, but the emotion of the moment was overwhelming. The tears streamed from her eyes as she watched her father take her mother's hand into his. She wanted so to be with them…to go with them. In an instant, her father and mother were disappearing, weightlessly drifting through a continuum of light and time.

A touch to her shoulder caused her eyes to blink open. A nurse in a crisp, white uniform whispered softly. "Wake up, Alexandra. I'm afraid that your mother has passed. I'm sorry, my dear. Spend all the time with her you feel you need to. I'll come back in a little while." Alexandra gazed around the room as if something was…but yet wasn't…there. She was all alone. The finality overwhelmed her. She turned to her mother who now looked peaceful and rested. She leaned in and kissed her forehead and softly stroked her hair. She laid her head on her mother's shoulder and whispered, "No more pain, Mama, no more pain."

***

The hands on the old Caledonia clock her mother had left her struck twelve, and the familiar St. Michael's Chimes interrupted the intersection of dreams and reality and startled her awake. Chester's ears perked. He barked twice at the noise, then settled back. Alexandra gazed at the picture of her father which held a place of honor on the mantle. *I miss you both dearly.* She wondered if they could hear her thoughts. The chimes coming from the clock seemed more calming than the sound coming from the television replaying Auld Lang Syne in Times Square from the night before. *How nice it is to be home*, she thought. *I'd rather be here than out there with hordes of drunken fools trying to find their way home.* "Isn't that right, Chester?" She sipped her wine and thought about John lying unconscious in the hospital. *If it weren't for his accident*, she thought, *I'll bet he wouldn't be alone.*

She didn't know him, but somewhere deep inside, she felt that...somewhere, somehow...she had.

***

New Year's had come and gone. The pandemonium at Scottsdale Memorial had finally subsided. The expected but unplanned events had been sorted out and divided up. The most critical patients, those still in life-threatening, critical-care situations like John, were still being processed and given priority care. It was standard procedure for Scottsdale Memorial's Administration Department to do record searches on persons being admitted with no known medical history. There were no previous admittance records for John Henning. Fortunately, however, he had had the foresight to include in his wallet the names of those to be contacted in case of any emergency--Karl and Laura Henning.

***

They were all gathered in the patient visitor's lounge. Karl had received the call from the Scottsdale police just as he and Laura had called it a night. They had rushed to the hospital and had been there ever since. Karl nervously paced the floor. Laura and Jessica were sitting next to each other, trying to reassure one another that everything would turn out fine...while Gary absentmindedly perused the well-read magazines that scattered a table top.

At the end of a hallway to the left, double doors opened automatically as a short, portly man in a crisp white coat with short, dark hair graying at the temples breezed through and made his way down the hall to where they were. He introduced himself as Doctor Balk. Laura stood up slowly from her chair, and John's father stepped up to wrap an arm around her shoulder. As the doctor began to describe John's condition, Laura dabbed at her eyes with a tissue and silently prayed.

Peering over the bifocals balanced on the end of his nose, Doctor Balk said, "At this point, John is stable. However... he's been unconscious since the paramedics brought him in last night. We've tried to wake him but have been unsuccessful in doing so. In essence, John is in a coma. We don't know the severity or the underlying cause for his present condition, but we are doing further tests."

Laura gasped and turned to weep on Karl's shoulder. Gary couldn't believe it. *How could this have happened to my best friend?* Jessica was in shock, staring blankly into space. It was all a horrible nightmare.

Karl said, "Doctor...is my son in any pain?"

Doctor Balk removed his glasses and shoved them in his coat pocket. "No, Mr. Henning... John is not in pain...that much is certain."

The doctor went on to explain the varying levels of unconsciousness through which patients may or may not progress. While John's mother listened, unable to fight back tears, his father drifted in thought. Karl couldn't handle the possibility of losing his only son and pondered how iniquitous it would be that he should still live. Karl had suffered two heart attacks--one at an early age, which was assumed to be stress-related, and one at fifty-five due to excessive drinking. That one forced him into early retirement. Karl had always thought his son would be the one to bury *him*.

In that compassionate tone of voice that doctors use with their patients, Doctor Balk said, "The good news is the trauma to John's head did not cause edema or, in simple terms, brain swelling. The MRI scan was normal. That would mean brain damage is highly unlikely."

Laura let out a big sigh of relief.

"However," Doctor Balk said in a cautious tone, "the physiological process that keeps a person conscious is the transfer of chemical signals from the brainstem to the cerebral hemispheres. That might have been interrupted and could be the reason John is in this state of unconsciousness."

Gary got to his feet, stepped up beside Karl, and rested a hand on his shoulder. "If I may," he said evenly. "I apologize, Doctor...but my knowledge of all this medical terminology is sadly wanting. Are you telling us that there is nothing seriously wrong with John?"

"Basically, yes." Doctor Balk replied as he reached for his chirping pager and looked down to study it. "Sorry about that. Anyway...other than a good-sized gash on the side of his head that took twelve stitches and a separated shoulder, John should be responsive. This so-called mild coma generally does not last for more than a few days to a few weeks but..."

Suddenly, out of nowhere, Jessica lost it.

"What do you mean a few weeks?" she interrupted, jumping to her feet. "When can we talk to a specialist?"

"Excuse me?" The doctor responded, looking over at her.

"Well..." she said, glancing at the others, calming the obvious hostility. "Sorry for the outburst, but I was just wondering if a specialist has looked at John yet."

"I'm a board-certified neurosurgeon," he said, with a condescending smile that put a deep crease in his chubby cheeks. "I'm afraid I'm as special as they come around here...and you are?"

"Jessica is John's fiancée," Laura supplied, in a gentle tone.

With his attention drawn back to Karl and Laura, he glanced at his watch. "Well...OK then. If you wish, Mr. Henning, you and Mrs. Henning may go see your son now. Over the next few hours, John will be closely monitored. The medical staff will frequently be in and out of his room, checking vitals, drawing blood, etc." He then turned to Jessica and Gary who were standing side-by-side. "I don't recommend any other visitors at this time," he said firmly. "I don't want to risk any interruption of the monitoring process. I have to run now. It's been a pleasure meeting…all of you. Mr. and Mrs. Henning…your son is in room thirty-two."

Chapter Five

Alexandra arrived at the lake before Susan did. She sat patiently in her Toyota, sipped on Starbucks and watched as the rising sun's reflection off the Tempe Town Lake widened. The water was glassy calm. The early morning air was a little bracing for January, but conditions were perfect for rowing. It was now a tradition…the fourth year in a row that Alexandra and Susan would meet in the early morning hours the day after New Year's and row the lake while others were still in bed, nursing sushi stomach-aches and alcohol hangovers. Susan McAdams, Alexandra's closest friend, had talked her into rowing while they were in college…where they met and had been roommates for two years.

Susan needed easy access to the lake for her thirty-foot double racing scull. Renting a space in the boathouse served that purpose. Packing, unpacking and transporting the equipment was becoming a pain in the ass. Susan's schedule was far too hectic. She taught physical education at a high school five days a week; and, on weekends, she worked as a weight trainer at a local gym. Getting a space in the boathouse wasn't easy, but Susan knew just how to charm old man Simon, the boathouse keeper. He had promised to call Susan once a space became available. Simon would get his rocks off just thinking about having in his possession the cell phone number of such a gorgeous woman as Susan McAdams.

The doors to the boathouse swung open and out walked Simon. The aging boathouse keeper wore a stocking cap, which covered most of his snow-white hair and his ears, and what appeared to be an old army field jacket.

He slid a sign out of the slot located on an outside wall, turned it over to read 'Open for Business,' then slid it back in its place.

***

Minutes later, Susan pulled into the space next to Alexandra. She jumped out of her car, tossed Alexandra a thumbs up and headed towards the boathouse. Her pale gold, narrow profile gave her an attractive side view against the rising sun. Her short blond, classic bob, which normally caressed the sides of her high cheekbones just below the widely-set brown eyes, was neatly tucked under a ball cap.

The black and yellow uni-suit Susan wore fit her like a glove. Her body was about as hard as it gets, ripped thin and all muscle. Susan could easily be featured on the cover of AXL magazine. A year earlier, she took her appearance up a notch with perfectly-placed, beautifully-formed breast implants. When Susan walked into a crowd, the guys wrenched their necks to get a look, and she liked it. Matching her stunning features was a well-developed liberal ego which only enhanced her image.

***

After jogging the parking lot to get their adrenalin pumping and stretching to get their legs loose, Alexandra and Susan carried the scull to the dock. They attached the oars and pushed off. Ten minutes into it, they reached a long, steady rowing interval. Susan's place was in the bow of the scull. Suddenly, she noticed Alexandra's technique had slowly deteriorated and her stroke become erratic. At one point, she hit her knees. Her hands got tangled and she "caught a crab," which meant that her oar got stuck in the water during the recovery phase of her stroke.

Just then, a commercial jet took off to the east from Sky Harbor Airport. The huge turbofan engines swallowed the morning air, and the noise it generated seemed to cascade through the lake and surrounding areas.

"Hold up, Alex," Susan called her. "Hold up, girl. Weigh enough!" she yelled, leaning forward. The oars feathered until the boat was drifting with the breeze. She tapped the back of Alexandra's shoulder. "What's up, girl? You lost it there for a while." After a pause, Alexandra shifted on the slide seat to glance back at her.

"Nothing's up," she replied, shifting her eyes away from Susan's gaze.

"Come on, Alex," Susan insisted. "Remember...no secrets? Was it one of those dreams again?"

"Yes," she said, gesturing widely. "Last night"

"Did you catch him this time?"

"Nope," Alexandra replied sadly. "He's falling and I'm still waiting with my arms out...same ole thing."

For a moment, Susan studied her.

"Damn it, Alex!" she said, clearly irritated. "I told you that you needed to see someone about this problem. It's starting to consume your life. You're my best friend but you're really starting to piss me off...and scare me, too. Yes...I will admit...it's really terrible to have lost both your parents at a young age, but don't you think they would have wanted you to start living your life by now? Look at you," she continued, with a tone that was growing impatient. "I'll pull no punches. You have your work and you have your rowing but there's nothing else...no boyfriend...no social life...no nothing."

"Save it," Alexandra shot back. Susan had preached the same old sermon a dozen times before, to no avail. Alexandra has the dream. Susan watches Alexandra get depressed. Susan counsels.

"By the way," Susan said inquisitively, "when *was* the last time you had sex...the last time you had a m..?"

I've been waiting for this one. "Let's not go there again, Susan," Alexandra broke in.

"Listen, Alex. Whether you believe it or not, you're falling into an endless pit to nowhere. You're teetering on the edge of a meltdown. You think that making believe there's nothing wrong with having recurring dreams about saving your father and believing it is normal isn't treading on dangerous ground?"

"Dangerous ground...meaning what, might I ask?"

"Danger, Alex," Susan replied, in a forceful tone of voice, "...danger of jeopardizing your whole future by allowing these demons to take over your mind. You've got to talk to someone, damn it! Find a demon executioner or something."

There was a long period of silence as Alexandra reached down and skimmed a hand across the ripples of cool water. "You know what, Susan?" she said lifting her head and gazing out towards the shore. "I hate where I am right now."

"I'm sure," Susan replied.

"Things should really be great...shouldn't they? I love working rescue and the people I work with. I have you as a friend...at least sometimes, that is," she continued, grinning as she drew in a deep breath. "The both of us, out here watching the sun rise, rowing on the lake. How does it get much better?"

"It doesn't, Alex."

"Then why do I hate where I am, and how do I get to some other place?"

Another moment of silence passed. Susan softly laid a hand on the back of Alexandra's shoulder and said calmly. "Alex...do you remember the time when we were in college and Anthony Rizzo made the touchdown that gave the Sun Devils a victory over the Wildcats for the championship?"

"Uh...yes. I remember. But what does..?"

"I'll tell you what it has to do with...being some place at the right moment in time," she interrupted. "Anthony threw the football into the bleachers where thousands were sitting and guess who caught it?"

"OK, so what? It was just a lucky catch."

"Oh...no," Susan said, gripping an oar with one hand as she wiped away a lonely tear with the other. *Wow...am I getting emotional here, or what?* she thought. "It wasn't just a lucky catch. Don't you see? It was meant to be *you*, Alex! Anyone else would have mounted that baby on a wall in their game room and gawked at it for all time. But two years later, when Anthony made pro and blew his knee out...never to play again...you went to the hospital and handed it to him. You have always been in the right place, Alex. You've always been there. You just need to get your head on straight. And... just maybe get laid in the process. Yes...that would probably help in a big way."

Alexandra looked surprised. "Wow...I've never seen your emotional side creep out like that. It was nice of you to say those things. I really treasure your friendship." As they made their way back to the dock, Alexandra thought about Susan's comment on getting laid...and she smiled.

Chapter Six

January 7

A week had passed since John's accident. He was still lying in a hospital bed at Scottsdale Memorial, unable to speak. Fortunately, he was showing signs of improvement, which was encouraging to Karl and Laura, but he was still in and out of consciousness. Stitches mounted horizontally on the right side of his partially-shaved head were covered with a gauze bandage. The skin around his cheek bone was still dark, swollen and stitched from a deep glass cut. The ball of his humerus had been reset. The extent of damage and potential effects on his physical, intellectual or psychological behaviors caused by the head trauma were still unknown. When John was awake, he didn't respond to the medical staff providing his care. He didn't interact with those who came to visit. His eyes were vacant, staring into space. He seemed to be suspended in time, waiting to be released from the silence and memory loss that entrapped him. Laura, fearing that John wouldn't do anything more than lay there like that forever, stayed by his side…going home only when coaxed by John's father.

***

For four days, Jessica manipulated clients and schedules to be with John. She was hoping for his swift return to consciousness while the words of her father, Lawrence, and his venomous speech about the Compton project loomed in the back of her mind. Jessica remembered the last one-on-one meeting she had with him. He was impatient, displeased and enraged about her lack of attention to Crawford Investments' failing business...and was quick to let her know.

"Time is money, Jessica," Lawrence said, leaning forward in the overstuffed executive chair behind a solid cherry desk with an expensive leather top. Lawrence was always formal with her. As a child, he always called her Jessica...never 'sweetheart' or 'daddy's girl'...just Jessica. Lawrence had wanted a son who would eventually stand by his side in the twenty-four by forty-eight portrait hung center-stage on the far wall of his company's conference room. The portrait was there, but Lawrence stood alone in his charcoal-gray suit, white shirt and a gray silk tie...a stone-faced, heavy-set man in his late fifties with several chins. The full head of white hair was cut short on the sides and around the nape. The angst in his life and years of smoking and drinking had left him with the look of a cold, serious man. The creases in his skin naturally pulled his mouth downward at the corners. The white bushy eyebrows rounded over his eyes made him appear sad and lonely.

Although Lawrence had never openly faulted Jessica for what had happened, deep inside she knew he'd blamed her as much as he blamed her mother. His second child, Lawrence, Jr., the son he had dreamed of, had been abducted from a shopping mall when he was just 13 months old. Jessica's mother, Marion, had briefly taken her eyes off little Lawrence... who, at the time, was strapped into the stroller just inside a costume shop. Jessica had been causing a ruckus over a princess costume she wanted to wear for Halloween. After an expensive and exhaustive search, their son was never found. Both the police and the private detectives Lawrence, Sr., had hired all agreed that their son was likely abducted to be raised by someone desperately seeking a child of their own. Jessica's mother would always be reminded and continually blamed for the disappearance of their son, and she eventually broke down. Five years later, she was committed to a mental facility where she bled to death after gouging her wrist with a letter opener.

"You know the financial position we are in, Jessica!" he said, slapping his half-full glass of Jack Daniels down on his desk. "This company has borrowed millions to purchase speculative property that we haven't been able to turn. With interest rates going through the ceiling and the inventory of property and homes rising, speculators are facing tough fundamentals. Our back is against the wall. Do you understand? Answer me, Jessica!" he shouted, demanding her to acknowledge him.

Jessica's reaction to her father's tormenting outburst was a timid, blank stare. Years of subliminal guilt about her brother's abduction had been driven deep into her subconscious and the constant pressure for her to be the son he had lost made her appear strong and cunning in the business world but weak and controlled in his presence.

Lawrence reached into the drawer in front of him, pulled out a folder and placed it on the desk. The folder contained confidential information about Project Desert Highlands Promenade, the development of a thirty-acre parcel in Scottsdale in a location yet to be determined. Lawrence had obtained inside info by paying off his source in the government zoning and land development office. Compton Investments Real Estate Partners planned to purchase thirty acres of land in a strategic area of Scottsdale, which would ultimately be a key component in the landscape of a newly-developed area of downtown Scottsdale. The fourteen-story, mixed-use project would include 330 residential condominiums, boasting views of

Camelback Mountain on one side and the skyline of downtown Phoenix and South Mountain on the other, as well as hotel units and upscale shops and restaurants. The project in the planning stage had been presented in private meetings with local attorneys, pertinent city planners and... Carriage Brokers.

John Henning was the primary agent for Carriage and was in the middle of working a contract to secure the land and spearhead the community relations activity to address any controversial aspects of the plan when his accident occurred.

Lawrence took a big swallow from the glass of Jack. "Now listen to me, Jessica," he said locking eyes with her. "Our company needs this contract. Compton was talking to your lover boy, John...and for now, he's out of commission. This is our chance to slide in. Get my drift?"

"Excuse me, Daddy!" she said, drawing back. "I can't do this...I can't do this to John. You're asking me to do devil's work. I'm going to marry the man, for God's sake."

Lawrence said calmly, "You still don't understand, Jessica. That beautiful condo you live in belongs to the bank, and my company is still paying for that expensive car you drive. If we don't take advantage of this situation now, all of that AND this business will flush out."

"But, Daddy..." she said with tears streaming down her face, "Is the company that bad off that you would want me to deceive John like that? How *could* you ask that of me?"

"It's very simple, Jessica," he responded, leaning back in his chair. "(A)...It's a matter of mathematics, and (B)...our creditors are getting ready to invade us because we're up to *our ass* in debt. Is that so hard to understand? That's why I needed John to work for us--not Carriage Brokers. We desperately need that Compton project. Besides, Jessica," he went on, sarcastically, "I'd hoped that your dear John, the man whom you say loves you so much, would have joined our company by now. But, no...Jessica, instead...he's still working *against us*."

"But, Daddy, it's just not fair to..."

"It's war, Jessica!" he corrected her and slammed the side of his fist down on the desk. "And you know what they say...all is fair in love and war."

Chapter Seven

The second 9-1-1 call of the day was the kind the rescue team dreaded most. It was an incident that should carry some kind of legal liability but is often viewed as just another senseless, needless accident. The gate in the fence around the swimming pool had been propped open, and the toddler wandered through the gate and fell into the pool while her mother was inside the house talking aimlessly to a girlfriend on the telephone. Alexandra exhausted her abilities trying to save the little girl. The mother was screaming hysterically as her two-year-old daughter was lifted into the emergency vehicle.

Local news channels gathered at the house and the hospital to scoop the story for their five o'clock news broadcasts. An unattended child falling into a swimming pool, tragic as it is, was like blood to sharks when it came to attracting the media. Cameramen with their reporters waited anxiously to find out the little girl's name, age, hair color, eye color, even her favorite toys...anything to describe the poor little girl, anything to develop a competitive storyline.

The triage team, prepared for the worst, waited with their equipment at the ready. When the ambulance coasted to a stop, the colored lights on top of the vehicle were still rotating but the siren was now silent. The rear doors swung open, and a swarm of medical personnel began aggressive resuscitation. All the medical personnel, equipment, preparation and training couldn't save her. The little girl was pronounced dead shortly after the ambulance arrived at Scottsdale Memorial. Protocol and specific procedural requirements made it mandatory that life-saving efforts be continued until the time of death is declared and documented.

Alexandra held the IV bag above the level of insertion and helped push the gurney up the ramp until the exchange was final. This would be the last she would see the little girl until her picture, along with all known details of how this tragedy had occurred, would air on local television stations. While the media looked for someone or something to blame, the rescue team grieved another useless death of a young, innocent child.

"All in a day's work," Tucker said, ripping the rubber gloves from his hand. "How old was she?"

"Believe it or not, Tuck…she was a New Year's baby that had just turned two."

"Hmm," Tucker's shoulders dropped as he let out a weary sigh, shaking his head. He glanced over Alexandra's shoulder to where the little girl lay covered with a white sheet. "What a shame. How are the parents taking it?"

"Hysterical, as you would suspect, and on their way here," Alexandra replied, gesturing towards the black and white that had just pulled up to the curb outside. "They don't know yet."

Tucker glanced at his watch. "What do you know…one week, two days, sixteen hours and twenty minutes into the New Year and already a child dies by drowning in a swimming pool. There's nothing like getting a jump start into summer to make one feel like shit, you know?" He reached for the pen in his coat pocket and put it to paper. "Listen, Alexandra," he said while jotting notes. "I have to record the child's time of death and attempt to console the parents. It's the part of my job that I hate with a passion, but someone has to do it. I should be finished in about twenty minutes. If you want to hang for a few, you can ask me about the guy named John you brought in on New Year's. Are you at all interested?"

Alexandra drew back. She was surprised he would even bring it up.

"Well...uh...yeah, I guess," she replied gazing around the ward at nothing in particular. It was obvious that she would have preferred not to answer. She jabbed a hand in each back pocket.

Suddenly, the pager on Alexandra's hip started making an irritating, vibrating sound. "Sorry...Tuck. Duty calls," Alexandra said, studying the text. "If it's OK with you...I'll come back later."

* * *

It was eight p.m.... and no word from Alexandra. Susan had called her several times and left messages. One message Susan left earlier in the evening was merely a tease to remind Alexandra to buy a gift for Susan's birthday. The other message was to find out why Alexandra hadn't shown for the rowing team's seven o'clock meeting to discuss the upcoming San Diego Crew Classic.

What Susan didn't know was that, during the five o'clock rush hour, Alexandra's unit and several other response units were summoned to a pile-up on the 101 North involving a moving truck, several cars and a motorcyclist. The motorcycle had plowed into the rear of the moving truck which had swerved into the inside lane to avoid hitting a mattress that had blown off the bed of an old pickup. The accident set off a chain of events that ultimately sent several people to the hospital...with the motorcyclist being pronounced dead at the scene. Traffic was tied up for hours.

* * *

As Alexandra finalized her report, she thought about what Tucker had said before she left him earlier.

The words played over and over in her head like a broken record. 'Are you interested?' *Sure I'm interested, but why?*

***

Alexandra maneuvered her way through traffic on her way back to Scottsdale Memorial to see Tucker. Her mind was occupied with thoughts of how accidents happen every single day and, in her line of work, the only thing that matters is the initial interaction with those needing help. *Just the act of getting people from the streets to the medical facility alive is often a miracle. What happens after that had never been a consideration for her.* That thought kept flashing through her mind as she wondered why she felt different about this guy, John Henning. It was a feeling that sent a passionate ache to the middle of her stomach. She just couldn't figure out what was different about *this* guy as she searched for some mysterious kind of answer or closure. She was so caught up in her thoughts that she nearly missed the tail-end of the ring tone from her cell phone that was buried in the bottom of her bag under all the junk. With one hand on the wheel and the other fishing, she grabbed the phone and flipped it open, all in one motion. Susan was hollering from the other end of the line. "Holy, shit, Alex! Where in the hell are you?"

After a pause, Alexandra said calmly. "I'm on my way to Scottsdale Memorial. Why do you care, and why are you yelling at me?" Everything seemed to close in around her…the stress from the pile-up on the 101 to the nerve-racking questions bombarding her mind about John. "Sorry, Susan…I didn't mean to snap at you but I've got a lot on my mind; it has been a hectic day."

"You must still be working," Susan replied, in a cautious tone of voice. "You do sound stressed out. If you are still working, I understand your frustration...it's late. But if you haven't been working, I'll be pissed because you missed our important meeting."

"Uh...let's see now...meeting?" Alexandra swallowed hard when it hit her. *Oh, shit. That's right...the meeting. That explains it.*

It was a meeting called days ago to discuss Kristy. Susan, as the lead, needed the full support of all the team members at the meeting to chastise Kristy for gaining weight and placing the team in jeopardy of being disqualified from participating in the San Diego Crew Classic in March. Kristy couldn't hide it. It was obvious and, even though the girls hadn't yet mentioned it, it showed a little when she wore her rowing attire. All weigh-ins of lightweight rowers and coxswains would take place at the Regatta site prior to the race. Each member of the team had the responsibility to weigh in at 135 lbs. or less, or the entire rowing team would be disqualified. They had been noticing the increase in Kristy's weight over the last two months and were ready to confront her at the meeting.

"God, I'm sorry, Susan," Alexandra said in earnest. "It's been hell on wheels today. You know what I mean...blood in the streets, so to speak."

The other end of the line was silent.

"Well...what did she say?" Alexandra asked.

"What did who say?"

"Kristy," Alexandra responded quickly.

"Oh, yeah," Susan said, after a few seconds of trying to dismiss the entire matter of blood in the streets from her mind. "Hold on to your steering wheel, Alex... Kristy's expecting."

"What…a baby?"

"Yes, a baby! How about that shit?"

"Who's the unlucky guy?"

"Could be anyone," Susan put in, sniggering. "You know Kristy."

"What now?"

"She's out."

"Who's in?"

"That's one we have to resolve," Susan said. "Hence, the meeting you missed. We have two months before the race, so we have a little time to find someone suitable. By the way," she went on, abruptly, "are you or aren't you off work?"

"Off."

"Then why are you going to the Scottsdale Memorial? Meet me for a beer instead."

"Can't, but thanks for asking. See you at the lake Saturday morning?" Alexandra put in quickly to avoid giving Susan any chance for further cross-examination.

"I wouldn't miss it for the world…maybe then you'll tell me what you're trying to avoid telling me now. Don't forget," she chuckled, "no secrets."

***

Tucker sat in his cubicle sipping coffee, finalizing patient reports and reviewing the previous day's after-hours' cases. He kept checking his watch and keeping an eye out for Alexandra. *Finally*, he thought, as the glass doors automatically opened and she walked into the reception area.

Tucker stood up. Towering over the top of the green-carpeted panel wall, he gave a shout in her direction. "Hey, kid, over here." Tucker reached into the next cubicle, grabbed an empty chair and dragged it back to his desk just as Alexandra walked up. "Sit. OK, then," he went on, "let's see. I'll bet you're here late because of the pile-up on the 101, right?"

"You heard." she replied, with a sobering gesture. "The scene was pretty damn horrible."

"No one was shuttled our way," he said, stroking his chin. "So I figured they all went to Banner...not that I'm complaining, you understand."

"Don't tell me you are concerned. Not enough blood and guts here today?"

"Absolutely not," he responded quickly, his brow knit into a single dark line. "We were swamped."

"Banner was the closest hospital to the scene, Tuck," Alexandra said. "Dispatch informed us that Banner had told them that they had no problem taking in the slew of injured."

Tucker didn't respond. He appeared to be drifting in thought. Alexandra snapped a finger to get his attention. "Well ... I'm here!" she reminded him.

"Oh, oh yes...John," Tucker said, discreetly scanning the area to make sure no one else was listening. "Sorry. By the way, how *did* Banner's emergency handle all the chaos?"

Alexandra stared at him. "Tucker, will you forget about Banner. I'm here, remember...the Henning guy?"

"OK. OK," Tucker replied. "Just relax, will you."

Tucker looked around again, straightened his coat, smoothed down the hair on one side of his head, rested his forearms on his thighs, leaned in and started whispering. He told her that John had been unconscious for four days and that the diagnosis was sketchy at best. He said there were no visible signs of brain damage. He went on to say, based on rumors, the doctors were puzzled and had no clue as to why he was in such a deep sleep most of the time.

"Earlier today, a nurse told me that one of the night nurses attending to John had told her that, four days ago, when she was checking his vitals, he opened his eyes and scared the hell out of her. She said it was ghostlike. Since then...he's been in and out of conscious-ness...mostly out."

"I see..." Alexandra said softly. "But isn't that normal in these cases?"

"Yes, sometimes, but listen up. Here is the weird thing," Tucker continued, as he re-set his glasses and locked eyes with her. "The family, the fiancé, his best friend, and several others have been coming to see him...but he doesn't remember any of them. Who they are is a mystery to him. They stand right in front of him...he opens his eyes and sees them but they are strangers to him. How about that shit?"

"You're not serious," she replied. "Not even his parents?"

"No one," he mused, gesturing widely. "No one."

"Where is he now?"

"He is in the next building...room two-forty. If you want, you could wander on over. He probably won't have any visitors this late. Satisfy whatever curiosity that's been bugging you since you brought him in here."

Should I really go see him? What if someone is there, like maybe his fiancé? Why would I go see him anyway? "I'll think about it, Tuck."

"It's up to you, lady. I'm just the bearer of the confidential information that could get me fired if some-one finds out."

Chapter Eight

Alexandra walked down the hallway as if she was supposed to be there, headed towards room two-forty. Visiting hours had been over for an hour. Televisions on low volume were still on in some of the rooms she passed. *Would the television be on in John's room and would he be able to hear it?* she wondered. Curtains on overhead tracks formed circles around the patients' beds just inside door openings. The smell of freshly-brewed coffee came from a break room where two nurses were getting their caffeine fix to help them through the night shift. Two other nurses and a nurse's aide sat at their station drinking coffee and chatting. They noticed Alexandra slowly walk by but didn't acknowledge or question her. Alexandra figured that there would be no reason for them to wonder why she was there or what she was doing. She was still in uniform, which made her appear perfectly natural to the environment.

Two thirty-six...four more. Alexandra stopped. *Wait, what if there was someone still visiting? I can't just barge into the room as if I were part of the family.* She started to get cold feet. On one hand, she was getting close to convincing herself to do a cut and run. On the other hand, she thought, *it's going to be now or never.* Suddenly, a soft tap on her shoulder startled her. Alexandra spun around to find a nurse standing behind her. She had a warm, gentle smile.

The nurse said calmly, "Can I help you find a particular patient, Alexandra?"

"How did you know my name?"

"It's stenciled above your left pocket."

Alexandra glanced down and then up again. "Oh, yes, of course..." she giggled, somewhat embarrassed for asking the question. "You're right." *What's the matter with me? Calm down, girl, you've done nothing wrong.*

Alexandra took in a breath, paused, and then introduced herself as a member of the response team that brought John Henning into the emergency room on New Year's Day...and how the circumstances that night left her wondering how he was doing.

"I just happened to be finishing up here tonight and Tucker Potts, in Emergency, informed me that Mr. Henning was in two-forty, and since I was..."

"Look, sweetie, don't you fret," the nurse interrupted and laid a hand on Alexandra's forearm. "I trust you have good reason for wanting to see him...so go ahead. Nobody's with him now, and the last I checked..." she continued, as she adjusted her spectacles and then reached back to secure a loose hair clip from the back of her wavy, gray hair, "he was asleep. Just try not to wake him. He's been in and out of consciousness all day, so sleeping straight through, at least until it's time to check his vitals, would be good for him. You decide, sweetie." She smiled again...then walked away.

Alexandra waited a moment. She watched the nurse turn into her workstation then contemplated her cut-and-run idea again. "Oh, what the hell," she said under her breath.

Convincing herself not to worry about what was right or what was wrong was winning. She thought about the fact that she had a perfect right to be interested in John's condition. *Jesus, I was the one who kept him alive, who comforted him, and cared about him when he needed it the most.* She inched her way to two-forty, glided softly through the open door and peaked around the curtain surrounding John's bed. *Try not to wake him. He's been in and out of consciousness all day.* The room was dreary and dark, much like the room Alexandra's mother, Ruth, died in. The same eerie, glimmering, dim flashes of monitoring equipment were a sad reminder of that horrible morning when the nurse woke Alexandra from her dream to tell her that her mother was gone.

John, lying motionless and slightly elevated in the adjustable hospital bed, looked very peaceful. Walking on the tips of her toes, she moved closer to the bed, but not too close. *Even with the side of his head bandaged, he looks extremely attractive...so handsome,* she thought. *What am I saying?* Alexandra wanted very much to touch him but felt she had no right. Even though, on that rainy night at the intersection of Twenty-Fourth and Oak, there was justification when she covered his mouth with her lips to save his life, it didn't matter anymore. *I want to press my lips to his, right now, this moment.* She glanced around the room and noticed the flowers and pictures of people she didn't know but was sure he knew...pictures of family, friends and a lover. She was certain that they wanted him more than she. *They all want him to remember and to come back to them. I just want him. Why am I saying this? It's that darn Susan putting words in my head.*

Alexandra wanted to speak to John but again reminded herself of the nurse's request not to wake him. *What would I say if he did wake up?* She really wanted John to know she was there...next to him. *It may not be fair to his fiancé; but right now, it doesn't matter,* she thought. *Why am I having these thoughts?* She wanted him to know that she couldn't sleep or function just thinking about him. She wanted him to remember how close they were when he opened his eyes for a moment that night in the intersection. She moved to the other side of the bed where a chair seemed to wait for her and sat down next to him. It was quiet and late and, as time passed, her eyelids began to droop.

***

She was standing in the water that was running down the street, coming from the water hoses pointed at the building. The sounds of people screaming seemed to echo all around her as the fire shot dark, flaming ash into the night air. Alexandra looked up at her father, hanging from the window as flames shot out directly above him. She could barely hear the woman standing in the bucket screaming over the sirens of the emergency vehicles speeding up the hill. The woman was screaming, "Save him! Please, somebody save him." Suddenly, everything around Alexandra seemed frozen in time. People who were once scurrying around now moved in slow motion...frame by frame. Alexandra could see the panic on the faces in the crowd. Their lips were moving but the words coming from their mouths were out of sync. Her father was hanging far above her, but it seemed as though she could reach up and touch him. With her arms extended, she yelled at him to let go. "Let go, Father! Let go and I'll catch you! Please...let go..."

***

A sudden beeping sound coming from the monitoring equipment caused her body to jerk back in the chair, interrupting her dream. Her eyes opened wide, and at that moment, she was looking at John...whose eyes were now open and staring back at her.

"It's you..." John said softly, with a groggy, surprised look.

Alexandra's perfectly-shaped eyebrows angled inquisitively. She glanced over her shoulder expecting to see someone standing behind her, but saw no one. She looked back at John and pointed at herself.

"Me? You remember me?" she asked, as her body trembled slightly.

"You've been in my dreams. I've seen your beautiful face in my dreams."

Alexandra's heart skipped a beat. *He's probably delirious.* "Do you know why you're here?" Alexandra asked. "Here, in the hospital?"

"I think I do," he said gazing around the room as if almost seeing it for the first time. "It takes a while for me to get focused. They tell me that I was in a terrible accident and almost died."

"That's true," she sighed. *Thank God you didn't.* "Things were pretty dicey inside that Porsche of yours, you know. You survived. However, the Porsche didn't."

"How did you know that?" he asked.

"I was there when it happened," Alexandra replied. "How do you feel?"

John paused. He angled his head and thought about her question. "To tell the truth...I feel like a stranger in a strange land. And I'm hungry. What do you *mean*...you were there?"

"At the scene of the accident," she said, removing her ball cap and pulling off the band that kept her hair in a ponytail. "It was pure luck that we were at the same stop light."

John grinned..."Maybe I should call you...my guardian angel?"

"Just Alexandra will do," she smiled.

"Hmm...I like that name," he said with a satisfying smile..."Alexandra."

The nurse tapped twice on the door and rolled in a portable blood pressure device.

"Well..." she said, looking at John. "I see that you are awake again. Wonderful. Do you remember me?" she quizzed.

"I do," he replied, pointing. "You're, uh...let me see. You are...Hazel, the nurse."

"Good guess, Mr. Henning," she said with a bright smile.

"No guess, Hazel," John replied, pointing at the white board on the wall. "See...it reads 'Hazel...nurse on duty.'"

Alexandra covered her mouth to keep from laughing.

"Well, Mr. Henning," Hazel said, "your blood pressure, your temperature...and apparently your sense of humor...are all very good."

John and Alexandra smiled at each other.

"If you need anything, John, just press the call button and I'll be here. I'll see you in four." Just as quickly as Hazel had entered the room, she left, pushing her equipment cart in front of her.

"I guess she means she'll be back in four hours to repeat the process. I hope you will still be here, Alexandra?"

"John," Alexandra replied, glancing at her watch. "I think that four hours would be way past my bedtime." *I should lay down right next to you.* "I presume it would be past your bedtime as well."

Don't go yet, Alexandra. Not now. "Then at least stay a while longer."

***

Over the next two hours, they talked. Alexandra tested Tucker's source...the one who had told him that John remembered no one...and that source was right. The recollection of anyone in his life and what life was prior to the accident had been mysteriously erased from his mind. They talked about the people in the pictures and the people who had visited him in hopes of being recognized for who they were in his life. John told her how his father, Karl, kept thanking God that his injuries were not life-threatening.

"I could tell that he couldn't handle the fact that I didn't know who he was. I could see that the stress was getting to him."

He told her how his mother, Laura, who he felt was a warm and kind woman, kept trying to say and do things that mothers do. Laura wouldn't accept that she was like a stranger in John's new, temporary world. She brought his favorite cookies to the hospital...the ones she made during holidays, which she said John would remind her to make weeks ahead of time.

John went on to say that his mother would show him family albums filled with memories of the past and present. She would show him pictures of their fishing and camping trips. She showed him the pictures of their cabin in Munds Park, near Flagstaff, and pictures of the party Gary threw for his engagement to Jessica.

"When my mother thinks I'm sleeping, she'll sit where you are sitting and pray that I'll wake up with a smile and call her Mom."

Alexandra fought the urge to cry but couldn't hold back the tears. He reached out his hand and touched hers. He felt an overwhelming sense of warmth and compassion rise up inside him. He pulled her closer and pressed her slim, silky-smooth hand to his heart.

"Do you feel that?" he said, looking at her long and hard. "I know that it's only beating because of you, Alexandra."

Alexandra put on a bright smile and slowly drew her hand back. "That's really sweet, John," she said earnestly, wiping away a lonely tear. "But I just happened to be in the right place at the right time. There were others more responsible for getting you here than I was."

Alexandra reached for the picture frame that sat on the night stand next to the bed. *This must have been taken in Hawaii or on a beach somewhere in Mexico,* she thought. She pointed to the guy standing on one side of a girl wearing a bikini and a floppy straw hat.

"Who's this?"

"That's...uh, Gary. Gary Mathews. Supposedly, we work together at a place called Carriage Brokers. He's been here a lot...I like him. My mother told me that Gary and I are best of friends. I wonder how it could be that I don't remember him."

"I'm afraid that goes with the territory when you temporarily misplace your memory."

John smiled. "That's a gentle way to describe it."

"And how about her," Alexandra said, pointing at the striking young woman in the middle. "Who is she?"

This isn't going to go over well. "The girl I'm supposed to marry...Jessica," he said noncommittally.

Alexandra paused before saying, "It must be hard for both of you. I can't even imagine how something like this would affect me if *we* were going to marry and you suddenly didn't know who I was. But, I'm sure things will change soon enough, and everything will be back to nor-mal...back to where they were before the accident. You probably love this Jessica very much."

"Jessica's very beautiful...but when she visits me, I get uncomfortable...you know... I get the feeling that she's very impatient with me. I don't know what that means. It just feels weird."

"You mean Jessica makes you feel different than the others make you feel when they come to visit?" *Damn, am I getting too personal? I'll get off the subject of*

Jessica. Maybe he'll forget I asked. "Tell me about Gary…what is he like?"

"Yes…to your question about Jessica. It *is* different with the others. And with regard to Gary, he knows a lot about me…perhaps a little too much. But I think I can trust him. He's a good guy."

John told Alexandra that, ever since he had regained consciousness, Gary would come to the hospital every day and show him documents from Carriage Brokers that pertained to something called the Compton Project. "Gary thinks that, if he keeps talking to me about work, it will stimulate the neurological nerve endings, or whatever, that are attached to my brain and reverse the whole process of memory loss."

Alexandra smiled. "Maybe Gary should have been a doctor."

"That's what I told him…as long as he never practices medicine on me," John laughed.

John went on to say that Gary was worried that other real estate firms would now try to take advantage of John's situation and try to steal the 'Compton Project' away from Carriage Brokers.

"As Gary put it, the so-called 'monster' land deal."

"Does this threat worry you?"

"Not really…but I wish it did. That would mean that I was back in control of my life and the blocked memories would be past me. What really worries me, Alexandra, is that I don't even know my father and mother. I see the pain in their eyes when they are here, and it makes me feel helpless. But look, enough about me," he said, slowly turning onto his side. "Tell me about Alexandra."

"Well," she said, shifting slightly in the chair. "There's really not much to tell. You already know what I do for work and that keeps me real busy. Besides that, other than rowing competitively, I lead a pretty boring life. Unlike you…I have no parents. My father was a fireman who died during a rescue…and my mother died of cancer not too long ago."

"I'm sorry to hear that, Alexandra," John said sympathetically.

"It's OK now. Well, rather…it's really not OK," she replied, shifting her gaze away from him. "My father died when I was very young and Mom is in a better place now than she was in her last days on this earth. Anyway," she continued, "I try not to think of them being gone." *Stop rambling, Alexandra.*

"John, you know what? I better go. You need your rest and it's getting late." Alexandra began to rise from the chair.

"Wait…please…stay a while longer," John said reaching up to grab hold of her hand. "What about brothers or sisters?" *What about a boyfriend?*

I'd stay all night if you wanted me to. "Only child," she replied, slowly sinking back into the chair. "It's just me and Chester…my Silky Terrier."

Keep talking and she'll have to stay. "I like dogs…Tell me about the rowing."

"My best friend, Susan, introduced me to rowing while we were in college. We have a team, well…now one member short of a team. But, anyway," she went on, "we compete in Regattas about four times a year."

Alexandra told him how she would meet Susan on weekends at the Tempe Town Lake and how the two of them would row the lake in Susan's double scull while solving the world's problems. She talked about the upcoming San Diego Classic and John just gazed at her as she spoke. *I love the way she moves her lips when she talks!*

They even laughed and joked about the recent dilemma the team was in, the limited time they had to re-

place Kristy, and the details of Kristy's current circum-
stance.

Suddenly, there was another rap on the door, and
in walked Hazel with her cart. Alexandra glanced at the
clock on the wall and stood up. She had already been
there four hours.

"My goodness, John, look at the time! It's really
getting late. I don't want to be accused of impeding the
recovery progress by keeping you up all night. Besides,
Hazel will hate me."

John reached for her arm again, but this time got
air. "Will you come back?" he asked anxiously. *Say yes!*

"If I do, John," Alexandra replied, "and by then
you've gotten back your memory...only to remember
everyone but me, what then?"

Hazel pushed her cart against the wall and fiddled
with medical gadgets, pretending not to listen.

"That won't happen... I promise."

"You don't know that," Alexandra replied, swallowing hard.

"Watch this," John said, reaching for the pen and
pad from the stand. "Tell me your phone number?"

Alexandra's eyes widened. "Why would you want
it?

"Trust me, Alexandra," he mused. "It's all part of
my healing process."

Hazel giggled quietly.

"980-5324," she said. "Cell phone."

"I'm writing a note to myself. Look, Alexandra...read it," he continued with a grin, and handed the
pad to her.

She gazed at the note longer than she had to. She
looked at him and smiled.

"Oh, this ought to do it," she said, and read the
note out loud. "Remember beautiful Alexandra, 980-
5324!!!"

Alexandra leaned down towards him with a wide smile and pressed the note into John's hand. "The three exclamation points at the end add a nice touch," she said, then kissed him on the forehead. "Sweet dreams, John," she whispered. "Sweet dreams."

Chapter Nine

Saturday morning

January 13

The morning breeze was warm and the sky over-head was clear. The light spray of water coming over the bow of the scull was refreshing. It had been an hour of swift, intense rowing. Alexandra and Susan were rowing in perfect sync...just as they had practiced. Alexandra's arms and shoulders burned, which was a clear sign that she was pushing the limit. They raised the oars as they approached the end of the dock.

Susan said, "Much better than last week. Now we can talk."

"Talk about what? Kristy?"

"Yeah, that too. But first, let's talk about why you couldn't have a beer with me the other night."

"Oh...that?" Alexandra said nonchalantly. "It's was no big thing. I went back to see a guy we brought into Scottsdale Memorial on New Year's."

"Who is he?"

"Just some guy in a Porsche I witnessed getting broad-sided on my way home."

"Since when do your victims get a visit from you a week later?"

Alexandra hesitated. "Since the last time we talked...now what's the plan to replace Kristy?" Alexandra hoped that Susan would dismiss the matter and move on to discussing the meeting.

"Not so fast, Alex," Susan said. "First tell me about the guy. Who is he, and why the interest?"

"If I tell you, you'll just think I'm crazy and tell me to see a shrink again."

"Scout's honor," Susan replied, raising two fingers. "I promise not to be judgmental."

"Let's get the boat back first."

They carried the scull back to the boathouse. Simon marked the log and, as usual, peeked over his clipboard at their asses as they walked towards the parking lot. Without looking back, Susan asked Alexandra if she thought Simon was getting his battery charged again.

"No doubt about it," Alexandra said, grinning. "Who knows what he'll do inside that boathouse for the next fifteen minutes!"

They both laughed.

For the next thirty minutes, they leaned against Susan's Jeep Cherokee talking. Alexandra told Susan about John, the accident, and the time she spent with him in his hospital room.

Susan said. "OK, Alex. I get the fact that, because of the circumstances surrounding his accident, you would be curious about his condition. However, I don't get all the gooey stuff about the hands to his heart, the note and the kiss to the forehead. The guy's *engaged* to be married, for Christ's sake!"

"I knew you wouldn't keep your word."

"Look, Alex, I said I wouldn't be judgmental but I have to say this for your own good. If you fall for this guy today and he comes to his senses tomorrow, your mind will really be fucked up. I mean...come on. Don't you think that trying to get past the saving-your-father thing is enough for you to deal with? Please...when I said you need a man, I meant a single guy; there are thousands of them out there that are chomping at the bit to get even a glance from a girl like you."

'You've been in my dreams. I've seen your beautiful face in my dreams.' After a moment of silence, Alexandra crossed her arms tight to her chest and shrugged. "You're right, Susan, but I did try to stop myself from seeing him…and the more I tried to convince myself not to, the more it seemed like I was supposed to."

"OK, OK, then." Susan responded coldly. "You went and you saw him. Now that you know he's alright, you forget about him and go about the business at hand. Help us find a replacement for Kristy. There happens to be some good rowers out there. They are on other teams that are not planning to go to San Diego. Let's find one," she continued, glancing at her watch. "Damn. I've got to bail. Got a client waiting at the gym, and she's an impatient one."

***

Susan left the parking lot while Alexandra sat in her car contemplating the things that Susan had said. *Susan is right*, she thought. The issues surrounding John's situation were much too complicated to get involved in. The rationale for getting drawn in wasn't worth the effort or the possibility that she might mess up something in his life that he was expecting to eventually turn out right.

Chapter Ten

Monday

January 15

The lobby created the image of wealth and luxury. Gary nervously waited on an elegant, pinstriped sofa in a quiet rotunda with marble columns connected by a bronze railing, all resting on contrasting shades of marble flooring. Gary Mathews had arrived at Compton Investments fifteen minutes early for his meeting with Mr. Robert Johnson. Johnson was the principal decision-maker and one of the top dogs with whom John had developed a business relationship early on in the deal making. Carriage Brokers had handed off the Compton Project to Gary while John was recovering from his injuries and loss of memory. Gary was given the task of settling all outstanding issues in what would be Carriage Brokers' largest contract ever.

Twenty minutes had passed when the impeccably-dressed receptionist walked over and politely handed Gary his second cup of coffee. She apologized again for Mr. Johnson's previous meeting running over. Although John, in his current state, couldn't help Gary with the possible handshake agreements and various nuances not documented that might have taken place (Gary discussed this with John at his bedside) in the Compton Project file, John seemed to feel confident that Gary could fill the void and close the deal with the information at hand. It all sounded good to John as he laid there and listened to Gary lay it out.

Gary glanced at his watch for the fifth time. It was thirty minutes past the time of his scheduled meeting. Suddenly, from the left hallway, he could hear voices and footsteps echoing off the marble floor which seemed to be heading in the direction of the lobby. *It's time*, he thought, *to put on a business face and represent Carriage Brokers on the biggest deal ever for their company. It's time to make John proud.*

Gary brushed a hand through his light brown wavy hair, adjusted his taupe, rectangular-shaped metal glasses, blindly felt for his tie to center it, and stood with his briefcase at his side. He managed to display a crooked smile, bending the attractive, neatly-trimmed mustache that complemented his long narrow face, until he spotted Jessica walking alongside and brushing shoulders with a man Gary surmised was Robert Johnson. The image of Jessica with Johnson caused his knees to wobble slightly and the smile on his face to slowly melt away. At first, Jessica didn't see him. She had turned to offer Robert her hand, and he took it...only to hold on as if parting were some sad event.

Jessica wore a dark business suit complemented by an expensive beige blouse. It opened just enough to expose a thick, shiny, silver necklace that hung just above the crease of her cavernous cleavage. After several soft-spoken words, Robert turned back towards his office while Jessica spun around and locked eyes with Gary. She was as surprised to see him as he had been when he spotted her. The situation was awkward at best. *Is this time for war, or was Jessica there for reasons other than the Compton Project?* Gary thought as Jessica crossed over to where he was standing.

"Jessica," Gary said, tossing her an icy look. "What brings you here?"

Jessica didn't hesitate, stutter or flinch. She was as cool as old man Crawford. Jessica knew she had been caught red-handed. She knew that Gary wouldn't, for a second, believe some trumped-up story about why she would be meeting with John's client. She threw her shoulders back, looked Gary straight in the eyes and said calmly, "Compton might be interested in our company's property for their new project."

That's bullshit, lady! "Is that so," Gary chided, tapping his briefcase. "In here is John's file...and no-where in here does it indicate that there's any acreage other than what was previously selected by Carriage Brokers and Compton Investments. The contracts are drawn and ready to be finalized and signed. Believe me, Jessica. There are no documents showing land owned by Crawford anywhere in this case."

I won't back down from this weasel. "Look, Gary," Jessica countered, "my father expects me to follow through on business he starts and ..."

"Business *he* starts!" Gary interrupted, lowering his voice to a whisper and leaning in towards her. "You must be nuts. How could you do this...and what the hell do I tell John?"

"Mr. Mathews...," echoed a voice from across the room, "Mr. Johnson will see you now." Gary turned, forced a smile to his lips, and nodded in the direction of the receptionist.

"Wait, Gary." Jessica said, clutching his arm. "Meet me at Anderson's on Fifth for a drink at six o'clock tonight and I'll explain everything."

"Don't screw with me, Jessica," Gary said pointedly. "You better have a damned good story."

***

Johnson treated the meeting with Gary as if it were just a follow-up to previous meetings with John concerning Crawford's property. *Must have been one of those off-the-record conversations.* Gary could tell he was being played or stalled until another meeting could be scheduled. Gary left the building even more pissed at Jessica, if that was even possible.

***

Six o'clock rolled around and Gary was ready to do battle. He passed the keys to the valet at Anderson's, marched through the crowd and straight into the lounge area where Jessica sat at the bar, already working on a glass of Cabernet.

"How was your meeting with Johnson?" she asked, peering back at him through the mirror between shelves of liquor bottles hanging behind the bar.

She can't even turn and look at me straight in the eyes. Gary said acidly, "Let's don't play games, Jessica." *Your father is sick and twisted.* "It's because of your father's vindictiveness that Compton now wants me to explore the viability of building the Promenade on *Crawford's* property. What were you doing to him while he leaned back in that comfortable chair of his?"

"Oh…that's real rich, Gary! I didn't do anything," she said coldly.

"*Whatever*…Johnson gave me the copy of the subdivided layout you left and has *commanded* me to consider your father's property along with the land options my company has already recommended. Johnson also wants me to do a study of demographics and a comparison between properties of the view of downtown Phoenix."

"You see, Gary," Jessica responded quickly, turning to face him, "and you suspected I was trying to steal John's client away. I was doing no such thing," she went on. "Nothing changes in that regard. We have no interest in managing the project. It's just that my father believes that the property Crawford Investments owns is more suitable for the Compton Project requirements."

Gary ordered Sky Vodka on the rocks with an olive. Jessica pushed her empty glass towards the bartender, "Another Cabernet, please."

Sorry, John. But this girlfriend of yours is a devious bitch! "I hate to burst your bubble, Jessica," Gary said with a sneer, "but the file indicates that John had already considered *your father's* land along with a few other *undesirable* sites and determined it was a no-go. And, furthermore, John didn't even include these parcels of land in the final proposal."

Jessica shrugged and took a sip from the Cabernet. "Well, *I* looked at the requirements and *I* think our parcel of land meets all requirements. So...you better get to work, pal."

Screw you! "Now you listen, Jessica," Gary said, balling his fist below the top of the bar, fighting the urge to throw a punch. "My guess is that John only looked at your father's land because of you." *You're my friend, John, but you're a sucker!* "If Compton was originally my client instead of John's, based on what *I* see, I wouldn't have given your father's land a second thought. Your old man should consider himself lucky that his land even got a look. So, Jessica," he went on, "you wanted to know how my meeting went. Well...it didn't go as well for me as your meeting with Johnson went for you. And one more thing, I couldn't even debate the subject with Johnson because I wasn't sure what kind of *arrangement* you made with him...if you get my drift. It looked to me, when you two parted ways this afternoon, there was some sort of intimate goings-on."

Jessica stared at him long and hard. "First of all...asshole," she shot back. "I resent the inference. If you think for one minute that I would prostitute myself to sell my father's land, you're sadly mistaken. I love John and he knows it. My father is a shrewd man and you know that. OK. OK...So what if my father wanted the whole enchilada, management of the project included, *I* talked him out of it!"

"The fact is, Jessica, in John's condition, he doesn't know anything about your love. And I hate to say it, but you're really lucky his memory *has* escaped him for the time being. Oh...and another thing you should know," Gary continued, as he slid off the stool and took a deep swallow from the glass of Sky. "John told me all about your father's offer letter which you presented him with at your little surprise dinner. Don't you think I know how to put two and two together? The whole thing is bullshit!"

Jessica hesitated. "Please, Gary," she said, grasping his forearm to the point her nails dug in. "You've got to work with me. Just present our land to Compton. It is prime acreage, and I'll make sure the price per acre will be much lower than the other properties being considered."

"Oh, now I see," he replied jerking his arm from her grip. "And how do you suppose this happens? Next, I suppose you're going to want me to disclose the competitor's price to you guys so you can beat it. In legal terms, I think that would be called some sort of illegal price manipulation bullshit that could cause all kinds of havoc. Well, no thanks to that idea." Gary took the last swallow from the glass and popped the olive into his mouth. "Jessica, you are your father all over again." He tossed a twenty on the bar, turned and strode out without another word.

Chapter Eleven

The police didn't know what to make of the situation. A man was lying on his back at the bottom of the stairs. A pregnant woman was sprawled out on top of him. They were both dressed for a formal night on the town. The baby sitter had made the call to 9-1-1 after she heard a sickening thumping noise coming from the stairs off the hallway. She left the two-year-old child playing with dolls in her room and hurried in the direction of the noise. That's when she spotted the man and woman at the bottom of the stairs. She told the police that, when she found them, the woman was moaning and moving her legs but the man was still and quiet. It wasn't long after the police had responded to the scene that the fire department and Bob Collins' emergency response team pulled up. Moments later, Alexandra's team arrived.

This scenario was one the response teams dreaded. It involved an unborn baby. It was determined that the man had broken his neck after falling head-first into the oak base of the railing on the second tier of stairs where the staircase made a sharp turn down to the tile foyer. The woman was lying on her back on top of the man. Her right arm was broken and twisted behind her. Her dress was ripped at the bottom…which led the police to believe that somehow, as they were walking down the stairs, her dress got tangled on the heel of her shoe causing her to lose her balance and fall. They theorized that her husband may have turned to stop her from falling but her momentum drove him backwards to his death. The heel had separated from her right shoe and was found teetering on the third step from the top.

En route to the hospital, Alexandra attended to the woman without knowing the actual condition of the baby inside her. The familiar wailing of the ambulance sirens and the rotating, colored lights warned moving traffic in front of them as it weaved from lane to lane at a high rate of speed. Alexandra knew that minutes wasted outside of the triage unit could prove detrimental to both the mother and her baby. The vitals on the baby, cushioned by the amniotic fluid within the uterus, were encouraging. In Alexandra's mind, however, she was afraid that a severe fall, such as the one the lady encountered, could easily prove fatal to the fetus.

The woman was in excruciating pain. Alexandra wasn't sure whether the pain was caused primarily by possible internal or external damage from the fall or from the broken arm or possible complications with the baby. At this point, she couldn't tell the condition of the woman's pelvis or if a possible placental separation from the uterus had occurred. The woman groaned and screamed all during transport...which Alexandra thought was a good thing. It kept her conscious. The woman had no idea what condition her husband was in. At this point, she was too delirious and in too much pain to ask. Even if she weren't, Alexandra was not about to tell her he was dead. It was the baby the woman was hysterical about.

"My baby!" she screamed. "My baby! Is my baby dead?" She kept crying out the same words over and over.

"The baby is fine. Calm down. Your baby will be fine."

Alexandra, well-trained for this kind of situation, lifted the woman's dress and looked between her legs for signs of bleeding or fluid. *What a relief,* she thought. *There is no sign of blood or fluid coming from the vagina.* The likelihood of ruptured membranes was slim.

Tucker spotted the ambulance as it pulled up and rushed out to assist. Alexandra leaped from the rear of the vehicle and unlocked the gurney all in one motion. Tucker had gotten the call from dispatch that they were headed his way with a pregnant woman who had taken a bad fall. His team stood ready to take the necessary action to save the unborn baby first.

"What do we know?" Tucker shouted over the loud, thumping noise from the rotor blades of an air ambulance that was taking off from the helipad. Alexandra, bent over the gurney, turned to look up at him.

"Tuck! She fell down a long flight of stairs. She's pregnant and has a broken right arm. I couldn't give her meds because of her condition. She's in lots of pain. I checked for blood or fluid coming from the vagina twice on the way here, and there were no signs of it. Her vitals are stable."

"That's good," he said. "Good."

Tucker pushed his glasses to the top of the bridge of his nose, lifted the woman's dress and bent over to look for himself. "You're right, Alexandra," he confirmed, "no sign of problems, but we won't know for sure until we get her to X-ray."

The woman was rushed into emergency with orders from Tucker to get her stabilized, start the appropriate IV, take X-rays, and perform an ultrasound to confirm the vitals and position of the baby.

Alexandra's heart rate finally started to decelerate. *Thank God, it's over*, she thought. Tuck was in control of the situation, and for that she was grateful.

Now…she thought, she could sit quietly and fill out the EMS forms and not think about bad things. She would think only positive thoughts, positive things about this mother and her unborn baby. Completing the forms was the last thing Alexandra would have to do involving this case. Recording a brief summary of the incident, what happened during transport, and the transfer of care to Scottsdale Memorial took all of forty-five minutes.

"Finished with your paperwork?" Tucker asked, leaning over. He planted his palms flat on the top of the desk and peered down at Alexandra, who was sitting in his chair.

"Uh, sorry, Tuck," she replied, and quickly shot up.

"Oh, sit down," he put in, reaching for her shoulder to push her back down. "You need time to chill after that run you just made. Oh...by the way," he went on, "the mother AND the baby are going to be fine."

Alexandra breathed a sigh of relief. She removed her EMT cap, jerked the rubber band from her hair, and dropped her head in her hands.

"Does she know about her husband?"

"She asked, Alexandra," Tucker replied. "I had to tell her."

"How'd she take it?"

"How would you take it?"

"You know what, Tuck," she said, with a strained smile.

"What's that?"

"He saved their lives. Her husband saved their lives."

Tucker reached around the desk and pulled two glass coffee cups from the bottom drawer. He grabbed the pot that was half full of coffee he had made earlier, filled both cups to the brim, handed her one, and sat in the chair across from her. "You're getting *too* emotional ...and I'm not going to let you drag me down with you. My shift is almost over, you know...so salute to a successful run," he said as he raised his cup.

"Tuck...this stuff looks pretty black and sticky to me," Alexandra said, holding the cup up and inspecting it.

"I suppose if I drink this...I can forget sleeping at all tonight. I'm only three hours away from my usual bedtime hour, you know."

"Drink up," he replied, grinning. "It's decaffeinated. Say," he added, "I've been meaning to ask you something."

"Ask me what?"

"That guy, John ...you know...the one you didn't want to get emotionally involved with? Hazel tells me you made it to his room."

"Oh...Hazel, the night nurse. Nice lady... but demanding."

"That's why she's considered one of the best."

"As a matter of fact, Tuck," she said, "I did. I went to his room, we had a nice chat and that was that. Seemed like a nice guy. It's too bad that he doesn't remember his friends or loved ones."

"Well, guess what?" Tucker said, after taking a swallow of coffee. "He still doesn't remember."

"Is he still here?" she asked. "I'm just curious, you understand."

"*Sure* you are," he mused. "Nope...he was released two days ago. I heard his parents wanted him to stay at their house until he made a full recovery, but the doctors recommended he go to his house...the place that would be most recent in his memory."

"Wow," she said, shifting nervously in the chair. "How is his girlfriend taking all of this?"

"What's that?" he replied, leaning forward. "Girlfriend? You don't really expect me to know everything, now do you? There are things you'll have to find out on your own going forward. That is, however, only if you are still...'curious.'"

Chapter Twelve

Friday

January 19

When Karl and Laura drove John home from the hospital it had been three weeks since the accident. Over the last week in the hospital, John had gone through various extremes of elaborative encoding therapy. As a result, he was showing signs of memory restoration. The doctors believed that John's lack of memory was due to some disruption in his D1 receptors, which are just one of five known dopamine receptors that control the memory function. Names, faces, places and different spaces in time triggered vague recollections by the end of the last session. His memory loss was so selective that, to some degree, it was baffling. But at the same time, it gave them confidence that complete memory retrieval could be days, if not hours, away.

It was as emotional as the scene in 'Miracle on Twenty-Fourth Street' when Natalie Wood saw her dream house...or when Jimmy Stewart regained his memory in 'It's a Wonderful Life.' John was riding in the back seat of his father's car as they turned into John's neighborhood. Everything changed when he spotted his house...it was like walking into a dark room, finding the light switch, and the whole room suddenly becomes visible.

Darkness turned to light. He fixed his eyes on his father and mother riding in the front seat, and there was no question about who they were...not like before, in the hospital, when neither of them had brought a feeling of closeness or meaning. His father pulled into the driveway while John sat quietly in the back, assessing his thoughts…trying to determine if what was happening was real and how much of his memory he had regained. Karl parked the car, turned in his seat, and looked back at John to see if something was wrong. John wasn't talking or moving. He just sat there staring through the window, out towards the house.

"John, is everything alright?"

"Yes, Dad," John said softly. "Everything is just fine now. I'm remembering things. I remember the neighborhood, my house, the cabin in Munds Park and other things that are now popping in and out of my mind in flashes. It's a weird feeling, Dad," he went on, turning to look at them. "But the best part is that you both are no longer strangers in my world."

Laura looked at Karl and began to weep. She couldn't control herself. The emotion was overwhelming. Karl leaned over, put his arm around her and looked back at John. Karl's eyes were beading tears. "You were never a stranger to us, son. Now come on. Let's go in the house and celebrate!"

"I'm sorry, Mother," John said, as they climbed out of the car. "I'm sorry for what both of you had to go through."

John wrapped the arm with the sore shoulder around his mother, grimaced a bit and held her closely. John's father brushed away a tear and moved in to enjoy the moment.

"It's good to have you back, son," his father said, wrapping an arm around John's shoulder. It was one big group hug.

"Your father and I always knew everything would be alright, John," Laura said, rising slightly on her toes to kiss him on the cheek. "We've prayed for this to happen."

Just then the door to the house flew open and Ofelia walked out onto the top step and hesitated. She wondered if John would remember her. She had been praying all along that things would be the same as when he left the house that night three weeks before.

"Buenos dias, Mr. John," she yelled from the doorstep, bringing her hands together as if she were praying.

"Hello, Ofelia," he shouted, smiling. *How could I ever have forgotten such a beautiful face?*

"Come, Mr. John. I made your favorite…tortilla soup."

"Now that's my Ofelia. Just what the doctor ordered."

They sat at the kitchen table talking as an hour passed. John downed one bowl of soup, then another, until the three of them finished the pot. Moments later, Laura noticed John's color turn pallid. He was losing his bearings, seemingly confused about his surroundings. She remembered the doctor had warned that, during transition of memory, there might be a tendency to become disoriented…but that it would only be part of the healing process and that they need not worry.

"You look tired, honey," she said in a calm but concerned voice.

Laura looked at Karl and he could sense her concern that John might regress mentally. Karl took hold of her arm and reminded her that the doctor had told them this could happen as John's memory restored itself.

"Give it time, Laura," Karl said calmly. "John has been through plenty over the last three weeks and look… look at the progress he's made. Now let's go on home and let John get some rest. Ofelia can tend to him."

"Dad is right, Mom," John put in. "I feel better now than I did a few minutes ago. I must have eaten Ofelia's soup too fast. You both should go home and get some rest as well. I'll be fine, you'll see."

"Now, John," she said, in a compassionate tone, "you know I'd feel better if I stayed with you, or we called Jessica to come over to be with you."

"Please, Mom," he said quietly, "don't call Jessica. What I need is some time alone...some time to think about things. Besides," he added, "right after I called you to come to the hospital to pick me up, I left Jessica a message on her home telephone to let her know the hospital was releasing me." *Thank God she didn't answer.* "She's probably working or something like that," he continued. "I'm sure she'll call when she gets the message. You guys go on. I'll be just fine."

John rose, gently gripped Laura's arm and guided her towards the front door.

"And, Mom...Ofelia is here...so you know I'll be in good hands."

"If that's what you want, John," she sighed. "You'll call if you need anything, won't you, son?"

"Yes he will, dear," Karl put in.

No sooner had Karl and Laura driven away than the phone rang. Jessica had been in Las Vegas working a potential Crawford client who'd been looking for investment property in North Phoenix. She had made several trips over a three-month period prior to John's accident.

Gary, although keeping his suspicions to himself, had thought Jessica was spending more time in Vegas than was necessary.

John, on the other hand, had been busy working Compton's Promenade project with Gary from his hospital bed and hadn't given it a second thought.

"Mr. John. Jessica es por teléfono para usted," Ofelia said, handing John the phone.

"Hi, baby, you're home. I called the hospital only to find out they released you this morning. I wish I had known," she continued, "I would have flown home to be with you."

"I left a message on your home phone around nine this morning," he replied.

"You could have called my cell phone," she countered.

"I figured you were busy and I didn't want to bother you. Where are you, anyway?" he added.

"Las Vegas," she replied.

"Then it's no big deal, Jessica," John said. "Consider us even."

"What are you saying, baby? What do you mean we are even?"

"You didn't tell me you were going to Vegas and I didn't try harder to reach you...so we're even."

"Spur of the moment, honey," she mused. "When things come back to you, you'll remember that I've been brokering a hot deal for Las Vegas Holdings."

"Things *are* back, Jessica."

It took a moment for John's words to sink in.

"You mean your memory's back?" she replied, excitedly. "Since when? When did it happen?"

"It happened on the way home from the hospital."

"Oh, baby, that's great news. I'll catch the next plane home."

"There's no need for you to rush, Jessica," he said softly. "Stay and take care of your business in Vegas. Besides...I'm not going anywhere. I'm in lockdown...doctor's orders. He wants me to rest. I'll be here when you get back."

"Rest?" she replied. "The doctor doesn't know you like I know you, baby. But if you say so, I'll see you in a couple of days. I'll call before I leave Vegas. I love you, John."

"Goodbye, Jessica."

***

Jessica pressed the phone to the switch-hook just as Keith walked in from the bathroom with nothing but a towel wrapped around his waist. After two hours of surrendering to each other, he had taken a shower while Jessica called home to retrieve messages. She didn't expect a call from John. Since his accident, even his mother hadn't received calls from him. There was no reason for Jessica to think he'd be calling her. She'd visit the hospital and seldom found him alone. Karl or Laura, or both of them, were always occupying space around his bed. Jessica called his room often but seldom found him awake. John's message had definitely caught her by surprise.

Sitting naked on the side of the bed, Jessica struggled to compose herself and act normal. She was struck with the guilt of infidelity, while the man she had been conducting business with finished running hot water over his rugged body—outrageously adorned with muscles. She had let wine and her emotions get the best of her, not to mention the animal magnetism of Keith Cantor, the handsome Vice President of Land Management for Las Vegas Holdings.

In Jessica's mind, legally it wasn't an issue. *I'm not married yet so screw it.* She tried hard to justify her actions...to satisfy the emotional rush that surged through her body...but it wasn't working. She still felt like an adulteress, nonetheless. Attempts to rationalize the events of the last day and a half were planting more guilt in her mind than if she had just chalked it up to a one-time fling and let it go at that. Cantor, on the other hand, showed no sign of guilt about the dalliance. The night before, over dinner, he had no qualms about telling her of his failing seven-year marriage and his two children. Jessica was sure she wasn't his first marital indiscretion.

'*You're just like your father.*' Gary's comment when they were at Anderson's flashed through her mind. *Maybe he's right,* she thought. *I am like my father.*

Their business meeting had culminated over dinner at Terrazza's Restaurant in Caesar's Palace. After great food and several glasses of wine, Cantor reached inside his coat pocket and took out two front-row tickets to the Celine Dion show. Over her last two trips to Vegas to meet him, Cantor had been dropping not-too-subtle hints that his intentions went beyond that of a business relationship. Jessica played along, thinking she could handle any situation that might get out of hand. This night caught her off guard. The wine, the action, the fact that Cantor was damned handsome wasn't making it easy to resist the temptation.

Her father had made it very clear that acquiring this client would secure future business for Crawford Investments outside the state of Arizona. He emphasized that kind of clientele was just what the company needed to sustain itself, and she should do whatever it took to close the deal. It was as if his blessing made everything alright. She was overwhelmed by Cantor's ability to show her a good time. The fact that it didn't seem strange to her that Cantor had procured a suite on the twenty-eighth floor and invited her up established her willingness to participate in a night that would end up with them in bed together.

It might have been the wine or the gambling or the Celine show after dinner that caused Jessica to totally dismiss John from her mind. It never occurred to her that John, lying in that hospital bed confused, might suddenly snap back to reality and ask for her. It wasn't enough that

Lawrence had coerced her into betraying John by pushing the sale of Crawford's property on Compton Investments, now the pressure was on her to be loose and creative to land the Las Vegas Holdings' deal. Over dinner, adding to the euphoria, Cantor had all but committed in writing to purchase the North Phoenix property from Crawford Investments.

When they walked into the Tower Suite, Jessica made her way past the plush furnishings to the picture window overlooking the Strip. The wine was creating havoc with her senses. Wasting little time, Cantor moved in quickly behind her and dropped the thin straps of her dress down below her shoulders. He gently caressed her bare shoulders with his strong, controlling hands, sending a warm tingle down her spine. He brushed aside her hair, revealing the beauty of her soft fragrant neck, and gently kissed it. He lifted her dress above her waist. She felt his tumescence grow hard as he pressed up against her. The urge to stop him wasn't as strong as the desire to totally give in to him.

He slid her lace panties down to her thighs, held her hands above her head pressing them against the window as he unleashed his passion for the all Las Vegas strip to see.

Chapter Thirteen

John's dislocated shoulder felt much better and the recollection of his past life had miraculously been restored. *Time to get back to work,* he thought, as he paced the house anxiously on Sunday afternoon. It had only been a few days since he'd come home and he was already getting restless. He tried to occupy his time by making conversation with Ofelia while she did chores...and glancing now and then at sports highlights on ESPN...but he still felt trapped in his own home. Regardless of the doctor's mandate for him to stay home with no strenuous activity for at least two weeks, he had other ideas. *Jessica was right,* he thought. *Rest just wasn't in the cards.* He was too antsy to obey any such orders. It was back to the office first thing in the morning...and that was that, he concluded.

***

Monday morning, Ginny was busy taking calls, checking calendars and setting up appointments. She was the first to arrive at Carriage Brokers and usually the last to leave. She wasn't your average, everyday, nine-to-five receptionist. Ginny was considered the company mascot and team mother and had the second longest tenure with Carriage. She was extremely good-natured and was always looking out for everyone. Most of the time, she felt she had to feed all of them. It was her contention that most of the staff in the office were too skinny to be healthy.

John leaned across her desk, gripped the soft, round hand, and blew a kiss. "Where is everyone?" he whispered low, gesturing with his hands as if using sign language.

Ginny was so happy to see John that she lost track of the conversation she was having with the person on the other end of the line. She smiled at John and then apologized to the caller. She removed her reading glasses and fidgeted with the crystal butterfly-style claw hair clip that held her gray hair in place. She squeezed the speaker on the headset with her thumb and index finger. "Gary's in his office," she whispered, looking up at him. "Fresh coffee in the break room, and there are fresh muffins. Welcome back," she continued, with a bright smile. "We really missed you."

John poured himself a cup of coffee, and then made his way down the hall to his office. There was a sign taped to the outside of his door...'Enter at your own risk!'

"I wouldn't go in there if I were you," Gary said, sneaking up from behind.

"And why would that be, buddy?" John replied, grinning. "Is there some sort of detonator tied to a bucket of paint hanging over the door?"

"Alright...go on. Enjoy the moment."

John hesitated, and then slowly turned the knob. He held back a bit and then swung it open...triggering music to start playing and confetti to fall from the ceiling. At that point, the entire staff came marching down the hall from the conference room singing, "For he's a jolly good fellow." When Gary informed the staff of Carriage Brokers that John had called and said he'd be in the office in the morning, they decided to send a few of the office pranksters into the office that night to decorate.

The moment was touching. It reminded John of all the reasons he liked working for Carriage and how tough it would be to leave if that day ever came. The celebration went on only as long as Ginny wanted it to, which wasn't that long. She finally nudged everyone out and then commandeered a few of the administrative workers to re-store John's office to its pre-celebration condition.

Meanwhile, Gary hurried John into his office, closed the door behind them and began to spell out the details of his encounter with Jessica at Compton Invest-ments...including their after-hours episode at Anderson's on Fifth. "I wished I had worn a wire so you could have listened to the bullshit Jessica was handing out."

"You and me both," John put in, crossing his arms. "Let's hear it all."

Gary went on to tell John how Jessica tried to get him to swallow a cock-and-bull story about her father's only asking that she push his land for the project, that Jes-sica had couched the whole thing by saying she was only trying to save the day, and that she had convinced her fa-ther not to go after the project management piece for John's benefit.

"That's bullshit...and she knows it!" John broke in, making no attempt to wash the bitterness from his tongue. "It wouldn't surprise me one bit if that dirty bas-tard, Lawrence, told Jessica to grab the whole enchilada. Jessica is just a pawn in his twisted, unscrupulous game; and now, I'm really afraid that his sickness is rubbing off on her. I wish you hadn't waited to tell me this."

"Wouldn't have made a difference," Gary replied. "I was afraid it would send you off the deep end while you were still at home, recovering so to speak."

"OH... I'm fully recovered now," John put in, thin-ning his lips, shaking his head. "This is on me now."

John wasn't about to let Lawrence's dirty little scheme succeed. He took the stack of Compton files from Gary, went to his office, sifted through unanswered mes-sages, and began the process of catching up on lost time.

***

Jessica knew John well enough to know that, if he was in any condition at all Monday morning, he would be in the office bright and early. She was concerned about how John would take the news from Gary, figuring that the Compton project would be the first order of business in his morning pass down. She fabricated a compelling story that would not jeopardize her position with Cantor or the land deal being consummated with his company and caught an early flight back to Phoenix.

***

Meanwhile, John reviewed the updates in the Compton file, leaned back in his chair and decided he was ready to confront Robert Johnson about the Crawford land option disturbingly proposed by Jessica. The only question in John's mind was the same question Gary had. Did Jessica make promises or establish some quid-pro-quo that might make his conversation with Johnson uncomfortable? Up to this point, John felt that his previous dealings with Johnson gave him no reason to believe that Johnson wasn't a man of high integrity...but right now, that was neither here nor there in the equation. He had revisited the land options documented in the file, incorporated the negative analysis of the Crawford property he had originally left out, and dialed Robert Johnson's office.

"Mr. Johnson, please. This is John Henning of Carriage Brokers calling."

"I'm sorry, Mr. Henning," she replied, "Mr. Johnson is in a meeting. Would you like to leave a message?"

"Uh...yes. Please. Could you have him call me? Or, better yet...it is extremely important that I see him regarding the Promenade project. Would there possibly be time on his calendar for me to meet with him sometime today?"

A brief pause...

"You're in luck, Mr. Henning," she replied. "Mr. Johnson did have a cancellation at two o'clock this afternoon. Does that work for you?"

"Perfectly. Thank you. I'll be there."

Suddenly, Ginny buzzed John's office. John jabbed at the speaker button.

"Please, Ginny," John said lightheartedly, "no more surprises today.

"Just one more, John," she replied. "Jessica is here to see you."

"No kidding, Ginny," he said flatly. "This doesn't surprise me at all. Make her wait five, then send her back."

What Gary told him earlier had given him still another reason to doubt his true feelings for Jessica. When his memory left him and everyone had seemed like total strangers, it was Jessica who seemed more distant than the rest. Now...it was Alexandra he couldn't get out of his mind...the attractive stranger who had entered his life in that intersection when life itself seemed to have temporarily abandoned him that piqued his interest. It was the girl wearing a uniform and a ball cap who had walked into room two-forty with that beautiful, yet timid and uncertain, smile. John knew at that moment that there was meaning to his existence. He saw her face every night when the lights went out. Remembering the past seemed to no longer be of any concern to him. Remembering lovely Alexandra is what seemed to matter most.

In those seconds after they drove into his neighborhood the day he was discharged from the hospital, John had total recall...past and present. And it was at that moment that Alexandra's words '...only to remember everyone but me...' flashed through his mind. He pulled the note from his wallet that he had written to himself that night and smiled. 'Remember beautiful Alexandra 980-5324!!!'

A feeling of warmth filled his senses. For a moment, the devious intentions Jessica displayed at Johnson's office, the meeting with Gary at Anderson's and even the file he had just reviewed didn't seem to set him off until, suddenly, Jessica came marching through the office door, interrupting his train of thought. Her decision to abruptly make the trip back to Phoenix hadn't allowed her the extra time she usually took to design her appearance to visually seduce any man at first sight. Instead, she appeared to be under pressure and in no way measured up to her usual flawless beauty. *She's looking a little worse for wear,* he thought.

* * *

Waiting to board her flight at McCarran Airport had given Jessica the chance to play several scenarios over and over in her head. *What would he want to hear, if anything, about my meeting with Robert Johnson? What should my response be to his questions? What would this do to our relationship?* The fact that she had had secret sex with a married man over the weekend wasn't as high on her list for damage control as the issue she was about to face. Explaining to John about her meeting with Robert Johnson wasn't going to be easy.

"Hi, baby!" she said, as she hurried around his desk and threw her arms around him. Her effort to plant a wet kiss on his lips was futile. John found the attempt aggravating. He wasn't taking what she was offering. He leaned back and held her at arm's length. Jessica knew at that point that his buddy, Gary, had already gotten to him. "I can tell that you're upset, baby," she said. "But I can explain everything."

"What's to explain, Jessica, that I don't already know?" he replied acidly. "I'm short of memory for what...maybe three weeks? Your father decides to seize an opportunity to steal my biggest client and, once again...he has you doing the dirty work."

"It wasn't that way, John," she replied, as her eyes began beading tears she conveniently manufactured to get him to ease back a little. She pushed his briefcase aside and positioned herself on the corner of his desk. "Didn't Gary tell you that my father had no interest in the project other than to offer up a great piece of property at a reasonable price?"

"Gary told me everything, Jessica," John responded with narrowed eyes, "including the cozy little departure that took place after your meeting with Johnson."

"Gary's full of shit!" she shot back as she moved off his desk. "The meeting was professional and above board. I even acknowledged to Robert that you and I were engaged to be married, and I had not had a chance to discuss the land with you because of your condition."

"It's Robert now instead of Mr. Johnson?"

Jessica scoffed. "Now you are really reaching."

"Did you tell all of this to Gary at your pub meeting?" John asked, leaning back and folding his arms defensively.

"Gary? ... Gary wasn't interested in hearing anything," Jessica said, rolling her eyes. "He had already made up his mind that I was fucking Robert Johnson as soon as he saw me there. Why would you believe him instead of me anyway?"

After a tense moment, John sat straight up, reached for the Compton file, opened it, and pointed to the study he had already completed on the Crawford's property. "The land doesn't meet the full requirements outlined in the prospectus," he explained, "and...to be more specific, it's the position of the land in relation to the view of downtown Phoenix that caused me to reject it from the beginning. There is too much obstruction of the view of Camelback Mountain. So I dismissed this property along with others that were in consideration. That's what I'm going to tell Robert this afternoon."

"I didn't know you had already considered my father's property until Gary informed me of that fact. That was after I met with Robert Johnson. So how could you think I was doing an end-around?"

"You know, Jessica," John said coldly, "right now, I'm having trouble thinking about anything good that involves *us*. You're not the same person I said I wanted to marry a year ago; and to tell you the truth, I don't think I'm the same person I was before the accident."

"Please, John," she replied, "you're talking crazy. Nothing's changed, baby. You're you and I'm me, and we're getting married," she went on, leaning in to put her arms around him again. "Isn't that right?"

"I can't think about this now, Jessica," he said, gently shoving her aside as he rose from the chair. "I want you to go now. Like I said, I'm meeting Bob Johnson at two and I need to figure out the best way to undo what you did, so please...go."

Jessica backed away, sulking on the outside and totally pissed on the inside about John's attitude towards her. Jessica wondered why this was really happening. *Why is he doing this? Something else is going on here... something strange,* she thought. She looked around the office at nothing in particular. She tried to think of what to say next that wouldn't set him off or make him more defensive than he was. She looked towards him only to see his eyes, cold and deliberate, staring back at her. She felt he was saying 'it's over' without verbalizing it. It was all happening too fast, she concluded. He knew nothing about what happened in Vegas. The thing with Robert Johnson she'd already explained fairly well.

"What is it, John?" she said, moving towards him, swiping at the little eye liner she had left that had not run down her face. "I won't leave like this. I can't leave thinking you might tell me at any moment that it's over between us."

"Jessica," he said, without hesitation, "it's not going to work so let's not pretend it will. You can keep the ring...I don't want it back."

"But I love you, John."

"Perhaps you do, but I've realized that I don't love *you*, Jessica, and it's taken almost getting killed for me to realize it. Things are different now. I was lucky to get a second chance at life, and it's important I don't screw it up this time. I thought about this all day yesterday, and my sixth sense tells me I'm right. It's better to break it off now instead of waiting until it's too late. It's over, Jessica."

Jessica could see the seriousness of his words etched on his face and they cut deep into her ego. She felt her father's presence even though he wasn't there, urging her to tell him to fuck off. She felt pressure building at her temples...memories of her father's neglect when she was a child...the years of watching and listening to her father torment and blame her mother for their son's disappearance...the illusion of seeing herself in the princess costume she had wanted so badly...and the knowledge that she was the one who had distracted her mother for that one second when her baby brother vanished...all of these thoughts were playing tricks on her mind.

John sensed that Jessica had been transported to a place he could not comprehend. She was standing directly in front of him, staring at him as if she were staring into a mirror, with a look of terror in her eyes...as if she were seeing horrible things.

She blinked herself back to reality and looked at John through eyes of despair. Her anger built to a boiling point. *At this point, it doesn't matter what I say,* she thought. There were no more words that could possibly change things, she concluded. She removed the ring from her finger and tossed it on his desk.

"If this is what you want, then this is what you'll get!" she said hysterically. "I'm sure you'll regret this after you think about it. If you change your mind and call me later with an apology...don't be surprised if my response is...it's too fucking late!"

She spun on her heels, opened the door, and slammed it behind her as she left.

Gary spotted Jessica stomping down the hall towards the exit. He assumed things got heated and hurried to John's office. He turned the knob, peaked in cautiously and spotted John standing with his back to the door, staring out the window.

"It seems as though Jessica's not having a good day?"

"Your assumption is right, my friend," John replied, turning around and snatching up the ring from the desk top only to juggle it in one hand in front of Gary.

"It's over, Gary. And...you know what? I feel good about it."

Gary repositioned the chair in front of John's desk and sat down. "Listen, buddy. Think of me as your consigliore. It would have happened sooner or later. I've seen the frustration you've been going through for quite some time. I assume you let her have it hard about meddling in your business over at Compton Investments...was that the straw?"

"Just everything," John replied softly, "just everything."

He slipped the ring into his shirt pocket, leaned back in his chair and put his hands firmly behind his head.

"Well...OK then," Gary said grinning, "So...how's the first day back going for you?"

"Very funny, ole friend," John replied as he leaned forward and flipped him a subtle middle finger. "Now get out of here and let me get to work fixing all the screw-ups you created while I was out there visiting some other galaxy."

Gary rose from the chair, turned to open the door, and looked back. "You were probably in a better place, buddy. Floating around in some strange galaxy seems like fun." The door closed behind him.

John leaned back, stared at the ceiling and wondered if Gary was right...then immediately dismissed the notion when *Alexandra* popped into his mind. He thought about the note he wedged in his wallet where it was visible every time he opened it. He wanted very much to call her but doing the right thing held him back. After all, he thought, he had to allow space between himself and Jessica to make the breakup legitimate. *Besides, what makes me think she wants to hear from me*? he thought.

Chapter Fourteen

February 3rd

Tempe Town Lake

Pre-regatta preparation was just as important as the race itself. Preparing in advance of the race gives teams a much better chance of getting focused and developing an edge for race day. Meg Webster showed up right on time, which was already an improvement over Kristy with her frequent excuses for not showing up on time. Meg was new to the Phoenix area and Kristy's replacement. As luck would have it, Meg was looking to join a team that participated in competitive racing. Although she was of questionable height compared to Kristy, her five-foot-three frame, coupled with huge thighs, calves and arms, more than matched strength with anyone else on the team and made her a perfect fit. Her massive crop of black hair, held back from her forehead with a bright red bandana, made her look even more tough and masculine. Meg came from Orlando with a high-performance rowing resume. She rowed with one of the most competitive amateur teams in Florida.

They had practiced partial strokes, used at the start of a race, through the high-ten and power-ten-to-twenty. Susan was overwhelmed with the team's performance. After two laps of the lake, the team was astounded at Meg's amazing strength and stamina. It didn't take long for her to settle in unison with the rest of the girls. The team was complete again. Two hours later, after rowing at all levels of cadence, they squared the oars in the water and drifted to the dock.

"Waist...Ready...Up," commanded Susan, and the shell was lifted to their waist. "Shoulders...Ready...Up," she yelled again, and the shell was lifted to shoulder height.

They carried the boat to its resting place in the boathouse, where the old boat keeper logged it in, took his usual 'dirty ole man's' glimpse at the ladies in tight suits, then disappeared into his office.

"Alex," Susan said, as they walked together through the parking lot towards their cars parked next to each other. "Is it my imagination, or have you been avoiding me this past week?"

"Not sure I know what you're getting at, Susan," Alexandra replied curiously, "but no...what makes you feel that way?"

"I've left two messages on your phone over the last three days and haven't gotten one response."

"Oh...yeah ... I know. I'm sorry for that, Susan. I've been getting home late...you know...the job... unpredictable as hell. There has been so much shit going on lately that it's been exhausting. To be honest," she continued with a somber look on her face, "if my messages don't have the name John Henning attached to them, I seem to lose interest quickly."

"See...I knew you were avoiding me, Alex," Susan said stiff-arming her. "So...no call from the coma guy yet...is that it?"

"Ugh...just frustration, I guess. Anyway, why should I expect a call? By now, John has his memory back...and he's engaged to be married. It's just as I thought it would be. Besides, who am I in his life? We only spoke for a while and that's when he could hardly remember his *own* name. Why should I think he'd remember mine?"

"OK...Alex," Susan put in, taking Alexandra by the arm and stopping her in her tracks, "Once again, I'm compelled to give you some smart, sisterly advice. You know I'm incapable of small talk...so get ready for a reality check. You have two choices. Don't hang on to the hope that he'll call. This guy and his wife-to-be are probably talking to a wedding planner as we speak. So as hard as it may be, it's time to *move on, girl!* That's the best advice I can give and it would be smart for you to take it. Or...have your friend Tucker sneak the John guy's number for you from the hospital records and *you* call *him*."

"You know I can't do the latter. Why is it I never look forward to hearing your so-called sisterly advice?" Alexandra shot back. "It never seems to make me feel any better."

"Maybe it's because you know I love you and, more than that, you know I'm right," Susan said, as she climbed into her car, fired the engine and drove away.

Chapter Fifteen

Friday

February 9

They had just placed their order for dessert when Karl grabbed his left shoulder and squeezed hard. Laura knew exactly what was happening. John thought he knew, but wasn't sure because he wasn't there when his father had the other two heart attacks. Laura moved quickly to keep him upright as he started to slump over onto the table, unconscious.

"Call 911, John!" she yelled in a panic. "Your father's having a heart attack!"

John jumped to his feet, helped Laura steady Karl with one hand, yanked the cell phone from his pocket and, within seconds, was speaking to the 9-1-1 operator. "It's my father!" he bellowed over the din that Augie, the strolling accordion player, was making as he played Italian songs from table to table. "Brunetto's Ristorante in Scottsdale," he shouted, for the second time. "My father's having a heart attack! We need help NOW!"

Laura sobbed as Karl, slumped in the chair, was turning pale. He looked unconscious but they weren't sure. Suddenly, from the other side of the restaurant, a man in dress shorts and sandals came rushing up to them.

"I'm a doctor," he said, moving in. "Help me get him flat on the floor."

John moved his mother aside, into the arms of a helpful lady seated at the table next to them. They moved

Karl from the chair to the terrazzo-tiled floor so that he was lying flat on his back. The doctor moved quickly and efficiently, doing what he could under the circumstances. John and his mother stood by...now holding onto each other...waiting for confirmation from the doctor that Karl was still alive.

In very little time, the doctor administered the fundamental first-aid techniques required to stabilize Karl until emergency services could arrive. His hands and his trained ability to diagnose by observation were his only medical tools. He checked Karl's chest to see if it was rising and falling, put his ear close to Karl's face to determine if he was breathing, and then placed two of his fingers on one side of Karl's voice box.

"We still have a pulse," he said, looking up at them. He gently lifted Karl's legs and extended them to rest on the seat of a chair to get them elevated. He felt a pulse, but Karl wasn't breathing. The doctor searched inside Karl's mouth with his finger and found no obstruction to his windpipe. He immediately placed the palm of his hand flat on Karl's chest just over the lower part of his sternum and began a pumping motion with his other hand.

Tables and chairs got moved around and people shuffled to one side of the dining room, clearing a path for the emergency response unit as they arrived. Everybody seemed to move in fast-forward mode.

Alexandra didn't notice John standing next to his mother, who was weeping into a red napkin.

John wasn't aware that it was Alexandra as she moved in with two colleagues carrying a light-weight spine immobilization board and other equipment. It was only when she stood up from a crouching position after huddling with the doctor and the other two members of the rescue team around his father that John recognized her.

"Alexandra?" John said, surprised, as their eyes met.

Alexandra, shocked to see John standing there, lost concentration for a moment then reached for his arm. "Do you know this man, John," she said, switching back to response mode.

"It's...it's my father, Alexandra," he choked.

Alexandra turned to John's mother. She remembered the picture of Laura propped up on John's bedside table at the hospital...smiling as she stood next to his father in the snow outside their cabin in Munds Park.

While another member of the response team worked on Karl right alongside the doctor, Alexandra's mother flashed through her mind. She remembered how happy her mother looked in the photographs hanging on the wall in her house. She looked down at John's father lying there on the floor, then back at John, then back to his mother to see the horrified look on her face. The thought of John's mother having to live a life as lonely as her mother had lived for all those years after her father died left a sick feeling in her stomach.

John took Alexandra by the arm and drew her between him and his mother. "You saved *me*, Alexandra," he said, "now please...save my father. I know you can do this."

Alexandra froze. Her heart pounded as though she were in the final lap heading for the finish line at a Regatta. She couldn't find any easy, comforting words to say to him. After hearing what the doctor had just whispered to her, she had little hope that John's father would make it further than the ambulance waiting outside, let alone the hospital. One thing she knew for sure, however, was there was no time for emotions or feelings or doing what she really wanted to do at that moment...which was to wrap her arms around John, hold him close and never let go. Right now, she had to focus on saving his father's life and that required swift action on her part in order to have the best chance of getting him to the hospital alive.

***

John sped through the streets of Scottsdale, negotiating traffic to stay close to the ambulance for as long as he could. His mother sat next to him, weeping, and rocking anxiously back and forth in her seat. She was terrified that the outcome of this heart attack might prove to be different than the last.

"Try to relax, Mother," he said, rubbing her forearm with one hand while steering with the other. He couldn't help but think about what was happening inside the ambulance. *Was he alive? Was he dead? What was Alexandra doing?* These questions played out over and over in John's mind as the street seemed to narrow with traffic jamming up in front of him.

Things suddenly seemed psychedelic-like. Starbursts from street lights, storefront signs, and blinking lights on airplane wings overhead as they lined up to land at Sky Harbor airport became maddening distractions. John felt he was losing his grip on reality right then and there. He shook his head from side to side to clear his mind and then realized he was losing sight of the flashing lights on the ambulance.

Suddenly, his anxiety and uneasiness abated. The horrible, tense feeling that was consuming his thoughts drained away. He felt eerily calm. A warm peacefulness flowed through his body and mind. Just knowing that Alexandra was there, inside the ambulance with his father, gave him assurance that everything would be alright.

"Don't worry about Dad, Mother," John said. "The girl in that ambulance taking care of him is the same girl that saved my life. She will do everything she can to save him...I know that."

John and his mother hurried towards the emergency entrance. The ambulance was parked in front with its rear doors wide open. One member of the rescue team was re-positioning an empty gurney. As they rushed past, Laura's stomach tightened. She grabbed John's arm and squeezed hard. John spotted Alexandra talking to a tall man in a long white coat with a stethoscope hanging around his neck. They were discussing Karl's status. John and Laura rushed up to where they were standing.

"Oh...John," Alexandra said, managing a smile.

"How is my husband?" Laura broke in with a strained voice, wiping tears from her cheek.

Tucker politely nudged Alexandra to one side and stepped in front of them. "Mrs. Henning," he said, tucking his clipboard under his arm, "I'm Tucker Potts, the attending R&O Physician. Your husband is stable but in critical condition. We believe he has had a substantial heart attack." Laura's knees buckled. "Under the circumstances, however, your husband is very fortunate that there was a doctor at the restaurant who was able to perform all the right procedures to keep his heart functioning. And...you can thank Alexandra here," he continued, glancing at John, "who did a great job keeping him stable on the way to the hospital."

John's eyes shifted towards Alexandra, who was staring at him. Laura gripped John's arm even tighter than before.

"We are taking him to the cardiac unit for observation and tests. I've ordered a CT scan which will give us detailed images of his heart and arteries in a matter of seconds. We should know the extent of Mr. Henning's actual condition real soon."

"Karl has had those scans before," Laura said, "the last time this happened."

"How many heart attacks has Mr. Henning experienced?" Tucker asked, making notes.

"Two before this," she replied.

"So...I assume he has a personal cardiologist."

"Yes, Doctor Thomas."

"Ed Thomas? Yes...I know him. He is a very good doctor. He's a resident both here and at Banner in Tempe. We'll notify him promptly. Meanwhile, Mrs. Henning, I need you or your son to complete the necessary admittance paperwork."

***

On weekends, Scottsdale Memorial is usually in a heightened state of pandemonium. Besides John's father, there were hordes of sick people hoping for attention. The tired look on some of their faces begged for some administrative person to get to them. Patients already checked into the system were waiting to be called by medical staff or someone who could at least administer pain relief. One man had injured his hand and was bleeding. He had a white towel wrapped around the hand, which was turning more and more crimson by the minute. Another man was given morphine to relieve excruciating pain from a kidney stone he was trying to pass. The first-come, first-serve rule only pertained to heart attack victims and pregnant women with babies making their way through the birth canal.

"Tucker Potts to radiology...Tucker Potts to radiology."

As the loud speaker blurted out Tucker's name, Alexandra snatched up the vibrating, alpha-numeric pager from the belt on her hip.

"I'm sorry, John," she said, looking at him, wanting to ignore the inevitable call to another tragedy. "This is a crazy night."

She wanted desperately to stay with John and Laura, but she knew she had to leave. John could see the distress in her face but didn't know what to say.

"You may as well go, Alexandra," Tucker said firmly. "Someone else needs help, and you've done all you can here."

Alexandra took one long look at John, then turned to Laura. Fighting to smile, she said, "Mrs. Henning...your husband is in good hands. Everything will be fine...I'm sure of it."

Chapter Sixteen

Alexandra didn't get home until nine-forty-five in the evening. She laid back on the couch in the living room and watched as Chester balanced on his hind legs, wagged his tail and begged her to take the little rubber ball from his mouth and toss it to the other side of the room.

"Not now, little guy," she said, looking at his droopy eyes. *It's late,* she thought, letting out a sigh. "I'm too tired to play rollover and fetch, Chester."

She eyed the telephone on the stand next to her. She was tempted to call Tucker's cell phone for an update on John's father but decided against it for obvious reasons. She didn't feel right calling him when she knew how busy he was, and asking for status on John's father or any person she took to the hospital wouldn't be something she would do under normal circumstances. It would have been obvious to Tucker that her emotional connection to John was much more than that of concern she felt for the wellbeing of his father.

The events of the day had finally taken its toll. Alexandra closed her eyes and her thoughts took her back to when she was in middle school and the nights she had spent sleeping over with girlfriends. She remembered how her friends always seemed to complain about how demanding and over-protective their fathers were...and how she envied them. She thought about how caring her mother was...and the times she felt resentful of her friends for having both parents. Now, thinking back at how hard her mother had worked to play the role of both parents, it made her feel badly for thinking that way.

She wondered what would have happened if she had never held it all in…if she had complained to her mother about the void her father left in her life…if expressing her true feelings back then would have made her life easier now. She wondered if her mother could have maintained the level of strength needed for both of them if she had complained about her lot in life. *Am I paying the price?* "Damn!" she muttered in despair and covered her face with both hands. *If only it were someone else instead of me who had to do without. If only I had had a father figure to protect me and help me through life's crises. Maybe then, I wouldn't have these negative thoughts about who I am and where life is taking me.* Remembering the past was exhausting. *I'm a strong woman.* She didn't want to succumb to what the devil was trying to put in her mind…that her life was meaningless. Susan told her that self-pity was going to get the best of her unless she went for professional help. Just maybe, she supposed, Susan was right.

Chester finally pushed the ball away with his nose, leaped up on the couch and nestled next to her, upside down, exhaling loudly. Alexandra thought about leaving John at the hospital, worrying about his father, the condition he was in, and if he would survive the night. *Be realistic,* she thought, reaching to scratch Chester on his belly. *I had no place in John's life before, and I have no reason to expect that I should have a place now. His soon-to-be wife has probably heard the news about his father,* Alexandra supposed, *and would she be there to comfort him and his mother as his father struggled to survive?*

Now it was the girl in the picture…Jessica…that Alexandra envied…not her girlfriends in school or the fact that her father wasn't there for her growing up. These things didn't matter…it was this moment in time that possessed her. *The past is the past*, she thought.

She looked at the old Caledonia as it struck ten-thirty. She remembered how she felt earlier when she was standing next to John...as if she were the only one in his life...and her pager went off. She wanted so badly to shut it off...to ignore it and stay there with him...but she knew she couldn't. Instead, she was pulled away to another tragic scene where she tried to assist several people who had been wounded or killed in a drive-by shooting. A van full of hooligans left their neighborhood in South Phoenix on a death mission or some gang initiation...determined to find a group of innocent people, kids who had it better than they did, and launch a senseless attack.

The incident covered a three-mile radius starting at a Multi-Twenty-Four-Screen Theater in Scottsdale. Witnesses reported that shots rang out, hitting several of the movie-goers. Bystanders immediately called 911 and reported a license plate number and description of a van carrying four Hispanic males. It wasn't long after the report that two officers sitting in separate cars at a Sonic drive-in on their break got the call and spotted the vehicle speeding down the street, heading south on Hayden Road. Within minutes, the chase was on. The police cornered the van in an alleyway, where several shots were fired. The kid driving the van was shot in the head as the rest of the suspects ducked for cover on the floorboards like cowards. They were all apprehended without further incident.

Alexandra grabbed the remote control and turned on the news. As if on cue, a reporter was describing the whole event. Behind the yellow crime scene tape, she could see herself attending to the wounded at the theater. Given everything that happened that night, it was too painful for her to watch. She had had enough for one day and quickly turned it off. She reached for the lamp and switched *it* off. She laid back and stared into darkness.

Peace and quiet at last, she thought. Other than Chester's wheeze every now and then and the ticking of the old Caledonia, it was eerily quiet in the house.

She squeezed her eyes shut and began to deep-breathe. She learned this technique when she first started rowing in competition. It's the Pavlov Method of breathing that helps athletes increase focus and eliminate stress. She needed to do this. She needed to focus on things to feel good about...like John's father lying in the hospital with improving vital signs...like things once again returning to normal in *their* lives. If she repeated this over and over in her mind, she believed, it would come true.

* * *

Alexandra watched from a distance...too far away to do anything to help. No matter how hard she tried, she couldn't find a way to get to her father. The crowd, the cars, the fire and police trucks all blocked her way. It was like being held back with an invisible rope or binding that wouldn't let her move in any direction. *This can't be happening,* she thought. She needed to get to him...like the other times. He hung from the window, fire shooting out above him, and everyone was just standing there--watching, screaming.

Suddenly, the burning building disappeared and she was looking at the image of her mother lying in the hospital bed, hooked up to all the tubes and monitoring equipment. It filled the space all around her. A sensation struck her like the hand of an evangelical holy-man striking down the curse of the devil in the middle of a healing. Suddenly, everything changed again. Above her, a small beam of light flashed, then quickly became bright and radiant. Through the aura surrounding the light, a fog-like figure slowly materialized and started moving towards her.

Alexandra was no longer in the hospital room agonizing over her mother's failing body. She stood in a shadow of darkness watching her mother, surrounded by a misty light, slowly come to her. Her gown was white. It flowed and waved like a flag in a gentle breeze. She looked more beautiful and younger than ever. She held out her hand, beckoning Alexandra to take hold. In a heartbeat...in some cosmic time machine with no mechanical controls...they were streaking through time and space into a time-changing continuum that revealed Alexandra's life...past and present.

She re-experienced the night at the college football game when Anthony Rizzo tossed the football into the crowd, and the day she gave it back when he was hurt and in the hospital. She had the vivid recollection of time spent with her high-school friends at parties and sleepovers and the awful feeling of loneliness that engulfed her during what was supposed to be the most wonderful years of her life. She relived the horrific night John's Porsche was broad-sided and the compelling need she felt to get to him...save him. She remembered the way he looked at her...with his eyes cutting through her. She watched herself press her lips to his and blow her breath into his body.

Suddenly, it was back to that that life-changing event that had haunted her from her early childhood. She could see her father hanging there once more. The building was burning like a gigantic candle lighting up the night sky. The ladder man was shouting while the man and woman, clutching each other, stood in the safety of the bucket, watching. He was falling again. It was her duty to catch him. "Mother!" she yelled frantically, "help me catch my father. I can't do it by myself."

In the blink of an eye, everything changed. It seemed that the universe had come to a dead stop. Her father was now suspended, standing in a cloud of mist. He hovered above them with nothing around them in motion. There were no more flames shooting out of a building...just the image of it...no more panicky people screaming and yelling.

"There's no need for panic or for you to be afraid, my darling Alexandra," her mother whispered. "Your father is here with me, and we are happy and content. We are a part of you always. We are in your thoughts, in your feelings and in your being...we love you always."

Her mother let her hand go and slowly ascended to where Frank was waiting. Alexandra watched as they both vanished into the warmth of light and time.

***

Chester tugged on Alexandra's sleeve, startling her awake, just as the phone stopped ringing. She shot up to hear Tucker's voice coming through the speaker of the answering machine. "Alexandra, this is Tucker. Just thought you'd want to know...John's father passed away an hour ago. Talk at you later."

Alexandra felt her heart exploding in grief. The madness didn't stop with Chester waking her from yet another endless, ongoing dream. The peaceful night's sleep she was hoping for now didn't exist. She panicked as if she should be the one by John's side through this time of tragedy.

Chapter Seventeen

The obituary in the paper was a moving tribute to Karl Henning. It gave a brief abridgment of his life and went on to mention that he was survived by his wife, Laura, of thirty-six years and a son, John...his only child. There was a picture of a handsome, much younger Karl who resembled John in every way.

As Alexandra read through the article, it gave her a sense of closeness...a surreal feeling that the loss of John's father had somehow impacted her life in a personal, spiritual way. She could not fully understand why Karl's passing meant more to her than it should have. All she could think of was that whatever feelings John had brought into her life had created some sort of mysterious connection to his father as well. It seemed as though she was riding on a confusing, emotional roller coaster that wouldn't stop.

That night in room two-forty was a memory Alexandra couldn't erase. She couldn't make sense of the connection then... and why it was happening. She thought about him as she lay in bed at night, waiting for sleep to overtake her. She thought about him at work...even in the middle of a rescue. She thought about him while she was rowing with the team at the lake...he seemed to consume her thoughts.

Many times, Alexandra pondered the fact that she hardly knew him, thinking that rehashing that idea would change things...but it didn't. The fact that John was only one out of hundreds of accident victims she'd transported to hospitals compounded her confusion. "Why is it I can't stop thinking about this guy?" she said, looking at Chester, who was sprawled out on the kitchen floor with his tongue hanging out the side of his mouth, waiting for a morsel of Alexandra's breakfast.

Trying to rationalize the situation seemed to make things even worse. She shrugged her shoulders, took the toasted bagel with cream cheese off the plate next to her cup of coffee, and took another bite. *One thing for sure,* she thought, gazing out the window, smiling, *John is honest and sensitive and more handsome than any other man I've ever encountered, even with bandages around his head, and bruises on his face and tubes protruding everywhere.*

After tossing Chester a piece of her bagel, she laid the newspaper down and leaned over to rest her elbows on top of the kitchen counter. She planted her cheeks in the palms of her hands, gazing at nothing in particular. *How much more confusing will this get?* Her thoughts about John continued to vacillate.

Again, she thought about being at the intersection that night, the right place at the right time, blowing her breath into John when he needed it to survive. She remembered telling Bob Collins to make up a story to the police so that she could ride in the ambulance. She remembered how she was a basket case in front of Tucker, trying to explain what had happened to John when Tucker knew how calm she had always been when it came to doing her job. *Was that night, waiting at that intersection, anything other than just a coincidence? Before I left the hospital, were those extra few minutes I took wishing everyone on the rescue team Happy New Year again really shaping some supernatural force playing out what was meant to be?*

Stop it! I'm torturing myself with all of this, her mind reeled. *I keep creating all these questions in my mind, and I know that no one forced me to go to his room that night.* "I'm going to drive myself crazy if I don't stop doing this," she said out loud, glancing down at Chester again. Chester looked up, wagged his tail and whimpered as if he understood what she had just said or was thinking.

She looked at the article once more. 'Services to be held in Scottsdale at Green Acres Mortuary on Wednesday, February 14, at 1:00 pm.' A tear trickled down Alexandra's cheek as she stared at the picture of John's father once more. He looked so young and handsome in his white shirt and tie…nothing compared to what he looked like lying on the floor of the restaurant fighting for his life. *Oh, well,* she sighed, taking in a breath and peering at the sun slicing through the spaces between cedar-wood shutters. *I've got the day off. There will be no emergencies or trips to hospitals today.* She wished that she could contact John to express her condolences on one of the saddest events of his life, but had no idea how to reach him and if she did…would she really?

Thinking back to that night at the hospital, Alexandra could have taken John's number as he had taken hers…but she knew it would have been too presumptuous of her, considering the state of mind he was in. She couldn't, in good conscience, look at Jessica standing next to him in that picture propped up next to his bed and then ask for his phone number. She sat and watched Chester gnaw on a dingo bone for the longest time… thinking…then yanked the receiver off the phone base and dialed.

***

"Please, Susan," she pleaded, for the second time in two minutes. "Won't you do this one little favor and go with me? You can go to work later in the afternoon. I just can't do it alone. I don't even want him to see me there."

"You know how I hate funerals, Alex," Susan said, switching the phone to her other ear, rifling through her makeup bag. "Besides, Wednesday mornings are busy...and what would I tell my students?"

"A death will do. How about an emergency? Something like that should work," she went on. "Heck, Susan...I don't know...you can think up something, can't you? You're my best friend. Can't you see your friend is in need?"

"Oh...now I see. A guilt trip," Susan shot back. "Why should I feel guilty here? I mean...I feel bad when anybody dies but I don't even know your guy, John," she went on. "Wait a minute...what am I saying? He's not even your guy; he's engaged to someone else."

"I know...I know," Alexandra murmured, "And you're right...he's not my guy. But you don't understand what's going on here."

"Well...you're right there, Alex," she said, in an incredulous tone. "And how am I supposed to ever know what's going on in your head? You're always having one of those mystical out-of-body experiences...those dream-scapes of yours."

"Doubt if I'll have any more of those," Alexandra put in.

"Oh...and why is that?"

"I had one the other night...the night John's father had the heart attack in the restaurant."

"And...what happened?"

"This time, my mother was there with me...as my father was falling."

"Was she a better catch than you? Or did you...?"

"You know what, Susan...I think I'll hang up on you," Alexandra interrupted, coldly.

"Alright, Alex," Susan quickly cut in, "I'm sorry. It was insensitive of me to say that. Please, don't hang up. Just tell me what happened. I'll be good...promise."

"Why is it that you like making fun of me?"

"Come on, Alex...I said I was sorry and I meant it... so let's have it."

"Well..." Alexandra said, dropping her voice to a low tone. "There wasn't much to it. My father was hanging outside of the window, the fire was raging and people were screaming...just like all the other times. He started falling towards me, but this time, he stopped falling and was just there...hovering over me. That's when my mother told me not to worry anymore. She said they were together, happy. She told me not to worry...then I woke up. That's all there was to it."

"That's it then," Susan responded quickly. "Your mother is right. They are happy, they are together and you'll never have those dreams again. That's great...don't you think? Now, Alexandra, you can focus on being happy...and possibly even getting laid by someone at some point."

"Oh, I see...trying to be funny again, is that it? Just for that, Susan, you have to go to the funeral with me."

"I give," Susan replied reluctantly. "You drive."

Chapter Eighteen

The Funeral

The weather prognosticators had predicted a calm, sunny afternoon, but they got it wrong. It was overcast, with wind gusts up to 20 miles across the Valley. The bright white sky intensified the colors of the flowers in the gardens around the mortuary. Cars lined the pathway leading to the chapel. Alexandra and Susan purposely arrived late to avoid being seen in the initial receiving line. Alexandra signed her name in the family guest book then moved inconspicuously through the inner doors. There were no vacant spaces to sit in the pews, which left several mourners standing in the back of the chapel when the service began, including Alexandra and Susan. Alexandra stood up on the tips of her toes and managed to get a glimpse of John sitting in the front row with his mother on his left and someone she presumed to be Jessica on his right.

Karl and Laura had always approved of Jessica and had hoped that she and John would reconcile whatever differences they had, reestablish their engagement vows, and at some point, finally get married. They weren't aware of all the issues causing strife between the two of them but knew there was something bad going on. John took the blame for the breakup. Jessica had used John's mother to get John to reconsider his position and take her back. Shortly after the morning Jessica tossed the engagement ring on John's desk, she had invited Laura to have lunch and go shopping. After that, Laura begged

John to give in and invite Jessica to dinner with them the night John's father had the heart attack. John yielded to his mother's plea and invited her. Because old man Crawford intimidated Jessica into attending a dinner meeting with client's which he said was more important, she had no choice but to do as she was told, which didn't bother John at all.

The pastor stood at the pulpit, glanced over the congregation and began reading passages from the Bible. Since grief is the natural consequence of loss, it wasn't long before his words and the soft sounds of music from the organist had the mourners wiping their eyes with tissues and holding each other's hands. Even Susan had tears in her eyes. As the pastor finished the acclamation, John stepped to the pulpit to say things about his father that he'd rehearsed ever since his father had had his first heart attack. As he somberly read from the notes he had pulled from his coat pocket, he stood straight and strong and sent a comforting message that had everyone there sobbing even more. Susan glanced at Alexandra, who had tears rushing down her cheeks. She was very puzzled at the depth of Alexandra's emotions as she put an arm around her shoulder, leaned in and whispered, "This is one of the reasons I don't come to funerals…too emotional. Can we go now?"

Before John stepped down from the dais into the aisle, he glanced towards the back of the chapel and thought he saw Alexandra standing there. She noticed his glance and slid behind Susan. John blinked and she wasn't there anymore…*Alexandra?*.

"I think he spotted me, Susan," Alexandra said, whispering into Susan's ear.

"Are you sure?"

"I don't know. I think so."

John was now standing in the aisle with the woman who had been sitting next to him in the pew. They were embracing as the pastor leaned over to console John's mother, who was still sitting.

"Let's sneak out of here," Susan demanded and grabbed Alexandra's arm to rush her out and down the steps.

"No gravesite, Alexandra," Susan said forcefully, as they walked towards the car. "I really don't do well around those things. Besides, if you really don't want him to see you, now is the time to disappear."

It was an unusually quiet ride to Susan's house. Little was said between the two of them, and Susan chose her words carefully. She had to settle on words that wouldn't upset Alexandra any more than she apparently was. Susan figured that the sight of John with his wife-to-be in his arms had cut deep into Alexandra's already dubious emotional state of mind.

"Listen, Alex," she said, now deciding to make a point but in a sincere tone of voice. "It's not the end of the world, you know. It isn't fair to think that that woman has no right to him. After all...she's the one with the ring; she's the one who's spent the time with him; she's the one that..."

"Alright, alright...enough already," Alexandra interrupted. "If you're trying to make me feel better, it's not working. Let's just forget it ...OK?"

Chapter Nineteen

Saturday February 17

Tempe Town Lake

It was late morning and a perfect day for the locals to be cruising the lake in rented paddle and light-powered motor boats. There were several people standing on the shoreline holding or casting fishing poles, hoping to catch the big one. Other folks sat around picnic tables, drinking soda or coffee, eating donuts, reading or just talking as their kids played in the grassy areas.

John parked his new Porsche on the north shore, close to one of the boathouses. He remembered Alexandra telling him that, on most weekends, she would either be rowing with her girlfriend, Susan, or with the racing team preparing for a Regatta that would take place sometime soon in San Diego.

This was John's first time at the lake and he hadn't realized just how big it was. He'd driven by it several times on the 202 freeway while heading for the other side of town, but looking down at the lake from that point of view, it seemed half the size. When he walked over to where the water met the shoreline, a young boy was fighting to hold on to one end of his fishing pole while something big was fighting to get loose on the other end of the line. As John got closer, he could see the two-foot carp that had surfaced on its side with a hook in its mouth.

"Hey, mister!" the boy yelled, as he reached into the water and yanked the fish out. "Would you mind grabbing my camera...there...next to my bag? Could you take my picture holding up this bad boy?"

John found the boy's request amusing and picked up the camera that was lying on top of a cooler next to the boy's fishing gear. The boy removed the hook from the fish's mouth, steadied the fish with two hands, and lifted it up as if he were holding a trophy. John snapped one picture off and watched the boy gently lower the fish back into the water and release it.

"Thanks for the picture, mister," he said, smiling. "Now my brother will have to believe me when I tell him what I caught...I'll have proof."

John smiled and set the camera back down on the cooler. He scanned the lake towards the west...then back towards the east. He noticed two rowboats out in the middle of the lake heading west down the lake...one boat had two rowers and the other had four. *A pair of binoculars would come in handy right about now,* John thought. He strained his eyes to see if Alexandra was in one of the boats. They were too far out for him to recognize anybody. All he could do at that point was to wait until the boats got closer. The bigger boat with four rowers was outpacing the other and continued down the lake as the smaller boat started its turn towards the shore.

After several minutes, they reached the halfway point between the shore and the middle of the lake. John used his hand to shade the sun, but he still had trouble making them out as the rays bouncing off the water distorted his view. He felt a rush of adrenaline. Just the thought of Alexandra being in that boat excited him. *I hope I picked the right weekend.*

***

It seemed like forever since that night in the hospital when Alexandra sat next to his bed...talking and laughing. He remembered every detail about her...her beautifully-formed lips, the perfect shape of her mouth, and her soft, delicate hands. As John waited for the boat to get closer to shore, his mind wandered back to his father's funeral, how difficult it was and the emotional toll it had taken on his mother. His aunt and uncle had made the trip from Texas and, although having them in town helped with some of the uneasiness, Laura still needed John at her side most every waking moment. He remembered how much he thought about Alexandra during that time. Since the day they laid his father to rest, his thoughts had been vacillating from the finality of his father being gone to wonderful thoughts about the girl who had saved his life in that intersection on a dark, rainy New Year's.

Standing dockside as the sun beat down on the lake, John's thoughts turned to Jessica and how annoyed he had become at the way she had made it a point to visit the house at every opportunity after his father died. Somehow, that alone had made him want Alexandra all the more. He hated the way Jessica had led his mother to believe that she was there to help her, to grieve with her over the loss of his father; but John knew it was only a selfish ploy to get him back into her life...another manipulative, tactical trait he knew she'd learned from her father, Lawrence. For two days after his father's funeral, while Laura laid down to rest, Jessica would park herself next to John in the living room and start a discussion about how good they were for each other. After the first day, John had found it very difficult to listen and politely tuned her out. In his mind, Jessica's only motive for being there was to attempt to restart a relationship that was already over-- she knew it, but just didn't want to accept it.

The more she talked, the more often John's thoughts drifted back to the time at the hospital, laughing and sharing with Alexandra. Although he tried to be cordial to Jessica for the sake of his mother, he simply didn't want to be around her anymore. After a while, Jessica finally had to admit to herself that John's head was somewhere else as their conversations always seemed to be one-sided. She had no idea that another woman was completely consuming John's thoughts.

She blamed his attitude towards her and his silence when she tried to talk to him on the grief he was dealing with over his father's death, the difficult time his mother was going through, and the fact that all this was keeping him away from work...so soon after all the time he had missed following the accident. Jessica finally realized that her plan to manipulate their time together to get him back to the place they were before the accident wasn't working.

For his part, John wasn't at all comfortable with the way he was acting towards Jessica. As much as he wanted to distance himself from her, he knew the callous way he was dealing with her was not right and it offended his innate sense of fair play...but he just couldn't help it. Jessica was really starting to get on his nerves. He just wanted to tell her to stop coming over, but decided not to for the sake of his mother and the condition she was in. The timing wasn't right.

As John leaned against the railing, still waiting for the boat to get closer to the shore, he thought about how unsettling it had been to him when, while his mother was napping, Jessica had suggested that he spend the night at her place. It seemed like a last-ditch effort on her part to convince him that one night together, alone, would make things whole between them. To dispel his concerns about his mother being alone, she suggested that his aunt and uncle stay with her one night...'to comfort her,' as she put it. Now, thinking back, he realized how shallow her attempt was to get him alone for one night, away from his mother's house, where grief overshadowed every moment they were together...distracting him. She said it would do him good to get away, when all along her motive was to seize the opportunity to get him into her bed where she could more easily manipulate his emotions. She knew just where to touch him, where to kiss him and how to relieve his tensions.

Suddenly, two kids riding bikes, chasing after a young girl on roller blades, sped by--almost clipping him. It diverted his attention back to the rowboat still headed towards the dock.

Again, John's mind wandered back to the previous day. Jessica's demeanor had quickly changed when she couldn't convince him to go to her house. It was though she had turned into a different person, traits of her father. Her tone of voice changed from loving to cold and callous. The look on her face transformed her from a beautiful woman to something almost frightful, unrecognizable. She lashed out in a furious rage, crying and screaming profanities, not caring who heard her then snatched her bag from the table and stormed out of the house.

He thought about how he rushed out the door after her, stopping her just as she approached her car. He wanted to calm her down, to stay rational about their situation. He was afraid that, if she got on the road in the frame of mind she was in, she would hurt herself or someone else. He wanted to end their relationship once and for all with a modicum of cordiality...certainly not while she was in this horrible fit of rage.

Suddenly, within seconds, Jessica's attitude changed again. She became passive, quiet. He watched and thought how very bizarre it was that she could go from one extreme to the other in the blink of an eye. He knew her mood swings but had never seen them this anomalous. Her anger had suddenly drained away as if the minutes before had been erased from her memory bank. It was at that moment that John realized he no longer knew who Jessica was or who she was going to be from one moment to the next. It was then he decided to stop leaving hope out there regardless of her totally irrational behavior.

"I want us to stop seeing each other...for good," he said, locking eyes with her.

"You really want this?" she replied calmly.

"Yes, I do, Jessica."

"Well..." she said evenly, "this isn't what I want...but apparently...what I want doesn't matter anymore, now does it?"

"Jessica, why make this any harder than it is?"

"I won't plead with you, John," she said, forcing herself to wash the bitterness from her tongue, as she fumbled for her car keys.

"I wouldn't expect that from you, Jessica. It's me; it's not you."

"Is that supposed to make me feel better?"

"No," he put in. "I'm just saying...it's not you...and it's not your father, if you're thinking that. There's something else weighing on me that I haven't been able to put my finger on. Ever since the accident, I've been feeling different about a lot of things... including us. I can no longer keep the commitment to you that I made when I gave you the ring."

Sure...who's the other woman? As she stood there, listening to him trying to explain the unexplainable, she kept her composure. On one hand, she was fighting hard not to do what she said she wouldn't do...plead with him to change his mind. On the other hand, her brain was inflamed with loathing and rage.

No matter how much Jessica thought she loved him and, even though John had no idea of her unfaithfulness to him during that weak moment when Keith Cantor wined and dined her in Vegas, she wasn't going to beg. Pleading wasn't what she was made of and she wasn't going to start now. It was that part of her personality over which her father had the most influence. She opened the door to the Escalade, climbed in and started the engine.

"My mother really cares about you, Jessica," he said earnestly.

"Save it," she replied, staring hard. "Obviously, she cares much more than you do."

***

It was the next morning, after John woke up, sometime between coffee and a shower that he decided to drive to the lake in hopes of seeing the extraordinary girl who haunted his thoughts. He hoped that he had been on her mind as much as she was on his. He was certain that Alexandra being among the first responders at the restaurant the night his father died was no accident

A 737 overhead snapped John out of his reverie. His eyes focused on the boat again, and then he saw her – Alexandra. All the thoughts that had been bouncing around in his head vanished. As the boat reached the shoreline, Alexandra glanced over her shoulder to gauge how close they were to the dock. He stood on the concrete walkway, leaned on the railing, and watched as they feathered the oars in the water and then gently glided in. Alexandra was preoccupied with Susan setting the scull and didn't see John watching them.

They glided in parallel and then placed the port-side oars on top of the dock until the scull settled. Susan climbed out, stood on the dock and steadied the scull while Alexandra removed the oars from the oarlocks and handed them over...then it was her turn to climb out. They grabbed the scull and lifted it up as if it were made of balsawood. John watched, amazed at their skill and mastery of movement, as they made their way towards the boathouse carrying the scull upside down on their shoulders.

It was Alexandra's beauty and confidence that had initially struck him that night in the hospital when she stood next to his bed in the uniform of her profession…but now he saw her, tired and dripping with sweat, in another kind of uniform. The striking curves of her body moved gracefully as she walked single file behind Susan toward the boathouse. *Out of all the beautiful women in the world,* he thought, *this one has something special…truly special.*

Chapter Twenty

Encounter at the lake

As they exited the boathouse and headed back to the dock to retrieve the oars, Alexandra spotted John standing by the railing and stopped in her tracks. Susan didn't immediately realize that Alexandra wasn't keeping pace, and when she did, she glanced over her shoulder.

"Hey, Alex!" she yelled. "You don't expect me to carry four oars back to the boathouse by myself, do you?"

Susan didn't get a response. Alexandra just stood there, staring towards the railing.

"Hey…!" Susan yelled again, heading back to where Alexandra had stopped. "Remember me?"

"It's him, Susan," she said, keeping her eyes focused on John.

"Who?" Susan replied curiously.

"John," she replied, making a vague gesture. "Over there…next to the railing, by the light pole."

Susan glanced over to look for herself. "Well…don't just stand here like a statue…staring at him."

"What do I say to him?"

"It seems to me, since you didn't invite him here, that would mean *he* came here to find *you*. It might be good just to put on a bright smile and let him start the conversation. Now, march."

John moved in their direction instead of waiting. The anticipation of seeing her and talking to her again exhilarated him. *What if she isn't as excited as I am?* he thought, sardonically. *I should have brought something for her...maybe flowers. After all, she did save my life.*

Even though they were only yards apart, by the time they reached each other, it seemed to John that he walked the length of a football field. They stood at arm's length and silently stared into each other's eyes. Susan stood to the side, feeling totally invisible. It reminded her of a tragic, romantic movie she once saw starring Mel Gibson...in which he had been dead for years, came back to life, and reunited with his long-lost love. It was obvious that there was a silent dialogue going on between Alexandra and John. *This is making me uncomfortable,* she thought. Susan cleared her throat twice, as if to say 'enough already,' but couldn't break the trance they seemed to be in.

"Uh, since you two *obviously* know each other, I'm Susan, Alexandra's best friend," Susan said, forcefully. "Sorry to intrude."

"Nice to meet you, Susan," John said calmly, reaching out to shake her hand, but never taking his eyes off Alexandra.

Anytime there were guys anywhere near where Susan was standing, they would always migrate to her. In this case, however, it was painfully obvious that she was the outsider.

"OK, then," Susan said, after a moment's pause, "you two just stay here and do what you're doing. I'll get the oars back to the boathouse myself."

Alexandra quickly snapped back to reality and reached over to clutch Susan's arm as if to say 'Don't leave...I need you.'

"Wait, Susan, I'll help you get the oars."

"Can I help?" John smiled.

Susan and Alexandra glanced quickly at each other, turned back to him and, in unison, said, "No!"

"Please, John" Alexandra said, swallowing hard, her voice quivering slightly. "Please...wait here; we'll be right back."

John, finding the whole routine somewhat amusing, smiled at them, crossed his arms and nodded.

As Alexandra and Susan walked towards the dock, any questions in John's mind as to whether Alexandra was excited to see him quickly washed away. Without being too presumptuous, it was just the confirmation he needed...that she wanted him as much as he wanted her.

As they hurried down the ramp, Alexandra looked back at John just to convince herself that this wasn't one of her dreams and that he was actually here. Suddenly, she felt like she was coming out of her skin. She was shaking uncontrollably.

"Susan, for some reason...I can't stop shaking."

"Well, you better do something...act normal," Susan replied. "You're starting to remind me of a bank robber caught red-handed with marked money."

"I can't help it."

"Calm down, damn it, Alex," Susan warned. "You're losing it and acting like a silly, fucking school girl. The last thing you want to do right now is to appear silly. Settle down and play it cool, girl, or I'll toss you in the lake. How stupid would that make you look?"

"OK, I can do this," she replied, drawing in a deep breath, bending to lift up two oars, one in each hand. "My knees were getting wobbly standing back there with him. I *had* to get away or I would have collapsed. Do you think he noticed that I was turning into a basket case?"

"I don't think so, but he doesn't know you like I do," Susan said, as they walked back up the ramp with oars teetering at their sides. "Now, look, Alex," she went on, "We haul these oars back to the boathouse, give Simon another look, then we'll head straight back to John.

At that point, you let me do the talking. I'll tell him you rode with me this morning, which you did, then I'll say goodbye and he takes you home. How's that for spur-of-the-moment planning?"

"It sounds good to me. Do you think *he'll* go for it?"

"Trust me, Alex," Susan put in. "The way he was looking at you...I wouldn't be surprised if he asked you to marry him today."

"I told you he's engaged."

"Oh, I see," Susan mused. "Then he must have come here to invite you to his wedding."

"Funny."

John spotted the old boathouse keeper peeking out at Susan and Alexandra as they left the boathouse.

"I think the old guy in the boathouse likes you girls," John said with a smile.

"He does that with all the girls," Alexandra said. "I guess it's his way of getting his kicks."

"Better than herding sheep...I guess," Susan mused.

"Susan's a comedian, John," Alexandra said grinning. "Can you tell?"

Intentionally switching subjects, John said, "I watched you out on the lake and the way you two handled that boat...wow...I must say...I'm impressed."

"Maybe we can get *you* out on the lake sometime to try it," Susan said, looking squarely at him.

"Yeah, why not...I'm game."

"Why are you here, John?" Alexandra said softly.

He looked at Susan and then back to Alexandra. "The truth is," he said, "I haven't been able to get you out of my mind since that night you showed up in my hospital room."

A moment passed before Alexandra, drawing a deep breath, replied, "Well, I've got you beat. I haven't stopped thinking about you since I was with you in that mangled car of yours."

"I thought I spotted you in the back of the chapel at my father's funeral…was it you?"

"Yes, John, it was. It was very sad," she replied. "I'm very sorry. I really thought your father would make it once we got him to the hospital."

OK, guys, Susan thought, *time to initiate the plan.* She could see that act one was over and that was her cue to leave the two of them alone.

"OK…you know what?" Susan said, tossing her bag over her shoulder, "I really have to run. You know…places to go; people to see…" she went on, looking directly at John. "Alexandra rode to the lake in my car. Do you mind giving her a lift home?"

"Only if she'll let me," he said, turning towards Alexandra.

"Bank on it," Susan, yelled, back-stepping.

Chapter Twenty-One

"This Porsche looks much better than the one I first saw you in," Alexandra said, with a strained laugh.

"It's amazing how fast insurance companies work at settling when you are the victim. Not that there has been a final settlement, but at least they got me back on the road."

John pushed the start button and the 3.6 liter, 530 hp, flat-6 engine roared to life. "If you don't mind getting a little wind-blown, I'll put the top down."

Alexandra gave him an intent look, smiled and said, "Ah, yes. This is going to be excellent. Go for it." She took off her ball cap and tugged on the band that was holding her hair in a ponytail until it came loose. "As it is…you caught me at a time when I look my worst. This is pretty much what I look like crawling straight out of bed in the morning."

"Is that so, Alexandra?" John said with a grin, "If you look like you do now when you climb out of bed in the morning, count me in for a sleepover…but I'm not suggesting that should happen anytime soon, you understand."

"I see," she said evenly, blushing, searching for the proper response. *How's your mother holding up would be one thing to say,* Alexandra thought, then concluded introducing that subject could be a mood-changing discussion and she wanted to stay on point. "Sleepover? Wow…I haven't heard that term since high school. But thanks…that was a really nice compliment." *Should I ask about his girlfriend, Jessica? Nope, bad idea.* Weighing the possible consequences of both subjects, she opted for the one of compassion.

"How's your mother doing, John?"

"I'm afraid she'll be in mourning for a long time," John said, turning onto Scottsdale Road, "but thank you for asking. Once my father retired, you could hardly separate them. It's been very difficult for her since he's been gone."

"It was like that when my Mom died. Oh…turn right on Heritage. Sorry about that, John," she went on. "Anyway, I miss her very much. It does get easier even though we miss them dearly. It *will* get easier for your mother as well."

Alexandra waited for a response, but John was quiet. *I knew bringing this up was a bad idea,* she thought, fidgeting with her hands. She glanced over at John wondering, *what is he thinking about?*

John was pokerfaced, his eyes fixed on the road. The silence hung like a cloud between them. She wanted to kick herself for introducing such depressing thoughts so early on into the conversation that had the potential to lead into some interesting prospects. *I've got to reverse what I did,* she thought. Although his feelings about his mother were important, that conversation should have taken place some other time, she concluded.

"John," she said, turning to him, "I'm sorry for bringing up your mother and her grief…but I really did want to know how she was doing. I'm sorry I made you uncomfortable. Bad timing."

"There will never be a good time, Alexandra," he interrupted as he reached across for her slim hand. "Please…don't apologize. One thing is for sure," he went on, drawing a deep breath, "there isn't anything we could talk about today that could even remotely change how wonderful this morning and this moment have been for me. I'm just grateful that you were at the lake today."

"Me, too," she replied, clutching his hand as if she never wanted to let go. She felt something happening inside her body. His hand was firm and warm and hers quivered just enough that only she could feel it. She took in a deep breath as the wind blew past her face and through her hair. He pressed down on the accelerator and sped around the car in front of them. She hadn't felt this excited, this engaged, in a very long time.

John was very familiar with McCormick Parkway and the picturesque condominium village he was driving into. He'd played golf several times with clients on both the Palm and the Pine courses surrounding it.

"My street is just a few blocks down on the right."

"Nice development," John said.

"Thanks...I bought in here after my mother died."

"It's funny," John said, "my house is not far from here...just off Lincoln."

"Well...what do you know," Alexandra grinned. "You mean we've been neighbors all along?"

"Yeah," he mused. "With only a few thousand homes and a golf course keeping us from finding each other...ironic, isn't it?"

"Is that what has happened here, John?" Alexandra said in a gentle tone, her eyes fixed on him. "We found each other?"

"I'm not sure," he replied, as they passed through the security gate. "It does sound like a cliché from a movie, but I don't know how else to describe it...how would you describe it, Alexandra?"

The question was straightforward but yet, to Alexandra, an answer seemed out of the realm of possibility... she could no more describe what was happening than she could change the universe. When Alexandra didn't respond to his rhetorical question, John quickly thought that he had crossed over some emotional line that had made Alexandra uncomfortable.

She sat quietly in her seat contemplating what to say next, worried about taking their conversation down another bad road. She wanted to ask what had happened to his relationship with Jessica, the woman he was engaged to marry. She wanted to know what would compel him to come looking for a girl that he really didn't know much about...a girl he'd encountered only briefly in a mangled car and in a hospital room for a few hours. She knew that, because of the accident and his state-of-mind, he might be confused about almost anything that was happening to him at this point.

When they coasted into Alexandra's driveway, John's thoughts were focused only on Alexandra, oblivious to anything else. He had no inkling that, ever since they left the lake, they were being followed by a light-colored Escalade that had now pulled over and stopped at the side of the road down the street from Alexandra's condo.

John activated the convertible top and it closed over them. Alexandra, lost in her own private thoughts, needed time to gather herself. John wondered if her silence meant that she was thinking that things were happening too fast. He wondered if he was being too presumptuous in his eagerness to pursue their relationship. He searched for words that wouldn't drive her further away...words that would bring them back to the place they were just twenty minutes earlier back there on the lake when they looked at each other as if they were alone in time. Alexandra could no longer stay silent. There was *that* question that had to be asked, here and now, before things went too far.

"John," she said, swallowing hard, "What is it that really made you come to the lake...? Why...?"

Before she could say another word, he reached over with his hand, covered her mouth and leaned in close to her. Caught off guard, she realized she'd been rambling on aimlessly, without giving him a chance to respond to any of her questions.

"I don't know, Alexandra," he said slowly. "I just don't know."

At that point, John tossed aside his thoughts, placed his hand on the side of her face, caressed her soft cheek and gazed into her eyes. "Right now, Alexandra, all I know is that I've never felt quite this way before."

The night of John's accident flashed through Alexandra's mind…that moment when John opened his eyes and looked at her with that empty, blank stare. This was oh-so-different. He was looking at her with warm, loving intentions. She let her eyes close when he pressed his lips to hers. Their mouths opened just enough to allow the warmth from the inside to pass through each other. As they French-kissed, he felt her body fall limp and her back become rigid. She gave in to him with all her sensual emotions.

There were no more doubts about why they were together. Her deep breath breathing took in his fresh, provocative scent which acted like an aphrodisiac… stimulating her fragile senses. She didn't want him to stop...she wanted his hands...his body...to dominate every inch of her. John began to pull back, but she wouldn't allow it. She grabbed his shirt and pulled him closer. The small compartment of the Porsche was cramped and prohibitive, but it didn't matter. His hand slipped down the curve of her hip, making her feel as if she were on fire beneath the insulated rowing suit. She wanted to tear it off and be free of any obstacles preventing him from taking her.

She grabbed a handful of his pants at the thigh and tugged. Suddenly, an untimely, annoying, beeping noise emanated from her bag. *Damn that pager!* Reluctantly, she freed herself from John's grasp, shifted in her seat, brushed a hand through her hair and scooped up her bag from the back.

"Horrible timing" he said, as he leaned back in the seat taking in a deep breath himself.

"This means trouble," she said, breathing hard. She snatched the pager from the bag, glanced at the screen and gave John a look of utter dismay. Then she reached back into the bag and grabbed her cell phone. The programmed speed dial connected her with the last person she really wanted to talk to.

"Alexandra…?"

"Bob?" she said back.

"Need you."

"Not today," she replied. "My weekend off…remember?"

"Denise called in."

"And why would this be my problem?" she shot back. "I'm…I'm busy."

"So are we, Alexandra, *you* know how it is on the weekends."

Alexandra pressed the phone against her chest, looked at John with a huge frown, and shrugged her shoulders. John knew what was coming next.

"OK…I'll be there in forty-five," she barked as she pressed 'end' and tossed the phone back into the bag.

"It's what I do, John," she managed, apologetically.

"Listen. You don't have to convince me how important your job is, Alexandra," he said evenly. "If you hadn't been there when *I* needed you, I might not be here today. We'll have plenty of time together later," he added, grinning, then put his business card in her hand. "How about tonight…like after you get off? My cell phone number is on the card. Just call me."

"I'll call on my way home," she promised, leaning in, putting her hands on his face, studying him with those beautiful sultry eyes. "John," she went on, "tell me I'm not dreaming…that you're really here with me."

Without hesitating, John drew her back to him. He gave her a long, slow, wet kiss…then he took hold of her hand and said, "Alexandra…this is as real as I had hoped it would be when I awoke this morning. We *are* here, finally…together."

He quickly kissed her again…then slid out of his seat, walked around to her side and opened the car door.

"You know, John," she mused, as she looked up at him and stepped out, "I can't *remember* the last time someone other than a valet or my high school prom date opened a car door for me."

"I'm starting to really enjoy your sense of humor," he smiled. He reached for her hand as she stepped out of the car, rose slightly on her toes and kissed him.

"Then I'll see you tonight." Alexandra said, tossing her bag over her shoulder, walking vigorously while backing up the walkway staring him down.

***

Jessica squeezed the steering wheel until the blood drained from her hands. It was all she could do to control her emotions as she watched the events unfold between John and Alexandra. Her skin crawled and her blood boiled. *So this is what it's all about,* she thought, *'something else weighing on his mind that he can't put his finger on'… my ass,* she concluded, peering through her sunglasses as she watched John get back in his car and drive away.

Chapter Twenty-Two

Barcelona's restaurant in Scottsdale was wall-to-wall people and, as usual, the guys outnumbered the gals. Alexandra spotted Susan sitting at a corner table and inched her way through the hoard of young vultures searching for fresh meat. Alexandra had told Susan that John was going to hook up with them but hadn't mentioned that he was bringing a friend.

It was early afternoon by the time Alexandra reached John to set a time for them to meet later that evening. During that conversation, which lasted until Alexandra got called away to another emergency, she mentioned that her friend Susan wasn't seeing anyone at the moment. John suggested that she bring Susan along with her, he would bring Gary with him and they would make it a double date.

There was no doubt in John's mind that when he gave Gary a detailed description of Susan, especially the top half of her anatomy, he would jump at the chance to meet her. Alexandra, on the other hand, knew Susan wouldn't go for it; she despised blind dates. Every time she went on one, the guy always ended up being some creep wanting only one thing or some guy who just came out of a relationship that the girl couldn't wait to end. Alexandra made John promise that Susan would never know that Alexandra had anything to do with Gary being there. There had to be a plan and they devised one. Susan would simply be told, by John, when they showed up that Gary had been working late with John and tagged along... simple enough.

When Alexandra told Susan she was meeting John that evening for drinks and needed her friend with her as moral support Susan didn't hesitate and agreed to go...she loved Barcelona's. Also, she was secretly curious about John and what he might be up to. It didn't make Alexandra feel very good... the veiled lie, leaving Gary out of the equation. It gave Alexandra a guilt complex only because they had never lied to each other, not even a little white one. She told Susan to meet her at seven-fifteen, knowing John and Gary wouldn't be there until fifteen minutes later. As it turned out, Alexandra altered the plan. Her conscience got the best of her when she met Susan at Barcelona's and she spilled the truth, to some degree. *Take some lumps now instead of later*, Alexandra thought.

"It's not a blind date," Alexandra insisted. *A little white lie never hurt anyone.* "It just happened to work out this way. It turns out that they were together most of the day, so John invited him. I knew that if I told you earlier, you might blow me off and not come. So here we are."

"Oh, no...*you're* here...*I'm* out of here," Susan replied and slid out of her chair.

"Well, looks like you're stuck." Alexandra grinned, making a gesture toward the door. "Here they come now."

As Susan turned to look, Alexandra grabbed her arm and pulled her back down into the chair. "Will you just relax? It's not that you're on a date or anything like that. Your weren't doing anything tonight, anyway. Besides," she said flatly, "after a few drinks, who knows, maybe your perspective might change."

"I seriously doubt it," Susan scoffed.

John pointed them out as they weaved their way to the high table near the corner with four stools where the two ladies sat, watching them . The closer they got, the more Gary was happy that he agreed to go.

"OK...This is good!" he nudged the side of John's arm. "I see the one that's mine. Your description fits her to a tee," Gary said loudly, with a big wide smile across his face.

John grabbed Gary by the arm to slow him down. "We're just having drinks, remember?" he said, speaking in a low tone next to Gary's ear.

When they reached the table, John leaned over, kissed Alexandra on the cheek and grabbed the chair next to her. Gary stood there, staring...totally captivated by Susan's looks.

"You can join us if you wish," John mused, snapping Gary out of his temporary trance.

Gary smiled as he took the chair next to Susan, somewhat embarrassed by what might have seemed like child-like behavior, hoping Susan hadn't noticed him staring and drooling.

"Gary...Susan...Susan...Gary," John said quickly, leaning in towards the middle of the table as if their meeting had only secondary value. He sat back on the stool and turned to Alexandra.

"John..." Alexandra said, nodding in Gary's direction.

"Oh...yeah...sorry about that. My mind was preoccupied. Gary...this is Alexandra!"

"Really nice to meet you, Gary!" Alexandra said with a smile, raising her voice to be heard over the noise generated by the crowd of voices and music. "John has said some nice things about you."

"That's kind of him. I will accept his compliments...*even though he acted as if I weren't here a moment ago*! he thought, glancing at John. "It's wonderful to meet you as well, Alexandra."

***

As the evening progressed, Gary was making points with Susan, but John and Alexandra weren't keeping score. They were caught up in a world of their own and hardly noticed they were there. The more John found out about Alexandra, the more he was convinced that his decision to break off with Jessica was the right thing to do. Their conversation mostly centered on Alexandra... her life, her job and her family. Their discussions gave light to obvious commonalities between them. The more they talked, the more John realized that their lives ran in parallel. Her life wasn't much different than his. She had no brothers or sisters. He had no brothers or sisters. She was without parents...he only had one left. She was dedicated to her line of work and so was he. The similarities were striking.

As they began to probe deeper into each other's psyche on a more personal level, Alexandra was puzzled as to why John didn't bring Jessica into their conversation. She wanted to ask, but figured he would speak about it in his own time...when *he* was ready. Earlier, Alexandra almost broached the subject outside her house, parked in the driveway. Things at that point were heating up, however, and it would have been awkward to bring up a wife-to-be at that point. But now, thinking back, she wished she had gone ahead and asked, even though John may not have been ready to discuss it.

By the time ten o'clock rolled around, the crowd had died down a bit. They were sitting around a table of empty drink glasses, laughing and having a good time. However, in spite of the camaraderie, the issue of Jessica and John's relationship with her, weighed so heavily on Alexandra's mind that she became totally distracted. As John, Gary and Susan talked laughed, Alexandra felt as though she were circling above, watching and listening to them getting acquainted. She was sitting at the same table, maintaining the appearance of being an interested part of the group; but deep inside, she was obsessed with the need to ask that unanswered question. The uncertainty of it made Alexandra very uncomfortable, and she was struggling to hide it.

Susan was right, she thought, as she recalled her earlier phone conversation with Susan. It was after she asked Susan to meet at Barcelona's that Susan asked her if John had ever mentioned Jessica while they were driving home from the lake. Alexandra remembered Susan's words just before they hung up. 'How do you know he isn't playing two ends against the middle?'

By eleven o'clock, John was ready to leave...to be with Alexandra in a more quiet setting. Gary and Susan were oblivious to their surroundings, still laughing and making jokes about real estate transactions and workout routines with overweight ladies dissatisfied over not losing forty pounds after working out for only a week. John was sure that if he and Alexandra suddenly left, it would hardly be noticed.

"I'm ready to leave," John said, whispering close to Alexandra's ear. "What do you think?"

"I'm ready if *you* are," she replied. "What about those two?"

"My guess is," he replied, glancing over at Gary and Susan..."at this point, I don't think what we do matters. They'll end up finding their own way."

"I brought my car," she said. "Susan met me here."

"Good," he said, tossing money on the table. "I rode with Gary...works out perfect for *us*."

They both slid off their seats. John broke into their conversation. "Hey, guys...we are leaving. Alexandra is going to give me a lift home and, whatever you do... don't follow us."

Gary looked at Susan and grinned, Susan looked at Alexandra...and they all seemed good with it.

"Now I'm beginning to enjoy *your* sense of humor," Alexandra mused with a smile as they walked towards the exit.

***

After a long four-hour wait, with the evidence of five cigarette butts lying in the street just below the car window, Jessica's persistence paid off. She watched as John and Alexandra walked out of the restaurant arm-in-arm and into the parking lot to a car that wasn't John's. Jessica had parked her Escalade in the shadows of a ficus tree growing next to the building. She managed to contain her wrath, but it took all the self-control she could muster to remain in her car and watch them leave together. What she wanted to do was get a tire iron, walk up the car and smash the windows with them sitting inside.

This is the final straw, she thought. *That's the same Betty he was with this morning. It was an outright lie,* she concluded. *That story about the accident, and the fact that he needed time to evaluate things...bullshit! All along, it was because of this other woman horning in. When did this start?* She beat herself up with the question. *I might have known it was her... the chick in the stupid-looking wet suit who had climbed into his car at the lake. She was the one who had made him violate my trust...she'll pay... somehow...she'll pay.*

Watching them leave together triggered the thought of what happened in Las Vegas when she drank too much wine and swallowed the business bullshit handed to her by that asshole, Keith, while he seduced her. She realized the feelings of guilt she had felt at that indiscretion were now feelings of justification...pay back for John's own obvious indiscretions.

She sat in her car, staring into the night lights, stunned by the events that were causing her life to crash down around her. A million questions cascaded through her mind. *How long had he been seeing her? When he made love to me, was he really taking advantage of our sexual relationship? Was he thinking of her when he was screwing me? Was he thinking he could make love to this other girl and, when it was convenient for him, break it off with me?*

Suddenly, she thought of her father and his infidelities with his secretary, Millie, before her mother killed herself. *Am I really like him?* she thought. *Ruthless and uncaring?* She thought about the pressure her father put on her to be callous...to succeed in business and look at life the way he does. She closed her eyes only to see images of her father sitting next to her at night on her bed, touching her. Horrible thoughts of him bathing her, still touching her in private places at the age when she was still playing dolls. She thought about the terrible things he said about John and the way he pressured her to steal him away from Carriage Brokers for his own selfish motivations.

She glanced up to see Gary walking out of the restaurant with a girl she'd never seen before. *If I had a gun, I'd shoot that bastard*, she thought. By this time, the extreme anxiety coupled with uncontrollable anger caused the hairs on her neck and on her arms to stand straight up. She could hardly restrain herself from charging like a cat in the wild after its prey. She hated him and believed that he was a nothing but a damned trouble maker who planted doubts about her in John's mind.

***

Later, at Alexandra's house, Chester lay patiently on the floor outside the bedroom door. Alexandra had shut it purposely to keep him from settling into his usual spot on her bed. She stepped out of the shower, turned and backed into the towel John was holding for her. He wrapped the towel around her clean, beautifully-curved body and drew her backside to him. The soft lighting overhead gave her hair a glowing, radiant appearance in the slightly-steamed mirror. With eyes half shut, she watched him and felt his warm breath caress her neck and ears until her body quivered. He turned her around and she let the towel fall to the floor. She moved close enough so that he could feel her firm breasts and hard nipples press up against his chest. He leaned in and she felt his thighs press hard against hers. This time there would be no pager or cell phone to keep him from taking her.

John carried her across the threshold of the bathroom door and laid her down on the pillow-top mattress. He moved gently over the top of her body. She moved her hands up his muscular biceps to his shoulders and pulled him down to her. Their lips came together as he slipped his hand underneath the small of her back and brought her closer. She felt his passion begin to strengthen and get hard as her body jerked…then became rigid, motionless. She breathed intensely, and gazed into his eyes as if she was waiting for him to say or do something other than take her. He looked into her eyes, wondering if he had done something wrong. *Have I been too aggressive…too premature?* he thought.

"Do you have a condom?" she whispered.

The question caught him by surprise, and he had an urge to delay a response. There was an uncomfortable silence that he couldn't help, and he knew he had a confused look on his face.

"A condom…do you have a condom?" she repeated.

"Don't you take the pill?" he replied, looking down at her.

"I hate pills," she said, her voice hesitant.

"Shit...I'm sorry, Alexandra," he said, reluctantly. "Bad planning on my part."

"Don't apologize, John. I'm glad you didn't plan for this to happen," she went on, lifting herself up to kiss his lips. "It means much more to me that it wasn't planned."

There was a moment of silence. "It...it would have been great, you know," he said dangerously, locked on her eyes.

"It still could be, John, " she replied...then nudged him over and onto his back and rested the side of her head on his hard, undulated stomach.

As her warm tongue passed the creases of his abdominal muscles, it gave new life to that which had been interrupted when she asked if he had a condom. Her mouth closed around him. He reached down to her shoulders and then to the back of her head and touched her soft-as-cashmere hair, lifting it in fistfuls then releasing.

Inside, her body ached for more. He maneuvered his body into position to give her the same pleasure he was getting and that she deserved. Her warm thighs pressed hard against his shoulders each time she felt the warmth of his mouth consume her until she couldn't keep the passion inside her from exploding.

***

As the morning sun began to shine through the bedroom window, John opened his eyes to look into the closed eyes of one of the most beautiful women he'd ever known. *I could do this for the rest of my life,* he thought, even though the sudden feelings for her seemed mysterious. He had always believed that falling in love was a process...something that more or less evolved over time.

He softly kissed her cheek, lifted slightly and gazed at her beautifully-tanned, smooth complexion, void of makeup or anything artificial. *From out of nowhere, you came into my life and changed it forever.*

***

Chester scratched on the bedroom door. John grabbed a towel, opened the door, and then watched him scamper past him to make a mad leap up and onto the bed. As he snuggled his wet nose under her arm, Alexandra's eyes opened. She noticed John standing there, looking down at her, smiling. She took in a deep breath.

"I liked it much better when you were in here with me," she grinned.

"Chester will have to do for now, Alexandra," he smiled. "You're not the only one that has to work weekends. I have a proposal that has to be finished Monday morning. I'm afraid it's off to the office for me."

Chapter Twenty-Three

Crawford Investments Corporate Office

Monday morning

"I'm here to see my father," Jessica said, prancing through the lobby.

"I'm afraid your father is busy, Jessica," Millie replied, "and he asked that he not be disturbed until eight."

"Well..." Jessica replied, tossing her a frosty look, "for your information...he's the one who woke me up at six this morning, and he's the one who wanted me to rush here at this ungodly hour...so...if you don't mind, Millie. Just tell him I'm here."

Millie Jones had worked for Crawford Investments ever since the doors opened, back when it was located in a small industrial park on the east side of Indian School Road and Hayden. At fifty-five years old, her tall, thin frame never displayed any carelessness of image. As the vanguard for Crawford Investments' clients, or anyone else of stature who entered the building, Millie always managed to appear elegant, stunning and professional. She had a style that only experience and maturity could bestow. She met Lawrence's every expectation... what he'd always demanded from her.

The tiny lines on her face and the diminutive wrinkles above her upper lip, brought on by smoking, did little to distract from her youthful appearance. From the silver shine of her hair to her buffed fingernails, she looked better than most women in their fifties. Although Millie projected a sweet, natural appearance of congeniality and beauty on the outside, she had a shrewd, manipulative side that appealed to Lawrence. Everyone working for Crawford Investments knew to be aware and very cautious of what was said in her presence.

She took copious notes about happenings around the office...including any gossip that she would glean through eavesdropping and the like. Even personal information about employees was fair game, and she felt no compulsion to keep it confidential. She felt it was part of her job to keep her finger on the pulse of the office and report to him, during their intimate sessions, any staff weaknesses or lapses in loyalty.

Jessica had suspected that Millie and her father had been lovers long before her mother died but had never brought up the subject. Even in their fiercest battles over their father-daughter relationship, Jessica kept her mouth shut about Millie. When Jessica walked into his office, Lawrence was standing behind his desk with his arms folded and his back toward her...staring out the window.

"Morning, Father," she offered.

He continued to gaze out the window without acknowledging her presence. She knew what was happening. This is what Lawrence did in preparation for a confrontation with whoever was in the line-of-fire or was going to be on the hot seat that day. The fact that Jessica was his daughter made no difference...it was his way of showing displeasure before the cross-examination.

After a minute of awkward silence, he turned on his heels and reached for the envelope that Millie had laid on his desk late Friday afternoon. It had arrived by courier.

"How do you explain this one, Jessica," he growled, reaching across the desk to shove it into her hand. Jessica opened the envelope and took out the letter.

Sitting down on one of the chairs facing the desk, she began reading to herself. The letter was addressed specifically to Lawrence Crawford, President, Crawford Investments, Inc., and began:

Dear Sir:

It is with regret that I must inform you that Las Vegas Holdings has decided not to retain Crawford Investments, Inc. as an exclusive broker for land to be purchased in North Phoenix for purposes of a proposed retail center project.

Las Vegas Holdings feels it necessary to keep their options open for the possible selection of other properties available in the Phoenix metropolitan area and will be accepting listings from other land brokers within the state of Arizona.

Unfortunately, there was no opportunity for further discussion or to begin the process of contract negotiations with Crawford Investments since your representative, Jessica Crawford, had to return to Arizona prematurely to handle more important business. Since that initial meeting, we have reconsidered our position as it relates to representation by a single land broker.

Sincerely,
Keith Cantor"

Jessica laid the letter on the desk, rose from the chair and began to pace the floor with her arms crossed.

Lawrence waited impatiently, staring, tapping his foot on the hardwood floor…another aggravating habit he had designed to demand attention quickly. His patience was running thin. In his mind, this was another deal that had gone bad and which put his soon-to-be insolvent company in even deeper financial jeopardy.

Jessica passed the front of his desk for the third time without saying a word. She was clearly puzzled. *How could that dirty bastard, Keith Cantor, turn on me like this after I gave in to his every whim?*

Lawrence quickly moved from behind the desk and cut over to head her off, grabbing her by the arm and spinning her around to face him.

"Just what the hell does this guy mean when he said you had to leave prematurely?" he sneered, causing the muscles around his jaw to tighten.

"I *had* to leave," she said, sarcastically. "John came out of the coma."

"Are you out of your *fucking* mind, Jessica?" he shot back, squeezing tighter. "I told you this company couldn't stand another lost business opportunity!" Yelling in her face now, he snapped, "How much clearer could I have made that to you?" Turning back to his desk, he gave her a shove in disgust.

"What would you have expected me to do?" she said, staring hard. "He was going to be my husband and I loved him."

"Going to be?" he replied tersely, bending his eyebrows.

After a tense moment, she couldn't look him in the eyes anymore and stared at the floor. "We've put our relationship on hold," she said softly, a frown marring her brow.

"Do you mean to tell me...look at me when I'm talking, damn it!" he said, angrily. "You mean to tell me that that asshole trader, who doesn't give a shit about our business, convinced you to leave Vegas in the middle of closing a big deal just to break up with you? How stupid can you be? I'll bet he's talking to this guy, Keith, as we speak."

"John doesn't have anything to do with Las Vegas Holdings, Father," she responded raising her voice, "When I left, I thought everything was fine with Keith and the sacrosanct deal we need so bad."

"Well," he growled, "evidently, you didn't do enough to satisfy him...now did you?"

Jessica couldn't take anymore. The room was closing in around her. Her eyes filled with hatred. Her facial features took on an evil appearance, and her fists clenched as she moved into his space.

"Enough, Father!" she yelled, moving closer, "I even slept with the unfaithful bastard," she went on, shaking a finger in front of his face, "...just to get you what you wanted."

"Apparently," Lawrence said in a sarcastic tone, staring callously at his daughter, "it seems you failed to impress him."

"Go to hell, Father," she replied acidly.

No sooner had she said it than Lawrence raised a hand and slapped her across the face, knocking her into a chair.

"Don't you ever speak to me in that manner again, young lady!" he roared coldly. "I've done everything for you," he went on, his eyes looking through red haze. "You owe your life to me. I forgave you for Lawrence, Junior's disappearance. I forgave you for what it did to your mother. I..."

"Stop...*Stop* it!" she yelled, interrupting him, gripping her hair and tugging.

Lawrence recognized the first signs of the emotional breakdown Jessica could experience at any moment and backed away from her. He watched as she rocked back and forth in the chair, mumbling words that meant nothing to anyone but her.

***

It had been several years since Jessica had her last real breakdown. It happened when she was twenty-five years old. She went berserk in a restaurant after a waiter had spilled a glass of wine on her new gold spaghetti-strapped dress and threw the glass over the bar into a row of bottles before slamming her fist into the waiters' nose. The police were called and Lawrence subsequently bailed her out of jail. After that episode, a judge, ruling on the matter, ordered her to resume therapy sessions…therapy sessions that stopped when she was nineteen.

John had no idea Jessica had such extreme tendencies. Less severe episodes, contained by prescription medication, had occurred at various stages of their relationship and were explained away as minor bouts of migraine headaches.

At one time when Jessica was younger, her therapist at the time had suggested in a private meeting with Lawrence that Jessica may have been subjected to some kind of mental abuse at an early age and inferred that Lawrence may have contributed to her mental frailties. Lawrence vehemently disagreed with the therapist's diagnosis, fired him on the spot, and hired another who was less aggressive at placing blame for Jessica's condition. Lawrence never once admitted to having any part in the cause of Jessica's mental problems and chastised anyone for inferring it. Jessica's mother, however, agreed with the therapist's assessment, but she was always afraid to say anything for fear that she would be subject to more of Lawrence's wrath.

In middle school, Jessica had been expelled for a week after attacking a girl who accused her of flirting with the boy she was dating…and her behavior had gotten worse over time.

*** *

Lawrence discompassionately moved back behind his desk and plopped down in the overstuffed chair to wait while Jessica worked herself out of her emotional frenzy. .

"You've got to pull yourself together, Jessica," he said, in an annoyed tone of voice. "You've lost sight of what's important. Look at you...you're pathetic. I taught you this business and how to handle yourself. I taught you how to be tough and shrewd...and now look at you! Just get out of my sight." he said, waving a hand towards the door. "I'll fly to Vegas and revive this deal myself. I'll make this Keith Cantor a deal on our property he won't be able to refuse."

"Go ahead, Father," she warned. "But...if you use the fact that I slept with him to get what you want, he'll just deny it."

"Go on...get out!"

Chapter Twenty-Four

Wednesday

Lawrence Crawford's House

Under the silvery light of a full moon, the clouds moved slowly...casting shadows on the tall trees surrounding the property. Jessica entered #9633 on the security keypad and the double, wrought-iron gates made a groaning sound as they slowly swung open. The Escalade rolled to a stop under the eucalyptus branches that hung over the circular driveway in front of the house. She detested the thought of being at her father's house again, even though her intentions this time were for very different reasons. It had been the horrible memories of being there that limited her visits...especially after her mother died. Jessica's mother was the one person that made visiting the old house tolerable. Being there on special occasions...like her father's birthday, when she'd bring a small cake...or at Christmas, so he would receive at least one gift from someone other than Millie...was usually more than Jessica could handle.

There was an intrinsic compulsion on her father's part to make it appear to the outside world that their relationship was normal when, actually, it was all a sham. Although Jessica was smart and had a natural aptitude, which she learned from her father, for the real estate business, her position in his company and their so-called father-daughter relationship around the office was nothing but phony.

She slid the key into the keyhole, turned, pushed, and the huge door swung open. She made her way to the security keypad on the wall and disarmed the system. For a moment, she stood quietly on the cold, ceramic-tiled flooring in the foyer looking from one side of the house to the other, taking in the musty odor of a place neglected. Slowly, she made her way through the house by the dim light of the moon bleeding through the huge casement windows partially covered by dusty red velvet curtains. She moved to the familiar circular staircase that she used to secretly slide down when her father wasn't home… because when he was home, he always yelled at her for doing it. She made her way up the stairs and walked down the long hallway to his office, which was located in the rear of the house.

Old man Crawford was out of town but Jessica could feel his presence as if he were standing next to her. The house always had an eerie quality that made it seem like a center for paranormal phenomena…some unexplained, supernatural activity that Jessica was sure involved her mother's suicide. It was like the years of stress and anguish that had occurred there had drained the life from the old house and left only emptiness and feelings of dread.

Regardless of whether or not Lawrence was at home, he always kept the door to his office locked. He had forbidden anyone, including Jessica's mother, to enter unless invited. Jessica had known for years about the key that hung on the hook…behind a large mahogany and glass table holding a bronze southwestern sculpture of a cowboy on a bucking horse. She knew it was there because she had once watched him take it when he was too drunk to notice that she was watching through a crack in the library door. She had always been forbidden to touch anything in the office with the exception of his overstuffed chair. As a child, when her father was a little more forgiving, she would follow him into the room and dash over to the chair, sit and swivel and laugh as if she were on a ride at Disneyland until he had enough of it and kicked her out. Any attempt to touch anything else was met with stern discipline...particularly the cabinet she was about to violate.

She lifted the key off the hook, glanced back down the hallway...then opened the door. She made her way over to the metal cabinet located in a corner under one of his many self-portraits hanging throughout the house. Her father's vanity and inflated ego was everywhere. There were four drawers stacked vertically against the far wall. She had no interest in the first drawer labeled 'Crawford Investments.' It was the third drawer down labeled 'Financial Files' that she was focused on. She took a penlight out of her bag, held it in her mouth like an experienced thief, and scanned the files for the one she wanted...'The Crawford Family Living Trust.' *Ah... here it is.* She yanked the file out and marked the exact spot she had pulled it from, raising the next folder in order. *It's time, Daddy,* she thought...*time to find out if I will get what I deserve after you kick the bucket.*

When Jessica decided to search her father's files, she had concluded that his endless speeches about the trouble Crawford Investments was in more than likely had nothing to do with his personal assets. She was sure that, as shrewd as her father was, there had to be plenty of money in investments and land not tied to the business, life insurance policies, and the old mansion which, alone, had to be worth at least three million. She carried the folder over to his desk, placed it on top, sat in the overstuffed chair, and briefly glanced around the room. She wondered if her father had tiny cameras installed just to catch her doing something like this...then quickly dismissed the thought. "Screw him," she whispered. She opened the folder and began to scan the provisions. Some of the legal jargon didn't make sense to her until she came to 'ARTICLE XII, TRUSTEES AND SUCCESSORS'. Her eyes opened wide in amazement as she read the text:

"Trustees and Successors: Upon the death, resignation or incapacity of Lawrence P. Crawford as Trustee, the successor Trustee shall be Millie J. Jones. Upon the death, resignation or incapacity of Millie J. Jones, the successor Trustee shall be Jessica M. Crawford."

That dirty bastard, she thought, leaning back in his chair running her fingers through her hair. *After all I've been through...and the grief I've taken from him all these years, he put that bitch, Millie, in charge of what should rightfully be mine.* "Well," she mumbled to herself, "I've got news for him...*and* her." As Jessica continued to read the documents, she became even more furious. Her father was leaving Millie the house, stocks and bonds, and one hundred ounces of gold bars, secured in safe deposit boxes at two banks. She found a term life insurance policy for half a million dollars with Jessica M. Crawford named as the beneficiary. "Son of a bitch," she said, scowling at the document, closing it and laying it down on the desk...then picking it back up and slamming it back down with both hands.

She sat there a moment, pondering the implications of what she had just learned. Then, she shoved herself backwards in the chair, rose and made her way back to the cabinet. She slipped the folder back in its proper place, turned and walked across the room to the old rolltop desk against the wall by the window. She rolled back the top, reached in and grabbed the metal box from the back, and pulled it forward. She lifted the lid and pulled out her father's old .22 caliber pistol and a box of ammunition.

Years ago, Lawrence had taken Jessica to Shooter's World for target practice. He enrolled her in the Children's Gun Safety & Awareness Class and seemed to be proud of her ability to accurately fire the weapon. She gripped the pistol, admiring the cold, black steel barrel. Before shoving it in her bag, she pointed it at his picture hanging across the room. "Thanks for the lessons, you bastard."

Chapter Twenty-Five

Wednesday

March 7

At seven p.m., Lawrence sent Millie around the corner to Ra Sushi Bar Restaurant to bring dinner back to the office. It wasn't unusual for Lawrence to stay after hours to review paperwork, dictate nasty letters to creditors... or just be there. For the most part, he'd rather hang around the office with Millie than go home to a dark, empty house with all its bad memories. He had just finished approving the final documents for a potential merger with Valley Investments Corporation, which was considering a secret offer that Lawrence and his attorney had prepared and submitted some months earlier. It was still another attempt to avoid the inevitable...Crawford Investments was sinking deeper into financial difficulty. The timing was good, and with Crawford Investment assets and some obscure, potential land deals in the pipeline, Lawrence's company, at least on paper, looked somewhat appealing to outsiders. Lawrence, however, knew that the appeal would be short-lived if any one of the land deals fell apart before the merger went through.

Millie had loved Lawrence for years but neither one of them ever talked about it.

Jessica, along with others, knew exactly how Millie felt and what was going on. However, they all kept quiet about it because they were well aware of Millie's reports to Lawrence involving office gossip and loyalty. Their relationship was all about Lawrence and what his mood dictated. A few times a week, after everyone else had abandoned the office, he'd buzz Millie's desk and beckon her in, expecting her to do what satisfied him… and only him. Intercourse in the office hadn't happened in years, but what did happen was indicative of his advancing years and selfish nature.

Lawrence's idea of closing out the day's business was lying back in his overstuffed chair, watching Millie give him oral sex. Unless she went to his house, which happened only on rare occasions, or if he dragged her along on one of his out-of-town business trips to some hotel executive suite, giving *her* pleasure was secondary. As the years went by, it got to be something she accepted, and it no longer bothered her.

***

At ten o'clock, Millie arrived at her condo just in time to take something for her headache, shower and climb into bed.

Jessica had followed her home and waited in the car until the lights in the house went out…with the exception of a glimmer of light in the upstairs bedroom and a light in the bathroom. Five days earlier, when Millie was away from her desk, Jessica had ripped off the ring of keys that she always left in her top drawer. After running down to the local hardware store to have a duplicate of Millie's house key made, she slipped the keys back into Millie's desk drawer without Millie ever being aware that they were gone.

Jessica stepped out of the car dressed in sweat pants and a hooded sweatshirt, glanced around, pulled the hood up over her head, and moved quietly up the walkway towards Millie's front door. A slight breeze rustled leaves on the trees surrounding the complex. A shiny black cat whose coat glowed from the soft light of a half-moon meowed then darted across the space between the solar lanterns lining the walkway. Intent on her mission, Jessica didn't flinch. It was all working out the way she envisioned it.

It was the third night in a row that Jessica had waited for Millie to come home, and each night was a duplicate of the previous. Jessica pushed the key into the hole, turned the knob, and let herself into the dark entryway… then quietly shut the door behind her. The jogging shoes she wore made no noise when she crept across the tile floor over to the shag-carpeted staircase. The volume on the bedroom television was just loud enough that Jessica could make out the voices of the local news anchors echoing down the hallway. She hesitated halfway up, gripping the metal pipe tightly in her hand, until she heard the sound of water running.

She waited until she was sure Millie was in the shower before making her way up to the top of the stairs, down the short hall and into Millie's bedroom. On the dresser next to the bed, she saw a picture of her father with his arm around Millie as they stood on the deck of a cruise ship. It infuriated Jessica to the point that she wanted to run into the bathroom and finish her off right then and there, but she resisted the urge. *A messy scene would lead police to believe that there was foul play*, she thought. *I have to make her death look like an accident.* Jessica had a plan and it meant having self-control while implementing it.

She stood outside the shower curtain and waited for the right moment…with her adrenalin flowing. She squeezed the pipe until her hand became numb. Suddenly, Millie shut off the water and reached out to the towel rack. Jessica threw aside the curtain and smashed a blow to Millie's forehead. Just as Millie's knees started to buckle under her, Jessica grabbed her arm and shoulder and yanked her out of the tub, smashing her head into the corner of the Victorian-style vanity. Millie lay motionless on the floor with the blood gushing from her head pooling up on the tile floor. Jessica's chest rapidly expanded and contracted as she leaned back against the wall looking up at the ceiling, the sweat trickling down her face like a flood of tears. She stood there a moment to make sure…to make sure that she was dead.

After a minute or so, she bent over the body, being careful not to step in the blood, and grabbed Millie by the hair, slightly lifting her head up. Suddenly, Millie's body jerked and her eyes opened wide. Startled, Jessica smashed her head onto the tile floor. It was the blow that would finish her.

Jessica glanced around as if being watched, then a calmness came over her. Gathering her wits, it was time for her to follow the plan and set up the rest of the accident scene. She rose from her knees, grabbed the shower curtain rod and pulled it from the wall. She positioned the rod across Millie's lower back. She took Millie's right hand and closed it around a section of the curtain, making it appear that she grabbed the curtain to break her fall. She then draped a bottom portion of the curtain across the tub shelf. She reasoned that it would be easy for a judicious investigator to conclude that Millie had slipped while getting out of the tub and grabbed the curtain for something to break her fall. After grabbing the curtain, the weight of her falling body caused the curtain rod to dislodge from the wall and come down on top of her. As she fell, she smashed her head into the vanity and the tile floor, causing her death.

Jessica took a last look at Millie lying there, bathed in her own blood, and smiled. *Got you,* she thought. *Got you, you bitch.* She looked around to make sure that she had made no mistakes and that everything was as she planned. Then she noticed that one of the gloves she was wearing had blood on it. "Damn," she mumbled, "blood from her hair." Jessica knew that traces of blood could not be found anywhere in the house but the bathroom, so she removed the glove from her hand and stuffed it into her pocket.

For five minutes she stood over the body staring into the vanity mirror, her eyes staring back like a wildcat eying its prey getting ready to pounce. All of her father's indiscretions, his abusiveness and disgusting mannerisms passed before her eyes. She shook her head quickly to exit the trance state she was in. She glanced down at Millie's battered head, soaked in blood, then back into the mirror at herself and smiled wide. A moment later, she made her way back down the stairs, put the hood back over her head and left the house, locking the door behind her.

As she drove away, the events played out in her mind over and over again. She grinned. *No mistakes.* She fired up a cigarette, took a long pull and let the smoke exit her lungs slowly wondering what Millie was thinking that split second after she saw the metal pipe aimed at her head. *Was there enough time for her to know what was happening*, Jessica thought. *I hope there was.*

You're not the only one to be punished for taking away what is rightfully mine, she thought, as she passed a Scottsdale police car pulling out of a Quick Stop. *The cutie in the wet suit will soon be meeting up with you, Millie,* she smirked.

Chapter Twenty-Six

Thursday
March 8

The news was devastating. The egotistical man with the strong will suddenly felt weak and bewildered. He placed the receiver on the switch-hook, turned in his chair and, with a blank look on his face, stared out of the window towards the vast Pinnacle Mountain area. The call from Donna, Millie's sister, informing him that Millie was dead as the result of an accident at home sent a shock to his body. She gave him all the gory details, starting with finding Millie's car parked in the garage when she arrived and continuing to the point where she found her lying face down on her bathroom floor in a pool of blood. When Donna stopped talking, about the only thing Lawrence could remember was that Millie was dead... At that point, everything was a blur.

The news took a relatively normal morning and turned it into an agonizing nightmare. Millie

was Lawrence's comfort zone. The thought of being without her struck him as unbearable. The only other time he felt himself sinking into this kind
of darkness was when Lawrence, Jr., was kidnapped. He swiveled back around only to stare at
another one of the self-portraits marking his territory. He thought about what would happen without Millie directing the activity in the office.
Glancing around, from corner to corner, wall to
wall, he began questioning the value of all his
deeds and accomplishments. His struggle to build
an empire around a life cursed with the loss of his
son, a wife gone mad and an unstable daughter
now seemed pointless.

Suddenly, guilt set in. He thought about the
way he had controlled Millie and their one-sided
relationship. He thought about how unfair he had
been, the things he required of her, and how she
did them without question. When he needed her,
she was always there…when he didn't, it was OK
with her. It was a relationship that, in a sense,
would have been much more meaningful to both
of them if he had only treated her differently.
Now it was too late. Although she never said anything, he knew, deep down, she would have preferred being married…sharing his big house and
being accepted by Jessica as her second mother.
But, now, that could never become reality.

For years, like clockwork, Millie opened
the office for business much earlier than any oth-

er employee would even think of getting there. She'd have Lawrence's specially-brewed coffee already made and sitting on his desk when he arrived well before the others, as well. It was only when something out of the ordinary happened...such as a doctor's appointment or the occasional vacation with her sister or the times that Lawrence took her on a trip...that someone else would be responsible for opening the office in the morning. He knew that being without Millie was going to be difficult...she was indispensable in every way. The late nights in the office, which usually left them alone for things other than business, would soon be just a memory...stored somewhere in the back of his dark mind.

When he awoke that morning, it was like any other morning... his tired bones climbing out of bed, a shower, a choice from the vast collection of designer suits that hung in a row in the closet, and the lonely walk through the empty house down to the car parked on the circular driveway where it had been left the night before. Climbing the steps to the huge, glass doors leading into the Crawford Building, he found it strange that the doors locked and, with the exception of the security lighting in the lobby, dark inside. He couldn't remember the last time he had to use his key to enter the building.

He rushed into his office to call Millie's house but got no answer. After calling her cell phone with the same result, he scanned the top of her desk for a note or some indication that she wouldn't be there to open up the office...but found nothing. Frustrated, he made his way back into his office, plopped back down and leaned back in his chair. He stared at the ceiling, trying to recall anything Millie might have mentioned the night before pertaining to an early morning appointment or any other reason for not being there. He couldn't recall anything.

Jessica, along with several others, came wandering in around their normal time. Jessica, carrying a large cup of Starbucks coffee, removed her sun glasses and stared at Millie's desk as if to say, 'so long, bitch.' The door to Lawrence's office stood wide open. As Jessica passed, she noticed her father sitting at his desk with his head firmly planted in the palms of his hands. She knew then and there that he knew. She tapped lightly on the door.

"Father," she said. "Are you alright?"

Lawrence looked up and motioned her in. "I just received terrible news from Millie's sister, Donna. Millie had a terrible accident at home..."

"My God!" she broke in. "What happened? Is she alright?"

Lawrence sat in silence, shaking his head from side-to-side.

"I'm afraid she is dead."

Jessica could have been auditioning for a role in a movie the way she reacted...anyone standing there would have accepted her display of sorrow and hurt upon hearing the news as genuine. She sighed loudly and moved around Lawrence's desk and began rubbing his shoulder. If there had been a mirror in front of Lawrence, he would have clearly seen the shit-eating grin on her face.

"This can't be true, Father," she said, in a convincing tone. "There must be some mistake."

"I'm afraid it is true, Jessica."

"But, how...how did it happen?"

Lawrence could hardly maintain his composure. He sat there listening to a rerun of Donnas' words in his head as she explained to him what had happened. What had gone over his head during the actual call was now playing back.

Lawrence let out a loud, long sigh. "Her sister found her on the bathroom floor. There was blood all over. According to the police, she had been dead for some time, based on the color of the blood and temperature of her body. Donna said it looks like she might have fallen out of the shower."

"That's horrible, Father," Jessica said, her voice lowering. "I'm so sorry."

***

It is factual that some killers are compelled to revisit their crime scene to satisfy some deep-rooted compulsion. Jessica, too smart to get caught, satisfied her urge for power and control when she slammed Millie's head to the floor. The first officer to arrive at the scene, along with the paramedics and fire department personnel, speculated the cause of death accidental. Given the position of the body and Millie's age and the fact that there was no evidence of a break-in, there was no reason to presume foul play. After arriving at the scene, the medical examiner came to the same conclusion.

Jessica's plan had worked out exactly as she had hoped it would. Donna and two police officers waited outside in the street as Millie's body, concealed in a zippered black body bag, was carted out of the house and placed in the transport vehicle.

Ironically, Alexandra's paramedical team was called to the scene. The situation, although sad, was nothing compared to recent calls. There was no crowd, no fleet of squad cars, no investigators scurrying around to secure the area with yellow crime tape…and no camera trucks situated in front of the house hoping to catch a story for local news stations. There were just a few neighbors curiously milling around and a short, stocky man with a cane and cropped, thinning gray hair who walked up to confront one of the officers.

"And your name is…?" asked the officer, lifting a pad from his back pocket.

"Tim…Tim Sullivan…they call me Sully," he replied. "I act as security for the condos in this complex. I retired from the Tempe Police Force five years ago, and I volunteer my time here for the owners. May I ask what your name is, Officer?"

"Connor," he replied, "Connor Hoffman."

"Hmm...Officer Hoffman," Sully said, scratching his head. "I don't remember you...anyway; can you tell me what went on in that house...? I'm official."

The officer took a step back and looked curiously at the man. "It looks like the lady who lived here met with an unfortunate accident," the officer replied, writing something on the notepad. "Did you know the woman?"

"Uh, yes," Sully acknowledged. "But only through the group meetings she attended every now and then. She was hardly ever home...you know," he went on. "Leaves early in the morning and comes home sometime after dark most every night. Is there anything I can do to assist?"

"Not really," the officer replied, glancing at his pad then back at sully. "Seems cut and dry. We'll be wrapping up here real soon."

***

John's cell phone chirped. He glanced at the screen only to see Jessica's name and number. He hadn't talked to her in three weeks and contemplated letting his voice mail take the message. At the last second, he changed his mind.

"Jessica?" he answered.

"Oh…John," she replied, in a distraught tone of voice.

"What's wrong, Jessica…? Are you alright?"

"No…not really, John," she said, her voice slightly broken. "There…there has been an accident. Millie, you know... my father's assistant, was found dead in her home this morning."

The news caught John by surprise. "What happened?"

"It was a horrible accident."

"That's terrible. And your father…How is he taking it?"

"Not good, John," she said. "You know how they were. He's in his office, won't come out, and won't speak to anyone."

"That would be his way of mourning…wouldn't it?"

"Maybe," she responded, with a strained voice, "but I'm having a hard time dealing with all of it. Can I see you?"

"Certainly," he replied, sympathetically. "Should I meet you at the Crawford Building?"

"No," she replied. "The restaurant around the corner. I need to get away from here."

"Uh…sure, OK," he responded, in a cautious tone. "I'll get there as soon as I can…but, tell me, what happened to her?"

Jessica said, "If it is all the same to you, John...can I explain when we meet? I'm too upset to talk about it right now."

John thought for a moment, then glanced at his watch. It was eleven forty-five. "Oh, shit," he murmured. He had planned to meet Alexandra on her lunch break at twelve-fifteen. He called her but got voice mail. It wasn't unusual for Alexandra not to pick up when she was working. Probably on a call, he thought. Leave a message.

"Alexandra, it's me. I hope you check this message. Something has come up. I won't be able to meet you for lunch. Call me back, or I'll catch up with you later...Miss you."

When he walked into Applebee's, he spotted Jessica sitting at a table in the back corner, sipping a beer out of the bottle.

"Beer instead of tea?" he asked, when he reached the table.

Jessica jumped to her feet and threw her arms around him. "Oh, John," she said, drawing a deep breath, "I'm so glad you could come. You know how hard it is for me to tolerate my father; and now that this has happened, I'm almost out of my mind."

"OK," he said, gently gripping her arms and pulling them down to her side. "Just relax and sit so we can talk. So what happened to Millie?"

"Her sister, Donna, said they think she slipped getting out of the shower and cracked her head when she hit the floor."

"When...this morning?"

"I'm not sure," she replied. "They thought she had been dead for a while, maybe since last night," she went on, her gaze shifting from his eyes to his mouth. "Do you want a beer... or wine or something?"

"Oh...no thanks, Jessica," he replied. "I really can't stay long. I've got an important meeting to prepare for this afternoon."

"Please, John," she said anxiously, "Can't you cancel and be with me this afternoon? We can go to my place and..."

"Jessica..." he interrupted in a calm voice, "you know that's not going to happen, so please don't ask. I thought you just needed someone to talk to...and I'm here for you."

Jessica tossed him an icy look, leaned back in her chair and folded her arms. He knew then that there was more on her mind than her father's grief over his deceased girlfriend.

Suddenly, as luck would have it, his cell phone began to sound off. He reached into his coat pocket, pulled it out and glanced at it. "Excuse me a moment, Jessica." John got to his feet and moved away from ear shot.

Jessica's eyes narrowed. This was not what she had planned. She overheard the name 'Alexandra,' not loud, but something definitely sounding like it. It must be the name of the bitch he's seeing, she thought, forcing herself to maintain composure. Moments later, as Jessica sat there steaming, John put the phone back in his coat pocket and walked back to the table. She shot him a long, hard look.

"And who was that?" she said, looking annoyed. "Your little girlfriend?"

"Jessica," he replied flatly. "Don't do this to yourself...or to me, for that matter. I told you we needed space...and nothing's happened to change that."

"Well...it sure didn't take you long to stick it into someone else, did it?" she replied coldly.

"How would you know what I've been doing?" he snapped.

"You must think I'm dumb...do you?"

"Jessica," he replied as he shot up from the chair. "I won't do this." He turned on his heels to walk away. In a calm voice, Jessica called out to him. He looked back. She flashed him the finger and mouthed, 'fuck you.'

John ignored the gesture, headed back to the work and went straight into Gary's office. Gary got a rise out of what John told him about his encounter with Jessica and snickered as he chewed on a salami-mustard sandwich.

"She actually used someone's death to lure me there! How bizarre is that?"

John's cell phone chimed...it was a text from Jessica. John studied the words before handing the phone to Gary. "Look at this," he said. "This is what I'm saying about her erratic behavior."

Text...'I'm sorry, John. I didn't mean to upset you. We can see each other tonight, can't we? Call me. I love you.'

"Wow...that woman's becoming a real psycho," Gary said, shaking his head.

John placed his hands on top of Gary's desk and leaned in. "She went psycho long before this. I just didn't see it."

"Must have been the sex," Gary mused.

John didn't find that amusing. "Get serious here, buddy." John said, running his fingers through his hair. "The bitch is stalking me."

"Don't you think you might be taking this to the extreme?"

"How in the hell do I know. I've never been stalked, but this feels like it."

Gary said, "Now that I think about it. What disturbs me is how did she find out about Alexandra?"

"Good question." John replied. "Good guess, maybe?"

"Maybe...maybe not. That girl is ruthless. You might be right. A stalker she could be."

John said, "Now it sounds like you might be taking things to the extreme. Maybe I should give her the benefit of the doubt... see if this thing, whatever it is, goes away."

"I'm not sure, buddy. If you had been sitting next to us at Anderson's, listening in...you'd realize that woman is malicious. I'll tell you...I'm thinking you can't put anything past her. Just in case, I would watch my back if I were you."

"What...?" John mused. "I should get a gun or something?"

Gary chuckled. "Maybe a can of mace."

John smiled. "Why am I standing in this office anyway? I've got real work to do!"

"Well...I'll tell you what I really think," Gary said, wiping the mustard from his mouth. "I think she's as dangerous and eccentric as her father...so do as I say...watch out."

Chapter Twenty-Seven

Alexandra's Condo

Friday
March 9

Warm air being pushed over a cold air mass coming in from the north had caused a gentle rainfall which had continued most of the day and into the evening. Jessica glanced at her watch to see how long she'd been there... it was seven-thirty. She leaned back in the leather seat of her Escalade, watching, gloating, as she recalled the horrified look in Millie's eyes in that split second when she realized she was about to die...and how gratifying it was that she knew Jessica was the one wielding the weapon. The thought caused Jessica to experience the rush of adrenaline all over again. She was now living in the same world of uncontrollable, inner turmoil that had manifested itself years ago. She had trouble controlling her emotions...a constant state of upheaval consumed all her thoughts.

Her sense of self was changing as the minutes passed. She was in denial about how evil she'd become. The bipolar-type illness led her to believe that what she was doing was justifiable. She grinned at the thought of the look on her father's face and how distraught he was after he found out about Millie's death. A normal daughter would have felt compassion for her father, but instead, his pain gave her pleasure. She wanted him to feel what she had felt all those years...the rejection, the blame, and the yearning for the person for whom she had a deep and profound love...her mother. He had taken her mother, whom she loved dearly, and burned her body as if she had never existed. Jessica couldn't stand the sight of him and simply couldn't tolerate working for him anymore...she had to win.

Screw the old bastard, she thought. It was Jessica's ultimate goal to see to it that her father suffered the way her mother did. One way or another, he had to pay. He would be the final challenge to clear the path for her to take what was rightfully hers--all of her father's personal assets...and John.

The light sprinkle dusting the windshield of her car didn't obstruct the view of Alexandra's condo. Looking past the reflection of the dim street lights, she could see the John's and Alexandra's shadows moving around through the window's half-open shutters. At that point, Jessica had been watching the house for about an hour.

Tailing John to Jessica's condo was easy. Sitting in her parked car, waiting it out, was killing her. Puffing on cigarette after cigarette only added to the anxiety that was sending her over the edge. She was a train moving down the tracks at eighty miles an hour and a mile down the road was a mountain of bricks in her path. Her blood boiled. She wondered if John would stay as late as he had the night before, and if she should wait it out. She wanted to confront him, let him know she was there for him...and then make passionate love to him, She was delusional and it was difficult for her to stay on track...to stick to her plan.

Jessica used every means at her disposal, legal and illegal, including the real estate property database, to find out more about the woman she felt was shutting her out of John's life. *Alexandra,* she thought, throwing her head back against the headrest, *a name that might be associat-*

ed with royalty or some prim and proper heiress. "Yeah, right," she whispered, "not her...she's just a common whore."

Jessica was having difficulty accepting anything other than black or white; there was no gray area. People were either good or evil, and in her mind, the woman in that house with John was as evil as they get. Jessica couldn't allow Alexandra's domination of him to continue much longer. She was convinced that John's accident had something to do with his current state of mind; otherwise, none of this would have happened. *Before that happened, everything was wonderful,* she thought, pulling another cigarette from the almost empty pack. Her thoughts took her back to their engagement party and how happy they were...with every one celebrating, toasting them, and dancing. She cracked the car window again, felt the dampness of the night air seep in and exhaled a deep draw of smoke.

A light gust of wind sent heavy drizzle and smoke back into the car. The smoke in her lungs made her a little lightheaded; she wasn't normally a chain smoker but, in her mind, the circumstances warranted it. She leaned her head back and closed her eyes. She remembered how they used to talk over dinner about all the things they were going to do and the places they would go on their honeymoon. She thought about how they rarely argued, the sex together (which was sometimes rough), and the objective conversations about life in general...it was all working out then.

She took in another draw, exhaled, and let out a huge sigh at the same time. *All in one night,* she thought, tossing the cigarette out the window...*in an intersection on another rainy night, it all changed. He forgot who he was, he forgot who I was, and everything else in between.* Thinking about what John and Alexandra could be doing in that house was extremely hard for Jessica to handle emotionally. But she had no choice. *I need to stay focused, strong,* she thought. *It would all be over soon, and John would thank her for rescuing him from the clutches of that evil woman.*

She sat there, watching, staring, waiting, contemplating her next move as it started to rain harder. She refused to believe that her relationship with John was over. *There's no way,* she concluded, twisting strands of her hair around her index finger, pulling hard. She was convinced that her lover and future husband was being taken advantage of by a woman who didn't really know him, who didn't know what he liked and needed. Her head started to ache. She rubbed her temples with the tips of her fingers, hoping the pressure would relieve the throbbing. *This was all my father's doings,* she thought, locking her jaws so tight they ached. *He's the one who drove John to break it off. He was the one who made me spy on the company John worked for. He was the one who pressured me into going after the Promenade project to undercut Carriage Brokers and work Crawford's property into the deal. He was the one who decided to make me secondary in his Trust.* She would never forgive him for any of it, including what she had now become…a murderer.

Suddenly, the headlights of a slow-moving vehicle reflected off her side and rear-view mirror. The car was moving down the street as if the driver was lost or looking for a particular address. As the car moved past the Escalade, Jessica slid down just far enough in the seat that she could still see but not be noticed peeking over the door panel. *It's a woman.* The car coasted a few yards further then stopped across the street, directly in front of Alexandra's condo.

The car idled and the interior light came on. The woman reached back and grabbed something lying on the seat behind her. Moments later, she killed the engine and stepped out of the car., She shielded her head from the rain with a big package, and quickly made her way across the street to the walkway leading up to Alexandra's condo. Up a few steps and she rang the doorbell.

Chester barked furiously, as he did anytime someone came to the front door.

"Quiet down, Chester," Alexandra said, grabbing his collar to pull him back as she opened the door. "Meg, hi," Alexandra said, smiling, as Chester continued to yip annoyingly. "I didn't know whether you'd make it tonight, you know, with the rain and all."

John, who had been standing near the fireplace, hurried over to where they were, bent down and lifted Chester off the floor.

"Hi...I'm John," he said, offering his hand as he tucked Chester under his arm.

"Oh... Hi," Meg replied, "I'm Meg Webster." Meg looked at Alexandra then back to John. "Rowing team member."

"Yes... I know," John said. "Alexandra told me you might be stopping by," he went on. "Alexandra has told me a lot about you and the other ladies on the team."

"Well," Meg smiled softly, glancing in Alexandra's direction. "I'll get back at her for that," she went on chuckling. "I wouldn't pay too much attention to what Alexandra says about us girls unless, that is, she includes herself in the conversation."

"I'll tell him the real stories later," Alexandra put in, grinning.

"I'm really starting to worry about what rowing does to you ladies," John mused, setting Chester back down on the floor.

"I was late leaving work, and it took me longer than I had planned to change," Meg said, handing a water-soiled folder to her. 'Sorry...didn't bring an umbrella. I'm meeting some friends, and I'm running a little late on that front as well, so I should get going."

"Thanks for bringing it over, Meg," Alexandra said. "If I hadn't left this in Susan's car, you wouldn't have had to bother."

"No problemo, girl," Meg replied. "I needed to get you information on the rooms at Mission Bay, confirmations, etc., and that info is inside the folder along with the up-to-date rules and regulations for the Crew Classic we all need to memorize...aren't we lucky?" she scoffed.

"Yes, we are," Alexandra replied. "We don't want to get disqualified in the first round." Alexandra opened the door to let her out. "We'll meet you in San Diego around noon-ish."

"It was Nice meeting you, Meg," John, said, speaking from the kitchen. "Good luck in San Diego!"

***

The engine on the Escalade turned over as Meg drove off. Jessica was now on another mission...to find out who the chick was who was visiting Alexandra. She followed close behind, with no idea where it would lead. The Escalade's windshield wipers activated as the rain intensified, throwing water in every direction. Jessica eyes stayed glued to the taillights on Meg's car.

"Where are we going, little-miss-friend-of-Alexandra," Jessica said, maneuvering the last cigarette from the pack. "I want to be your friend, too," she went on, sneering. "Just long enough to get what I want out of you."

Meg drove up Scottsdale Road to Bell, turned right and headed east. Jessica made the turn but got cut off by a guy driving a pickup truck. He swerved in front of her then slammed hard on his brakes, skidding on the wet blacktop…all in an attempt to make the next turn up ahead.

"Asshole!" Jessica yelled, then accelerated until she caught up with Meg who had been detained by a red light up ahead. Jessica eased up behind Meg's car just as the light turned green. A quarter of a mile up the road, Meg turned into the parking lot of the Arena Sports Bar and Grill.

Jessica's timing was perfect. As luck would have it, the space next to the spot Meg parked in was vacant. The Escalade pulled into the narrow spot while Meg was making her way across the lot. All in one motion, Jessica cut the engine, jumped out, and rushed up behind her.

"Uh…pardon me," Jessica said, walking up along-side of Meg. "I noticed you getting out of your car and thought you looked very familiar to me."

"Gosh…I'm sorry?" Meg replied, tossing her bag over her shoulder, picking up the pace to get out of the rain. "I don't think so," she went on as they both rushed for cover near the entrance of the club.

"Wait…I know," Jessica, said, snapping a finger, pointing. "I've seen you at the Lake, haven't I?"

"Tempe Town Lake?"

"Yes…that's it. That's where I've seen you"

"Are you a rower?"

"Me? Oh, no," Jessica replied, "but I have friends that do and I go there a lot to watch. Do you row?"

"Yes, I do. Our team is heading to San Diego for the Crew Classic in a few days."

"Why isn't that ironic! My friends have entered that race and I'll be there as a spectator. By the way," she went on, "my name is Kathy…Kathy Perry."

"I'm Meg…Meg Webster…Nice to meet you."

"When is your team heading over to San Diego?" Jessica asked.

"We are going next Wednesday," she replied, as they worked their way through the door of the club.

"Driving?"

"Huh," Meg said, distracted by the noise as they walked in. "Oh... two of us are flying," she replied, as she searched through her bag for her cell phone. "Alexandra is picking up Susan...I mean, the other two girls are taking off early in the morning. They're hauling the boat and equipment."

"Well, Meg Webster," Jessica said, putting on a bright smile, "maybe I'll see you in San Diego. It was nice to meet you."

Meg spotted her friends at a table in the back and headed in that direction while Jessica made her way over to the bar, sat on a stool, and ordered a glass of chardonnay. She looked around and saw no one she knew. The Arena Grill wasn't a place she would normally frequent anyway.

It didn't take long, ten minutes or so, before a predator occupied the stool next to Jessica. He was of medium height, sported a half-gray goatee minus a mustache and wore faded jeans and a western shirt. Jessica wasn't in the mood for the advance that she knew was coming in the next few minutes. She reached into her bag, pulled out a ten and tossed it on the bar top.

"Leaving so soon, sweetheart?" he said, turning to her sporting a crooked smile and raising a bushy brow.

"Unfortunately, yes," Jessica replied, looking into his eyes. "I'd like to stay, get acquainted, and take you home tonight, but I'm late for my porn shoot."

His eyes opened wide and his chin dropped. Catching a guy as full of himself as he was off guard made her feel good. She grabbed her bag and made her way towards the door, glancing around to look at Meg one more time before leaving. *The night turned out to be a productive one,* she thought, stepping over puddles of water to get to her car.

Chapter Twenty-Eight

Sully laid the detective novel on the table next to his chair. He eased himself up, grabbed his cane and the last beer from the six-pack he had started earlier, and staggered into the den. He made his way over to the video tapes stacked next to the monitor near the corner of the room, picked up the tapes from the last few days and selected the bottom one marked Wednesday, March seventh. He shoved it into the player, pushed the rewind button and plopped down in the easy chair positioned directly in front of the monitor. By the time the tape finished the re-wind cycle, which automatically activated the play cycle…he was fast asleep, snoring loudly.

Sully had lived alone since his wife had divorced him twenty years earlier. The divorce was the result of her no longer being able to deal with his job as a police officer, and his drinking every night after shift didn't help. One night, a hoodlum in a car chase aimed his gun out of the car window and got off a lucky shot. The bullet went through the windshield of his police cruiser and caught him in the right shoulder. One year later, as he struggled with a drunk driver on the side of a road, the driver grabbed the gun from Sully's holster. Before he could get the gun back, it went off, striking him in the leg.

Sully's wife went straight to an attorney the second time he got wounded. Sully couldn't blame her for wanting to leave; he even encouraged it. His job had become his whole life, and he just couldn't change that. The other thing that strained their marriage was the fact that she wanted children, something that he could not give her. A divorce was inevitable…reconciliation was an option that neither one of them would consider. Since the divorce, he had been forced into medical retirement and was now used to living alone in the small world he created for himself.

Most nights, Sully looked forward to peering into the lives of others. He would usually review the tapes after he'd spent the better part of the evening killing a few beers, reading, or watching 'Crime Scene Investigations' or 'Law and Order' on the tube. The condo owners had asked him to install the multi-camera security system a year earlier because there had been an up-tick in vandalism occurring around the condo complex. It was his responsibility to review the tapes, report any suspicious activity to the police, and then report his findings during homeowners' meetings. He liked this part of his job as it reminded him of his days back on the force. After only a year of retirement, boredom had been getting the best of him and taking on security duties for the condo complex was just what he needed. He had even tried using contacts on the force in hopes of getting an opportunity to donate time to the police Ride-Along program. However, his contacts couldn't help…the policy was very strict and clear. Since he'd been wounded in action, the only volunteer work they would let him participate in was answering phones at the station house, which he refused to do. He thought it was beneath him to just sit and take calls when he had always been actively involved in street work and everyday operations…where the action was taking place.

Almost every night since the system was installed, Sully would sit in his living room, suck on beer, gnaw on snacks, and watch portions of tapes which had been recorded on previous days until he'd fall asleep. It had soon evolved into eavesdropping on the tenants and their relatives and friends who visited the complex. He watched his tenants' daughters get fondled by their boyfriends in cars after being brought home from a date. He knew who came home late and left early. He knew who ordered pizza in, and from which pizzeria. He had direct video admission into the lives and homes of the tenants, where he clearly didn't belong. So far, reports to the Homeowners' Association had been nothing more than one failed attempt to steal a truck in the middle of the night and a few occurrences of kids from the school up the road ditching, making mischief, or tossing wayward baseballs through windows every now and then.

Sully woke up in the morning still dressed, slumped in his chair with his arms hanging over the armrests. He glanced at his watch as he rubbed the hair around the sides of his head, yawned wide, and dragged himself into the kitchen to make coffee.

I've got to start watching these tapes before midnight, he thought, shaking his head as he recalled that, once again, he had put a tape in the player then conked out before watching it. He grabbed a two-day-old cinnamon roll off the counter and took a huge bite. "Oh, well," he said, mumbling to himself. "So what? I'll watch it later."

Chapter Twenty-Nine

Tempe Town Lake

Saturday

March 10

After finishing the final at-home practice leading up to the San Diego Crew Classic, the girls carried the scull back to the boathouse and then gathered around the dock to go over the final details of their trip to Mission Bay, including meeting at the Bahia Resort Hotel as Meg had arranged. As planned, Susan and Alexandra would ride together, leaving early Wednesday morning around four. They would tow the boat trailer behind Alexandra's Toyota, then meet up with the others at Mission Bay around one o'clock for a late lunch. Although this would be the second year in a row that the team would participate in the race, it was Susan's duty as captain to make sure that the team reviewed, in detail, the race course traffic patterns, water safety laws and safety practices. There had been changes in the rules from the previous year's race, and the information in the manual was crucial to each team on race day.

"Now, remember," Susan said, addressing the group, "this is important. We'll be in San Diego for five days. On two of those days, we will be practicing in the North Pacific Passage. According to the new rules, only the coach and coxswain attend the Friday meeting. You guys will be responsible for getting the gear and scull inspected and in place no later than noon that day. Any questions before we adjourn?" A collective 'no' from the girls ended the meeting.

As Alexandra and Susan strolled together through the parking lot towards their cars, Alexandra spent fifteen minutes telling Susan all about the encounter John had with Jessica at Applebee's...that, and other details Susan was dying to hear about the budding relationship between Alexandra and John which had taken place over the last few days.

"Wow!" Susan said, showing a degree of concern in her face. "This Jessica woman seems to be a little unstable, don't you think?"

"Well," Alexandra replied, "she's just not willing to let go."

"And what's this thing about the dead lady?" Susan said, raising her sunglasses to the top of her head as she searched her bag for car keys.

"It was her father's girlfriend and long-time secretary. I was there."

"You were where?"

"There," she replied flatly. "My unit was called to pick up the body. Ironic, huh?"

"OK," Susan said, dropping her glasses back to the bridge of her nose. "Let me see if I understand this. Jessica's father's girlfriend dies. Jessica meets with John because she's distraught, then tries to get him to go home with her for a roll-in-the-hay."

"That's pretty much it," Alexandra said, shrugging her shoulders.

"Good thing he didn't go," Susan said..."or did he?" she continued as she opened the car door with the remote.

"No!"

"Good...Then score a point for Alexandra," Susan bellowed, as she climbed in the car and closed the door.

"Hey! Wait a minute, Susan!" Alexandra said, having to shout over the engine noise from a Boeing 737 airliner making its approach into Sky Harbor Airport. "How are things going with you and Gary?"

"He's a *sex machine*!" she yelled, pulling away. "See you at the Coffee Shop in the morning!"

***

Alexandra went home from the Lake, stripped out of her rowing suit, showered, and plopped down on the couch, waiting. Chester stretched out upside down in her lap. She gently rubbed his belly...Chester's favorite thing. She began to think about all the time she'd been spending with John over the past few weeks and how wonderful it had been. She took in a deep breath, and then let out a huge satisfied sigh. Chester whimpered as if he felt her emotion. She reflected back on how her personal life had been troubled and empty until now...the nights spent alone, the dreams of her father and mother that seemed so real and sometimes too painful to deal with. She thought about how quickly fate could change things. *Being in the right place at the right time,* she thought, as she rubbed Chester's belly. Being there for John, in that intersection, the night of his accident was just that...fate. Since then, there had been no more frightening dreams waking her up in the middle of the night. Chester let out another whimper as if he understood what she was thinking.

"Yeah, what about that, little guy?" she said, as a single tear trickled down one side of her face.

Chester glanced up at her and tilted his head from side to side before suddenly leaping off her lap onto the floor and bolting towards the front door, barking as he always did when someone approached the house.

John's knock on the door brought a smile to her face. She shot up off the couch and hurried over to open it. When she swung the door open, John was standing there holding a paper bag in his hand.

"How do you feel about roast-turkey sandwiches?" he said smiling, waving the bag in front of her. "Fresh from the Honey Baked Store."

"Turkey's great," she replied, grinning. "But what the heck took you so long?" Before John could say a word, she grabbed his shirt, dragged him into the house, and planted a long, wet kiss on his lips.

"Wow!" John said. "Can I get greeted like this every time you open the door?" She kissed him again. Chester tugged on his pant leg. "Had to stop by the office for a folder. And…just for your information, beautiful," he went on, "I almost got cited for breaking the speed limit getting here."

"You don't say," she grinned. "Just to see me?"

"Heck, no," he mused. "I couldn't wait to get into this turkey sandwich."

"Funny," she said, snatching the bag from his hand and giving him a gentle shove backwards.

They sat on the balcony overlooking the golf course, eating their sandwiches and talking. John tossed the ball back into the house, and Chester hurried through the door and dug his paws into the rug chasing it. Alexandra watched John interact with Chester, all the while reflecting on how happy she was and how much her life had changed since John showed up at the Lake that morning. She leaned in and softly kissed his cheek. Her eyes filled with tears of joy and the comfort of his being there, filling the void left in her life by the death of her father and then her mother.

"John," she whispered into his ear.

"What is it, my love?" he replied, angling his head to look straight into her eyes.

For a moment, the words 'my love' took her aback. She searched her mind for the thought she was going to share with him. He waited for her to say what she wanted to say, but he could see that she was struggling to get the words out. The look in those warm, sultry bedroom eyes drew him to her. They kissed long and hard.

Chester dropped the ball next to John's feet and tugged on his pants again, then picked up the ball and dropped it again. John drew back, looking once more into her eyes.

"Your dog just won't quit with that ball, you know," he mused. "All he wants to do is play."

"I've got news for you, buddy," she replied smiling wide. "So do I."

John chuckled at the remark, snatched the ball out of Chester's jaws and tossed it back into the living room. "I have an idea," he said. "After a quiet dinner, a glass or two of wine and a dose of nighttime sleep-aid for little Chester, here, we can play all we want. Now... tell me what it is that you were about to whisper in my ear a moment before I kissed you and you lost your concentration."

She paused a moment and let out an exhaustive sigh. "OK...but if I'm going to ask, you have to answer honestly...promise?"

"Do I really need to promise?" he grinned. "Promises make me jittery; it seems so final, no room for wiggle.

"Alright, funny man," she said. "I'm trying to be serious here...come on," she went on taking a light swipe across his arm with her hand.

"Sorry," John said. "Thought I'd lighten the moment. I'll tell you what, though, I won't promise...OK? But I will swear to be honest. So there, now I'm ready...shoot," he continued. "I've got my game face on."

"Well," she said, "it's like this...several weeks have passed since we began seeing each other and I haven't brought up the subject about you and Jessica, even though it killed me not to... I just want to know...I need to know, I guess...and don't ask me what's the point. What was it that caused your relationship to end?"

John looked at her intently, knowing there was a complicated answer to her simple question. Even though he knew at some point the subject would be front and center, he intentionally avoided preparing the answer. He preferred to focus on Alexandra every waking moment and not on the woman who had caused him so much grief.

"Alexandra," John said, in a serious tone of voice as he placed the palms of his hands gently against her cheeks, gazing with conviction deep into her eyes. "If I tell you the answer to your question, will you promise me that this will be the one and only time we discuss it... deal?"

She looked at him and grinned. "Making promises is good for me and not you? Just kidding," she mused, wiping the grin from her face. "We have a deal."

"OK, then...I have a very simple answer for you," he continued, slowly rubbing the palms of his hands together. "I wanted a love story...and frankly...I didn't have it with her."

Those tender words made Alexandra want to melt. *He wanted a love story,* she thought. What other explanation could she...or any woman, for that matter, in her position possibly need? But Alexandra's curiosity begged for more.

"But you put a ring on her finger, didn't you?" she said, continuing to press. "I mean...didn't you think you had a love story then?"

"Please, Alexandra," he replied, taking hold of her hands. "I thought about a lot of things near the end of my relationship with Jessica. My career taking off; Jessica

being in the same kind of business, working for her ob-
noxious, ruthless father who wanted me to either quit Carriage Brokers or get fired …either way, it didn't matter to
him. Listen closely…my love. The relationship between
me and Jessica was once good. That changed actually before I realized it. Gary warned me, and I didn't listen nor
did I see it happening until you saved me that night. My
life changed the minute you used that crowbar to pry open
the car door before you breathed life back into my body.
What I know now is that I love *you*. Can we forget about
Jessica and never think about her again?"

The tears found their way down Alexandra's
cheek. Whatever else she may have been thinking or
whatever else she wanted to know didn't matter. "Forgotten," she said, "I'll never bring her up again…and I *will*
promise."

Chapter Thirty

Sunday

The Coffee Shop

Alexandra took a table next to the window; Susan was late as usual. As she waited, sipping coffee and nibbling on a cream cheese bagel, from the corner of her eye, she could see the guy sitting at the table across the room looking her way. When she first walked in, he was fingering the keypad on a wireless laptop like others sitting around him...using the free Wi-Fi. Surreptitiously, he kept looking at her. She wondered if she had met him before but knew she hadn't. *Just some stranger making me very uncomfortable by the minute,* she thought. She avoided eye contact, but it wasn't easy. He rose to his feet and headed towards her table. Alexandra took a sip of coffee and shifted her gaze towards the window, hoping he would change direction. *It's too early for this,* she thought. *Where in the heck are you, Susan?*

"Excuse me," the man said, sporting a warm smile.

Alexandra turned, looked up at him, and in a polite tone of voice said, "Yes, can I help you?"

"In the chair across from you," he said, pointing. "Uh, the paper...do you mind if I borrow it?"

Alexandra sank an inch in her seat. *Am I touchy or what?* she thought, leaning over slightly to look. "Oh...sure," she replied, "by all means. It's not mine, anyway."

Susan strolled through the door and spotted the stranger hovering over Alexandra and quickly made her way over to the table.

"Excuse me," she said in her normal, overly-protective manner, "am I interrupting something?"

"Oh, no," he replied with a curious look. He grabbed the papers that were scattered on the chair and held them up in front of her. "Just the paper," he huffed as turned to Alexandra, smiled and nodded gratefully before heading back to his table.

Alexandra covered her mouth, holding back a giggle. Susan hooked her bag-strap over the back of the chair as tossed Alexandra a hard look before sitting down and crossing her long legs off to the side of the chair.

"OK, smarty-pants…that's enough," Susan warned. "How was I to know that he wasn't trying to pick up on some innocent, defenseless, homely-looking girl?"

"All guys don't have bad intentions, you know," Alexandra replied. She grinned as she took a sip from the quarter-cup of coffee she had left. "Anyway," she went on, "forget about that. What I'm interested in is that *sex machine* of yours…Gary."

Susan thought. "Sure, why not!" she replied with a smirk, shifting in her chair, anxious to put it all out there.

"Never mind," Alexandra said, shoving the palm of her hand out in front of Susan's face. "I was just kidding. Not really interested...your business."

"Come on, Alex...you know you're interested. You just don't want to admit it, do you?"

Alexandra didn't comment, hoping the subject would change on its own.

"The truth is, Alex," Susan continued..."I like Gary a lot. He's smart; he's not bad looking; he has a nice house; and he has money. I'll tell you the best part. He's never been married and...yes," Susan went on in a proud tone..."he is great in bed."

"One way or another, you were going to get that last part in...weren't you?"

"You bet, girl," Susan mused, "best part. I figured if I tell you mine, you'll tell me yours. After all," she went on, grinning, "isn't that why we meet here every week, to trade secrets?"

"Tell you what, Susan, let's make a deal," Alexandra offered. "If you get me another cup of coffee when you get yours, I'll think of some juicy details to give you about John."

"That is a deal, sister," Susan replied. She quickly slid her chair back, shot up, and grabbed her bag off the back of the chair. "Oh, yeah," Susan said, as if an afterthought had just popped into her head. "You got any money? I left my wallet in the kitchen this morning. No wallet, no driver's license...just lipstick and a cell phone. Is that dumb or what?"

"I'd say typical," Alexandra replied, shaking her head. "I should start writing you off as a dependent."

Susan made her way over to the counter. Minutes later, she returned to the table with a cup of coffee in each hand, Alexandra pulled the pager from her bag and threw her head back in disgust. "Ah, shit!"

"What's this 'ah shit' all about?" Susan said, standing there.

Alexandra lifted up the hand holding the pager, wiggled it in front of Susan's face, and put it down on the table.

"It's Bob... from work," Alexandra said, searching in her bag for her cell phone.

"Don't call, Alex. Doesn't he know you're on vacation for a week...that you're preparing for a big race?"

"Yeah, he knows all that," Alexandra replied, furious with herself for even bringing the pager with her.

"But Bob wouldn't call unless there was really a crisis. I can't ignore it, given the fact that I've already taken the page."

"You and your sense of loyalty is beyond belief," Susan replied, with a strained laugh. "I've got to hand it to you, girl."

Alexandra dialed the number. After one ring, Bob picked up. He didn't let Alexandra get a word in edgewise. Not what are you doing? Are you in a place that you can't talk? Nothing. All Alexandra heard was 'come now, big trouble. Tried to get a replacement but couldn't.' Alexandra gave in, as usual.

"Two people didn't make it in...flu going around, I guess..." she said, stuffing the phone back in her bag, "and I was the only one carrying a pager this morning."

"Lucky you," Susan replied, handing Alexandra her change. "Just make sure you're on time Wednesday morning. I'll have my bags sitting out on the curb."

"Not to worry," Alexandra put in as she snatched her coffee from the table, grabbed her bag, and turned for the door. "I'll be there at four-fifteen sharp."

"Hey, wait a minute," Susan belted out. "What about the juicy details?"

"Hold onto that thought," she said glancing back. "It will give us something to talk about on our ride to San Diego."

***

As his golf-cart made its way down the fourth fairway at the Biltmore Country Club, John's cell phone rang. Alexandra called to let him know she had been called in again, and the early dinner plans they had were not going to work out. It would have been the last time they would see each other until her return from the Crew Classic. Most of the Carriage Brokers' sales team, including John, were scheduled to fly out Tuesday morning to Chicago for a two-day seminar.

"I won't see you for a week, John," Alexandra said sadly, pressing the phone to her ear with one hand and steering with the other. "I wish you could meet me in San Diego after your Chicago business is finished."

"Believe me, Alexandra," he replied, tapping Gary on the shoulder, pointing out his ball lying next to the sand trap on the right, "there's nothing I would like more than to be there and watch you guys win. Unfortunately, when I get back into town, the whole week is filled with meetings. Besides," he went on, "if I *were* there, I'd probably distract you. Kind of like a prize fighter the night before a big fight."

"I get the analogy and I can't deny that," she replied. "You and me...in San Diego...I couldn't dream of a better place to spend time alone with you."

"Look, my love," he said. "Not good etiquette for me to be talking on a cell phone in the middle of a golf course, better hang up. But, think how great it will be when we see each other again. After being apart for a while, who knows what we might do."

"Just hearing that is enough to distract *me*; how you can play golf with that thought in mind amazes me. Have a good game...I love you, John."

John laid the phone in the golf cart's cup-holder and slapped Gary on the back. "Guess what, old buddy?"

"What?" Gary replied, pulling over next to his ball which was sitting on the lip of the trap.

"She loves me."

"That's wonderful, John," he responded, "but I'll bet those guys waiting behind us aren't feeling much love."

Chapter Thirty-One

Tuesday

March 13

Las Vegas

5:00 p.m.

Jessica handed the car keys to the valet, tipped the bellhop for taking her suitcase and made her way through the dark-tinted, sliding glass doors into the lobby of the Wynn Resort Hotel. She crossed the mosaic-embedded terrazzo walkway over to the reception desk and checked in. Thirty minutes later, she was in her room waiting for the bellhop to deliver her bags.

She pushed the auto button on the wall and sheer curtains covering the huge picture window automatically opened to reveal a breathtaking view of the Strip from the thirty-sixth floor. Ironically, it was available...the very same room where John proposed to her. The Wynn is where they always stayed when in Vegas. John enjoyed playing craps while Jessica stood at his side, drinking Chardonnay and chatting it up with the guys in dark suits walking around behind the tables. Jessica was very famil-iar with many of the pit bosses, even knew some of them by name. This trip, she made a point to specifically seek one out just to say 'hey' before heading up the west elevator to her room. She wanted to make sure he knew she was there.

A soft rap on the door signaled the bellhop had arrived. She smiled wide and let him in. He cordially greeted her as he removed the bag-stand from the closet. He positioned it on the marble flooring next to the wall and placed a suitcase on top of it. Jessica needed to make a lasting impression on him. She gushed over how polite he was and how wonderful the room was…then handed him a hundred-dollar bill.

"What's your name?" Jessica asked politely, cozying up to him.

"Uh…it's Roger," he replied nervously. His eyes widened when he noticed the tip she handed him and then stuffed the money into his pocket.

"Well, Roger," she said. "Thank you very much for being prompt with my things."

As she closed the door behind him, a sense of gratification came over her. She turned to the full-length mirror that hung on the wall to admire her reflection. "Roger… oh…Roger," she said, with a satisfying grin on her face and a gleam in her eye. "You certainly will remember *me*, won't you?"

Jessica unzipped the suitcase and pulled out the small bag inside. She carried it over to the bed, opened it, and took out a bulky, white towel. Gently, she unrolled the towel to expose her father's loaded pistol, a roll of duct tape and gloves. *I can't wait to see the look on little-miss-bitch's face,* she thought. She recalled the horrified look on Millie's face when the end came for her, and smiled wide. *This won't be any different.* She picked up the gun, shifting it from one hand to the other.

After carefully wrapping the gun and placing the towel back into the bag, she set it on the floor next to a table and went to the mini-bar. She opened a small bottle of wine and poured a glass. Sipping the wine, she sat down and gazed out the window rehearsing her plan from beginning to end.

Everything is coming together, she thought as she lifted a cigarette from the pack laying on the table, lit it, and took in a deep draw. *Drive five hours to Vegas, check in to establish an alibi, head back to Scottsdale around nine, wait for little-miss-bitch to walk out of her house-- then surprise the hell out of her. It's flawless,* she concluded, blowing a stream of smoke towards the ceiling.

She thought about catching a stroke of luck two days earlier when she drove south towards Tucson, searching for a place to dispose of the body, and found the old abandoned well just off a dirt road east of Casa Grande. She would be there in plenty of time before sunrise, enough time to dump Alexandra's body into the empty well. *No one will ever find her. It's the perfect resting place for her.* She checked her watch and decided there was enough time to make another round of the casino and talk to more people before heading back towards Phoenix. In her mind, backtracking to Las Vegas after dumping Alexandra's body was brilliant, the perfect alibi. *No one will ever know I was on the road ten hours. "It's all working as I planned," she muttered, swirling the glass once more.* She took the last swallow, snuffed out the burning butt of her cigarette in what was left of the wine in the glass, grabbed her handbag, and left the room.

Chapter Thirty-two

Tim Sullivan's house

Tuesday

March 13

9:00 p.m.

Sully dragged himself out of bed and made his way into the kitchen. After making himself a salami sandwich, he grabbed the first beer he'd had in three days. He'd been down sick with a cold...hacking and sneezing, living on soup and crackers. He finished reading the three-hundred-page mystery novel and had watched as much television as he could stand from a prone position. *It's time to see what was going on in the neighborhood,* he thought. He went into the den, pushed the video play button, and slumped down into the easy chair across from the monitors. He took a big bite from the sandwich and began to watch the surveillance video stream.

The date and time display in the bottom left of the screen indicated recorded activity on Wednesday, March 7th. The real-time images came from eight cameras mounted in various areas of the complex. Each group of four recorded simultaneously. Each camera represented images in four quadrants of the monitor. Sully had two monitors, one stacked on top of the other. He used the remote to fast forward the feed on the top monitor until he'd see something worth his attention. He had now forwarded into the evening and had yet to observe anything interesting. He set the remote down on the table next to the chair, picked up the sandwich and bit off another big chunk.

Suddenly, he glanced at the top monitor and noticed an image of a person with a hood covering their head moving slowly up the walkway to condo number two-forty-two, where Millie's body had been found. He quickly laid what was left of the sandwich on the plate, grabbed the remote, slid to the edge of the chair--then jumped up knocking his cane onto the carpet. He got so excited, he didn't bother with the cane and hastily limped across to get a closer look.

He watched the intruder reach the front door, insert what appeared to be a key, open the door and disappear inside. "Oh, shit" he whispered, clutching the back of his neck with his hand, then quickly fumbled with the remote to rewind the tape. As the replay showed the intruder reaching the door, Sully zoomed in. Years of police work had conditioned his mind to be suspicious. He knew that, whoever the intruder was, their method of entry would be crucial to any investigation. If a key was used to open the door, it might mean that Millie's death wasn't an accident at all, but a pre-planned robbery and/or murder. He pushed 'pause' as the object was inserted into the keyhole. The image remained frozen on the monitor, and Sully could plainly see that the intruder did, in fact, use a key and not some implement to jimmy the door open.

The sudden reality of it all caught him off guard. The lingering cobwebs left in his head as a result of being sick began to fade away. Different scenarios played out in his mind…things that the average person without investigative experience would not consider. *One thing for sure,* he thought, *that poor woman's death wasn't an accident.*

"Where did the key come from?" he mumbled, staring at the monitor. The fact that he now had information pertaining to a probable murder began to excite him. However, it was his job to keep close tabs on the neighborhood. Now, seven days after the fact, he finds out that he's sitting on information the police could have used to keep the crime scene open for purposes of investigating a possible homicide. Instead, at least outside the condo, potential evidence would now be considered contaminated.

Based on Sully's experience, he knew how important it was to keep information fresh in the minds of the investigator's in order to solve crimes quickly. He nervously fumbled with the remote to get it to the fast-forward mode, and then watched the time display tick off the seconds and minutes until the door opened again. The intruder peeked out the door through the hood that still shielded his/her identity and stepped through the door onto the doormat, closing the door and quickly moving down the walkway out of the camera's range.

Chapter Thirty-Three

Kingman, Arizona

March 13

10:00 pm

Jessica exited the highway at Andy Devine Avenue and turned left to the Chevron station just up the road on the right. She topped off the gas tank, bought a bottle of water and another pack of cigarettes. *Every detail had been worked out*, she thought as she turned back onto Interstate 40, east. Paying for the gas with cash instead of a credit card was part of the overall plan, which she now considered even more brilliant than she originally thought. There was no way anyone could trace a cash transaction at that time of the night so far away from where she was supposed to be. Driving the speed limit was another precaution of which she had to be mindful. Getting pulled over for speeding could have disastrous consequences, leaving a record of being in a place that didn't fit an alibi if she needed one. The intensity and anticipation of what would soon happen was mounting the closer she got to Phoenix.

Suddenly, her thoughts were being tossed every which way. She was going through a mental checklist. *Am I overlooking anything? Did I think of all the angles?* "Shit," she muttered, blowing out a stream of smoke. *Let's see now,* she pondered. *In the parking lot at the Arena Grill, Meg did say that Alexandra was picking up*

Susan. What if Susan decides to drive to Alexandra's house and leave her car parked there for the week...what then? Am I prepared to deviate from the plan and still pull it off? All these questions are a test of my resolve, Jessica concluded. *I won't let these damn demons fill my head with stupid questions anymore. If something goes wrong, I'll deal with it.* She flipped the cigarette butt out of the car window.

It took fifteen minutes to reach Junction 93 to Phoenix, the same road that Jessica and John took the last time they drove to Vegas. John had always hated that road. It is especially dark when traveling by night and a two-lane road most of the way...although recent improvements had made it safer. Passing lanes had been constructed every five miles. The only lighting on the road was the headlights of cars or trucks coming in the opposite direction or those coming up from behind. Luckily, this time of night, especially during the week, traffic seemed much lighter, and it gave Jessica more time to think without trying to anticipate what other drivers might do...like fall asleep. She recalled what it was like when they drove this road together...when John thought of nothing but her instead of the little bitch controlling him now.

Suddenly, in the rear view mirror, she could see the lights of a semi-truck barreling up behind her. *The bastard's not slowing down,* she thought, watching him while trying to stay focused on the road in front of her. "Slow down, asshole!" she yelled. It didn't take long for her to conclude he wasn't going to wait for a passing lane. The truck was going around her, no matter what. She could see headlights coming toward her about a mile up the road. "OK, asshole...you've got room...go around *now,* you bastard." She tapped her brakes three times, and the truck went flying around her on the left as if she were standing still.

**

Tim Sullivan's house

10:15 p.m.

Within minutes of watching the video footage, Sully called the police. Seven days had passed. Millie's death had been officially ruled an accident. What Sully had in his possession was incredible footage; it excited him, reminding him of the old days. What he had witnessed on the tape convinced him that Millie's death was no accident and that he was now in the middle of a homicide investigation. While waiting for the police to arrive, he popped the top off another beer, toasted himself for being so clever and stood by the window, peering out. Twenty minutes later, headlights from two squad cars came around the corner heading down the cul-de-sac; one parked in front of Millie's house and the other in front of Sully's.

A single officer exited each of the vehicles and walked towards each other. They just stood there, appearing to be waiting. Moments later, Detective Dan Michaels arrived, stepped out of the government-issued Ford Taurus and looked around. He deftly moved his jacket aside and tucked his shirt into his khaki slacks as best he could. Tightly cinching his belt just below his protruding belly, he made his way over to the officers. Moments later, the detective smoothed down his neatly-trimmed, gray beard, made his way to Sully's front door, and knocked.

Sully stood just inside the door waiting for his turn to take the stage. He opened the door, sporting a huge grin. They stood there exchanging glances. Sully looked like death warmed over. *Another one I don't know,* Sully thought. The detective smiled and flashed his badge.

"Come in, Detective...by all means." Sully said, clearing a path for the detective to get by.

Over the next few minutes, the detective found himself listening to Sully boast about his years spent on the force and how fortunate the homeowners in the neighborhood were to have him as their security provider. He couldn't tell that the detective was getting bored, being polite until his nerves couldn't take any more of Sully's gushing.

"Why are we here, Mr. Sullivan? You told dispatch that you have important information regarding the death of Millie Jones?"

"I sure do, Detective," Sully said. "And they say I can't work for the force anymore, huh?"

Detective Michaels had no idea what Sully was getting at and didn't care. "So...what is it?"

"Step right this way, Detective," Sully said. "This is where it all happens...my situation room, so to speak."

Sully led the detective into the small, cramped, dingy den and began explaining his setup. The detective cocked his head, mentally sizing Sully up. Sully wouldn't stop with the self-gratifying attitude. As he explained the out-dated monitoring system, his chest kept growing.

Detective Michaels had had enough. He glanced at a small end-table with three empties and one half-full bottle of beer propping up a bag of chips...wishing he had some duct tape to keep Sully's mouth from blabbering.

"OK, Mr. Sullivan," he said, interrupting him in the middle of his life story and the lesson in technology. "I get how all this works. You called and we are here. You claim to have information about the incident that happened a few houses from here, so what would that be?"

"Uh, yes" Sully replied, as if it were an afterthought, pointing with his cane, "Over here. I've got some video you will be interested in. There are cameras located in the neighborhood that I had installed—with the HOA's money, that is—which I monitor from this room. As I was viewing the stream from the day her sister found her, I realized that one of the cameras had picked up pictures of an intruder going into Millie Jones's house the night before."

Detective Michaels suddenly perked up. "OK... let's see what you've got." he said, stroking his beard.

Sully reversed and forwarded the tape at least five times as they watched the intruder go in and out of the residence. From the camera angle, there seemed to be no way to identify the intruder. It was too dark, and whoever was underneath that hood had been very careful not to get recognized...closing the hood around his or her head going in and coming out. The camera was positioned in such a way that it captured a wide angle and the front of several condos but, from that direction, it only caught the person from a slight side view.

"How many cameras do you have installed around this cul-de-sac?" the detective asked.

"Six," Tim replied, eyeing the half-full bottle sitting on the table next to the chair.

"The cameras, Mr. Sullivan...do they only take video of the houses in the neighborhood?"

"Oh, shit!" Sully responded, in a loud voice. "Two cameras get video of the street. I was so interested in the person who went in and out of the residence," he went on, "I forgot about the cameras filming the street."

Detective Michaels walked across the room, removed his jacket and draped it over a stool by the window. He noticed a small pair of binoculars sitting on the window sill, which didn't surprise him. He loosened his tie, which hung short, just above his belly. "Don't worry, Mr. Sullivan," he said, making his way back towards the monitors. "Shit happens. You can't think of everything, now can you? Why don't we just have a look-see."

Sully picked up the stack of tapes, gave them a shuffle, and ended up with the tape from the two cameras covering the street marked Wednesday, March 7th. He shoved it into the bottom monitor, grabbed the remote, pushed 'play,' and then started to fast-forward. The video stream zipped at a pace where images were still recognizable. However, to identify activity at any given point in time, the tape needed to be in normal-play mode for clarity and detail. Darkness came and went as the sun rose and set. The time display in the corner of the monitor changed quickly; the minutes passed in seconds.

Suddenly, a light-colored Escalade came into view from around the corner. Detective Michaels was right on it, but Sully had turned away seconds before.

"Wait, stop the tape!" the detective ordered, looking around for Sully, who was chugging what was left in the bottle of beer.

Sully was caught off guard. It took him a moment to recover and react to the detective's order. He hobbled over to the table next to the monitor's looking for the remote.

"There!" the detective exclaimed, pointing, "it's on the table next to the beer bottles." Shit, Jesus, buddy...the remote...get it."

Sully re-wound the tape to the point where the car appeared, then set the recorder to normal-play mode.

"Sorry," he said, suddenly feeling awkward. "I got thirsty...sorry."

The detective ignored his clumsy excuse and focused his eyes on the Escalade, which was now parked with the engine off. Taking into account that it was dark, he could see no movement inside the vehicle. They waited; minutes passed, and still no movement.

"Pause it, Sullivan."

Sully pushed pause. "Why do you want it stopped?" Sully said with a curious expression on his face. "It takes a few minutes before the driver exits the vehicle."

"I get that, but what I want to know is... is there a camera that monitors the entrance to the street?"

"Sure, I've got it all covered...why?"

That's the tape I want to see," he replied. "Where is it."

"Uh...let's see." Sully picked up the tape marked T-2 and shoved it into monitor. The sun rose and set...then suddenly the Escalade appeared entering the cul-de-sac.

"Bingo," the detective said, pointing. "Stop it right there." The video showed a clear picture. "It looks like we've got ourselves a license plate number."

The detective pulled a small note pad from the back pocket of his pants and a pen from his shirt pocket. "Let's see," he said, jotting down the number. "Arizona, 592PZZ. Now, start up the other tape again." he continued as he stuffed the pad back into his pocket and clipped the pen into his shirt pocket. "If you are right about someone getting out of that car..."

"Oh, someone will, Detective, I promise you," Sully interrupted, in a take-charge tone of voice. "Just you keep watching," he went on, sporting a confident grin.

The detective didn't like to be interrupted, but Sully hadn't picked up on that yet. He looked at Sully with an irritating look that could cut through granite.

"As I was going to say... if you are right about the person in that car going into Ms. Jones house at that time of night, you really might have something here, Mr. Sullivan."

"You're damn right I do," Sully replied, throwing out his chest.

"Let's do it...continue rolling the tape," the detective said, using a hand gesture. "Fast forward until we get movement."

The tape rolled. Suddenly, Millie's car entered the cul-de-sac, moved right past the Escalade and then went out of view. Sully switched to the side monitor and forwarded the tape to the exact time Millie drove up the driveway and into her garage. They watched the garage door drop down before Sully switched back to the other monitor, which he had paused, and activated the 'play' feature.

Sully said, "Back to the perp's car."

"OK, then," the detective said, folding his arms and shifting his balance to his other leg. "There is no reason to waste time waiting for them to leave the vehicle...just fast-forward until someone comes out of that damn Escalade." Two minutes later, a half hour in real-time, the door to the Escalade opened. Jessica stepped out, cagily looked around the neighborhood, then pulled the hood to the oversize sweatshirt she wore up over her head.

"Holy shit, Detective," Sully said, taking a closer look. "It's a woman!"

"I think you're right," he replied. "Go back and pause it...let's get a better look."

Sully rewound to the point where she stepped out of the car and momentarily turned in the direction of the light pole yards away which projected just enough light to confirm that the driver was indeed a woman. He paused the tape. Fortunately, there was enough light from the pole to bring her face into clear view.

"No doubt about it," said the detective, "...and a nice-looking, young one at that."

Sully went for another beer while the detective lifted the radio from his hip and called headquarters. The orders were direct and simple: run the plate number, get the name and address of the owner of the vehicle, put out an APB and bring her in for questioning. His final words were, 'Use caution...she could be armed and dangerous.'

"I'm going to need these tapes for evidence," the detective said.

Chapter Thirty-Four

Wickenburg, Arizona

1:00am

In the distance, Jessica made out the sign for Wickenburg. *Another twenty-two miles and I'll be in the biggest little town outside of Phoenix,* she thought.

***

Wickenburg is the place you drive through when you want to cut an hour and a half off the Vegas to Phoenix trip. Two gas stations, a Dunkin' Donuts, a MacDonald's and a few other establishments rounded out the town some seventy miles north of Phoenix. Big rigs working their way from Vegas to Phoenix gas up in Wickenburg before picking up their cargo in Phoenix. Then, they reverse their route back to Vegas so the mega hotels can continue serving steak and lobster to the few winners in their casinos as well as the losers hoping to make a final score before leaving broke.

***

Jessica eyed the gas gauge; quarter of a tank left. Stopping for gas wasn't what she wanted to do, but she had no choice. She couldn't take the chance of having to buy gas somewhere in Phoenix once the deed was done. Transporting Alexandra, bound and gagged in the back of her Escalade was going to be touchy. Making any kind of stop along the way before reaching the final destination might be risking it. *It's all part of the plan…do it.*

She pulled up next to the gas pump, stepped out of the car, and made her way into the store with cash in hand. Grabbing a bottle of water, she slid the cash through the opening under the bullet-proof glass, and then headed back out to fill the tank. Within minutes, the Escalade accelerated out of the Quick Stop and back onto the road heading for Phoenix.

The road was dark; no headlights or tail lights ahead or behind her. *Perfect,* she thought, *no other cars on the road but me, at least for now.* She switched to her bright lights for a better view ahead. She didn't want to take the chance that some animal might suddenly cross the road in front of her. Road kill just wasn't the kind of killing Jessica had on her mind. She glanced at the GPS time-display then pulled a cigarette from the pack that was sitting on the console. It gave her pleasure to know that her timing was right on. She smiled ruthlessly, and then pushed the tip of the cigarette against the glowing, red-hot lighter. The breeze filtering in through the half-opened window brushed at her hair and the car filled with cool, damp air. With her eyes fixed on the road in front of her, she recalled how easy it was to do away with Millie. "It's all in the planning," she mumbled, glancing up at her reflection in the rear-view mirror with a look of satisfaction. She leaned back and took the last draw from the cigarette before tossing it out the window into the darkness.

Cruising at sixty-five, Jessica thought about Millie's family and friends mourning their loss and accepting the fact that it was a tragic accident…likely praying for her soul. *I'm the only one who knows the real truth.* She started talking to herself. "I just wish, Father dear, that you could know the real truth…and that I'll stop at nothing to take what's mine…even smashing your mistress's head to the bathroom floor."

Her thoughts switched to Alexandra and how soon she would be gone. *How quickly John would forget about his brief fling with the bitch,* she thought. She couldn't wait until they were back to the place they were before the accident. She lifted her left hand off the steering wheel and gazed at her ring finger. She had a vision of the ring that was no longer there…but would soon be once again. She recalled that painful morning when she had yanked the ring off her finger and tossed it at him, and then thought about how wonderful it would be when he begs her to take it back. *When it's all over and that bitch is gone forever, I'll be sympathetic and caring,* she thought. As she stared, as if in a trance, at the intermittent yellow lines whizzing by, her mind kept whirring. *I'll put on such a show that John will know that I truly care about his feelings. I'll be oh-so-compassionate about the girl he had just met and who had gone missing without a trace.*

She thought about the adrenaline rush she got a week ago when she found the spot where Alexandra would take her last breath… a place south of Phoenix, ten miles north of Casa Grande, on a dirt road off I-10 that leads to nowhere. She was convinced that if anyone ever found Alexandra's body, it would be impossible to determine who had dumped her into that abandoned well with a bullet in her head. Another one of those terrible abductions you see playing out on the morning and evening news all the time.

***

Scottsdale Police Headquarters

3:00am

Detective Michaels obtained an 'Emergency Warrant' from a tired State official rousted from his bed to issue the search and arrest warrant. Once the paperwork was in place, and the all-points bulletin issued to all the law enforcement agencies in the state of Arizona, every on-duty cop would be on the lookout for a light-colored Cadillac Escalade and its registered owner, Jessica Crawford...considered a person of interest, possibly armed and dangerous.

***

Three squad cars pulled up to the front of Jessica's house. The officers moved stealthily around the residence, front and rear, with guns drawn, ready to use if necessary. With everyone in position, one officer knocked twice on the front door. Getting no response, two officers broke through the door with two more following behind. The first officer yelled, "Scottsdale police...Is anyone in the house?" Swiftly, they split up, moving from room-to-room in the darkness, yelling, "Clear! Clear! Clear!"

The officers methodically switched lights on in each of the rooms, their flashlights switching off one-by-one. The search began for anything of a suspicious nature that could tie Jessica Crawford to the death of Millie Jones. One officer pressed on the radio mic positioned on his shoulder and reported the house was empty. Meanwhile, neighborhood dogs barked, and lights from surrounding condos lit up. The neighborhood around Jessica's condo was now cordoned off; yellow tape strung every which way.

***

Lawrence Crawford's house

3:30am

With the shake-down underway at Jessica's condo, Detective Michaels pushed the button on the intercom attached to a brick wall and waited. A minute went by with no response. Parked outside the curl-patterned, wrought iron gate, he could see a dark-colored car parked near the front of the house. He hit the buzzer over and over again until his blood began to boil, waiting impatiently for someone's voice to sound out through the speaker.

The old mansion, on a hill overlooking the lights of Phoenix, reminded him of a haunted house setting. The house sat deep into the property at the end of a long, inclined, red-brick driveway surrounded by hedges and tall ficus and palm trees. No lights could be seen in any of the windows, which made sense at that time of the morning. The property leading up to the house was dark with the exception of old lantern-like fixtures positioned close to the ground lining each side of the driveway. The headlights from the undercover car aimed on a cast iron placard attached to the front of the gate which said, in raised lettering, "The Crawford House Built in 1925." Old man Crawford had bought the house from a prominent Phoenix banker who purchased it from the original owner in 1945, soon after the war ended.

***

"Who is it?" Lawrence asked, in a grumpy tone of voice reverberating through the speaker next to the keypad.

"Scottsdale Police, Mr. Crawford," he responded. "Detective Michaels."

"What is it you want at this time of the morning?" Lawrence said, in his usual intimidating, irritated voice as he grabbed his robe off of the bedpost and shuffled over to the window to peer through the curtains, out through the trees, down towards the end of the driveway. He could see one of the car's headlight's beaming towards the house.

Michaels, the seasoned cop that he is, had done this many times. He wasn't intimidated nor was he reluctant to face the issue head on; he didn't care who it was. Years ago, when the Mayor's son was involved in a drug-related hit and run, he rousted the Mayor out of an important council meeting, walked right up to him and whispered in his ear. This case had a similar sense of urgency...time was critical in a murder investigation.

"It's Jessica, Mr. Crawford...your daughter. Is she here with you tonight?"

"God, no, man! She doesn't live here. She's got her own house...try over there."

"We've been to her house, sir, and she's not there. Please, let's make this easy. It's very important that I ask you some questions. It's for your daughter's own good."

Lawrence didn't know what to think. He hesitated. "Oh, what the hell!" He pushed a button, then headed down the hall to the staircase. "What has she gotten herself into this time?" he muttered, walking down the stairs in his bare feet.

The gate made a groaning sound as it slowly swung open. The detective drove his car up and around the circular driveway until he reached the brick steps leading up to the house...parking behind Lawrence's car. Lawrence stood in the open doorway, cinching his robe.

Michaels flashed his badge before Lawrence allowed him to enter the house. Five minutes into the conversation, after the detective explained why he was there, Lawrence let out a deep sigh, bent his bushy eyebrows and sat down in an old velvet-covered armchair. He was stunned at the accusations being thrown out and just wasn't buying it.

"Are you out of your mind, man?" he said loudly. "My daughter has done a lot of things but...being suspected of murder...there's no way, I tell you."

"That is why I want to talk to her, sir. We have her on tape at the crime scene..."

"Bullshit! Millie's death was an accident."

"All the more reason Jessica's presence at Millie's condo that night leads us to believe something else is going on here. Can you think of a reason why your daughter might have been sneaking into Millie's house that night?"

"Sneaking?" Lawrence questioned.

"Like I said, Mr. Crawford; we have her on tape."

"Well, I want to see it...show me."

"Sorry," the detective replied, shaking his head. "The tape is now evidence in a crime scene. You'll have to trust me on this."

Old man Crawford sat there, silent and befuddled. Suddenly, he rose from the chair and made his way over to a cabinet located on the right side of the staircase, pulled out a bottle of Jack Daniels and poured himself half a glass.

He took a huge gulp from the glass and swallowed as if he were drinking water. "You actually think my daughter murdered my secretary?" he said flatly, "Is that what you're trying to say?"

"Mr. Crawford," Michaels replied, walking over to him, "right now, we are just interested as to why she would be at Millie's house the night before she was found lying on her bathroom floor in a pool of blood."

There was a moment of silence. Lawrence took another big swallow. The detective watched as a look of despair crossed the old man's face...as if he were deep in thought, thinking about something he wasn't willing to talk about.

"Look here, Detective," Lawrence said, setting the glass down and shoving his hands into the pockets of the robe. "I know my rights. I'm not sure what's going on here, but I'm not answering any questions until I talk to my daughter. As a matter of fact, Detective," he went on, "I'm going to wake my lawyer up right now and inform him what has happened here."

"Please understand, Mr. Crawford," Michaels replied, staring hard, "I don't like this anymore than you do." He pulled a card from his pocket and placed it next to the drink glass. "I know this is uncomfortable, but if you really want to help your daughter, you should cooperate with us. We *will* find her. And we all can only hope it is under good circumstances. Sorry to have bothered you at this hour of the morning."

The detective climbed back into his vehicle and lifted the microphone off its holder. "This is Detective Michaels...the Crawford woman...you got anything?"

Chapter Thirty-Five

Alexandra's condo

3:45 am

The garage door opened. Alexandra walked to the rear of the Toyota with a backpack thrown over her shoulder, carrying a suitcase. She opened the hatch and tossed both items into the open compartment.

Jessica had already been watching the house for over ten minutes, waiting.

Alexandra checked her watch and realized she was running late; she picked up the pace. She had committed to being at Susan's house around four o'clock or a little after. "I know," she said, as if Susan were standing next to her, "if I'm late, I'll be hearing about it for the first half-hour into the ride to San Diego." *OK, then,* she thought, making her way back inside the house. *One last walk through and I'm out of here.* The garage light automatically switched off. She made her way through the kitchen, and glanced at Chester's half-eaten bowl of dry dog food on the floor and frowned at the thought of leaving him in a kennel for a week. *I miss him already,* she thought, shaking her head...*and John too.*

Jessica stepped from the shadows into the dark garage and stood silently along the wall next to the door leading into the house. After making her way through the house, performing a mental check, Alexandra opened the door leading back out into the garage. Suddenly, like a vicious wildcat, Jessica attacked, smashing the butt of the gun against the top of Alexandra's forehead, knocking her backwards into the laundry room, up against a cupboard.

Alexandra's legs couldn't hold her up. She slid down the face-board of the cupboard, ending up in a sitting position on the floor. Stunned by the blow to the head, she was barely conscious.

Jessica moved in and stood over her. She scowled down at her victim with fiery eyes. Dropping her voice to a low tone, she snarled, "This is what you get, you bitch...for stealing my man." She raised the gun again and struck another blow to the side of Alexandra's head, knocking her flat onto the floor, out cold.

Working quickly, Jessica took Alexandra's wrists and bound them together with duct tape. After pulling her ankles together and binding them tightly, she took a strip of the tape and pressed it tightly over Alexandra's mouth. She rose to one knee, gloating over her accomplishment-- like a hunter standing over a trophy elk. Blood oozed from Alexandra's forehead onto the floor. The adrenaline rushed through Jessica's body like it had when she gave Millie the final blow that sent her to Jessica's hell. *There is one big difference,* she thought, pointing the gun at Alexandra's head.

"For now, you're still breathing," Jessica mumbled. "Sending you to hell will be with a bullet to the temple."

While Alexandra lay limp and lifeless, Jessica rushed out to the Escalade parked a few yards down the street, started the engine then drove the car into Alexandra's driveway. She opened a passenger rear door and quickly spread out the plastic tarp she had brought to avoid leaving blood evidence on the leather seat. She hurried back into the house, leaving the engine to idle.

Jessica's heart rate pumped furiously, giving her the momentary strength to drag Alexandra to the door leading into the house from the garage. She left her laying across the threshold and made her way out to the main garage door then looked around the neighborhood. She wanted to be sure there were no early morning joggers or neighbors who had a routine of walking their dogs at that hour. Another rush came over her, sending a barrage of endorphins into her blood stream. She rushed back, grabbed Alexandra by the arms, and dragged her to the open door of the Escalade. She placed Alexandra's arms across her body and, with some effort, hoisted her upper torso onto the seat. Looking around furtively, she hurried around to the other side, opened the door, reached in, and pulled Alexandra's body the rest of the way into the Escalade until she lay across the seat.

Jessica climbed in the Escalade and took a moment to go over the plan in her head. *No mistakes*, she thought as she put the shift into drive and sped off, leaving the garage door open.

The Escalade was quiet, quiet enough that Jessica could hear Alexandra faintly breathing. Then, five miles down the road, she heard a muffled groan coming from the rear seat. Alexandra was regaining consciousness.

***

The pain was excruciating. Alexandra's head throbbed, and her arms and legs felt numb all over. She had no recollection of what had happened but knew she was bound, gagged and being driven somewhere. She tried to think but, at that point, everything seemed in slow motion. Her head was still spinning, trying to clear itself. Through the car window, she could see the tops of light poles and signs passing by as the Escalade rolled down the freeway; she was terrified.

The emergency training she had undergone for her job, the weight training and the competitive rowing had never prepared her for what she was about to endure. She felt a breeze swirling around her filled with the smell of harsh cigarette smoke. *Who is doing this to me, and why?* She struggled to get free. She tried to quietly work her way into a sitting position but couldn't get the leverage.

From Alexandra's viewpoint, there was no way for her to tell who was driving; it was eerily quiet. A few minutes passed and her head began to clear a little...she could almost think straight. She tried pulling her arms free again, but the tape wouldn't stretch or give. She tried to do the same with her legs and got the same result. Moving cautiously, she slowly and quietly shifted her body a quarter turn to face the front seat. *It's a woman...my god, its Jessica*, she thought. Her body wrenched. *Oh, shit.*

***

Jessica glanced back and saw Alexandra glaring at her between the seats with wide eyes. "Well...little miss bitch," Jessica said coldly. "I see that you're awake."

Alexandra, still dazed, was hurting. *Why are you doing this to me?* Trying to speak, she could only mumble, *"Why? Why?"* She managed to wiggle herself into a leaning position against the car door. Jessica grabbed the gun from the seat next to her and held it up for Alexandra to see.

"Lay back down, you whore!" she warned, "...or you'll die now instead of later."

Alexandra worked her way back down flat on the seat, her body stretching from one door to the other, while trying to push words out through the tape over her mouth.

"Just lay there and be quiet," Jessica ordered, "or I'll put you to sleep again...but for good this time."

Alexandra squeezed her eyes tightly shut. *This can't be happening,* she thought, pulling hard on her wrists to get loose. *Maybe I'm having one of those dreams again...the ones that seem so real. Maybe John will wake me up and I'll be lying in his arms instead of on this cold, leather seat--on the way to God knows where.* "Please, someone," she mumbled, tears welling in her eyes and running down the side of her face, "…someone, please help me."

"Don't fight it," Jessica said nonchalantly, taking a pull from another cigarette. "You'll just make it worse on yourself. We've got about a forty-five-minute drive ahead of us so enjoy the ride…I will."

Chapter Thirty-Six

Alexandra's condo

4:30am

Susan couldn't stand still, pacing back and forth, in one room and then another, looking for Alexandra...horrified at the sight of blood all over the floor in the laundry room and tracks of it on the cement garage floor. For a moment, the trauma was too much to handle. It was all she could do just to maintain control. She wasn't prepared for anything like this.

Stay calm, stay calm... a voice in her head repeated over and over as she took short breaths, in and out, in ragged gasps. Images of Alexandra began to pop in and out of her mind... gruesome images of her body lying somewhere, in blood or mud or on a road somewhere. *Wait!* she thought. *Something happened. She somehow hurt herself and called an ambulance. Yes, I'll bet that's what is it is.* Still something wasn't right. She pressed the palm of one hand on the side of her head. *Why is the garage door open with no one around? The drag marks of blood on the cement...what about those?* Suddenly, reality flooded her senses. *What do I do? What shall I do? Call the police? Where is Alexandra?* The questions flashed through her mind faster than she could process.

***

Earlier, when Alexandra didn't show up at Susan's house as planned, Susan began to worry. She called Alexandra's cell twice, only to get her voice mail. The concern that something might be wrong escalated. At four-twenty, Susan had run out of patience. She grabbed her things, jumped into her car, and raced the five miles to Alexandra's house. She found the garage door open and Alexandra's Toyota still inside, easing her concern. Knowing that Alexandra was home and not injured or worse somewhere on the side of a road was calming. She slid out of her car and made her way up the driveway towards the garage. She tripped the sensor and the garage light clicked on. She noticed dark red marks on the cement but didn't think much of it until she turned into the doorway leading into the laundry room.

Susan was horrified by what she saw. Her body quivered and the hair on her arms stood straight up. She took in a deep breath, looked around and grabbed for a broom that was leaning against the wall next to the dryer. She held it out in front of her as if it were a weapon. If it weren't for the fact that Alexandra could be hurt, lying in another room, she would have darted out of the house long ago. Cautiously, she moved from room to room, switching on lights as she went. *Shit, she's not here.* She felt for her cell phone and realized she had left it on the console in her car. She rushed back through the house and out into the street. She reached through the car window, grabbed the phone and dialed 9-1-1, all the while looking around and shouting Alexandra's name, hoping for an answer.

Susan leaned up against her car trembling. Fear consumed her…she refused to believe that anything could be wrong with her best friend. Within minutes, squad cars were everywhere. Rotating lights, red and blue, reflected off everything in every direction. Curious neighbors peered out their windows, dogs barked and howled at the commotion, and she could hear the faint sound of more sirens in the distance.

As Detective Michaels pulled up and parked between two of the squad cars, he noticed a woman standing in front of an officer holding a flashlight under his arm. The woman was hysterical, waving her arms every which way. Within seconds, Detective Michaels was standing between them.

"OK...OK, lady. Now hold on here," he said, holding his badge in the air as if he were a coach holding up the runner at third base. "I'm Detective Michaels...now calm down, please, lady. Tell me your name and what do you have to do with this?"

"That's just it, Detective!" she shouted, "I don't know. I..."

"You don't know your name?" the detective quickly interrupted, bending his thick, salt and pepper eyebrows.

"Uh...no," she replied, "Uh...I mean yes," she went on, stuttering nervously. "I'm Susan, Susan McAdams."

"OK, then, Ms. McAdams, take a deep breath," he said. "Can you calmly tell me what you know?"

Susan paused, took in a deep breath, and then stiffened her arms down at her side. "My best friend was supposed to pick me up at four o'clock this morning. We were going to drive to San Diego...our rowing team is competing in the Crew Classic. It's a race that..."

"I'm familiar with the Crew Classic, Susan," he said, interrupting her again. "And your friend's name is...?"

"Alexandra, Alexandra Morgan."

"Uh...Detective," said an officer walking up to them, "There is fresh blood on the floor in the house. We've searched the premises, front and back...nothing sir," he went on, confirming with a head shake.

"Do we have a picture of her?" the detective asked, turning back towards Susan, as he wiggled his pad out of his pants pocket and lifted his pen from his shirt.

"There are pictures in the house," she replied.

"OK, then…" he said, turning back to the officer. "Get one, process it, and secure the scene. I want crime investigations here…pronto," he went on, making notes on the pad. "Oh…and I want the house, outside the house, every twig, rock and blade of grass carefully scoured for clues that might tell us something useful while we wait for the investigations unit to arrive."

"Yes, sir," said the officer, who made his way over to a squad car while barking orders at two others in uniform.

"What do you think happened, Detective?" Susan asked, crossing her arms, preparing for an answer that she wasn't ready to accept.

"I'm afraid that's something we won't know until we get more information," he replied, scratching his head with the pen. "So far, this has been one hell of a crazy night. I've got half the cops in Phoenix looking for some girl named Jessica Crawford and now the other half will be looking for Alexandra Morgan."

It took a moment for Susan to process what he had said. It was like this whole ordeal had her in some sort of trance. "Detective, did you say Jessica Crawford?"

"I did," he replied, tossing her a curious look. "Why? Do you know her?"

"Uh…not really. Other than…well…sort of, I guess."

"Well, what is it," he broke in. "Do you or don't you?"

Susan pondered a moment. "Jessica Crawford… Alexandra's boyfriend has an ex-fiancé by that name."

"Ex-fiancé?" he replied quickly, "Now, Susan," he went on, stroking his beard, "do you happen to know a Millie Jones?"

"Uh…no, I don't think so, Detective," she replied. "Should I?"

"Not necessarily," he said. "But, I have a feeling that there is a common thread that ties all these people together."

Chapter Thirty-Seven

John's House

5:00 a.m.

At first, it seemed like a dream. The phone ringing startled John awake. He moaned, rolled over and fumbled for the land line.

"Yes, who is it?" John said, mumbling as he glanced at the digital clock.

"John, it's me...wake up!" Gary said in a panic. "Something has happened to Alexandra."

All in one motion, John jerked himself up, swung his left arm around reaching for the lamp, almost knocking it off of the night stand. "Shit..!" He fumbled with the lamp, felt for the switch and turned it on. "Now, say that again."

"Something...has...happened...to Alexandra," he repeated slowly.

"What is it?" John said, running his fingers through his hair. "Is she sick or something? Wait a minute," he continued before Gary could answer. "How do you know something happened, anyway?"

"No...not sick," insisted Gary, rushing his words. "Trust me. Susan just called from her house and said the police were there. Susan found blood on the floor. You better get over there...quick."

"Get over where?" he replied, trying to make sense of what Gary had said. "Susan's house?"

"No, John," he responded loudly. "Not Susan's house...Alexandra's house. Susan is there with the police and... Alexandra is missing."

Confusion and fear flooded John's mind as Gary went into more detail. Beads of sweat laced his forehead. He hopped frantically on one foot, trying to get his pants on while holding the phone between his shoulder and his ear, listening.

Within thirty seconds, Gary had told John everything Susan relayed to him. John couldn't believe what he was hearing. It was the part when Gary told John that Jessica may have had something to do with Millie's death that drove him into overdrive, emotionally. John let the receiver drop, hanging by the coiled cord. He rushed down the stairs, grabbed the car keys off the counter, and made a mad dash to the Porsche.

"Son of a bitch!" The words echoed inside the car. Out of pure frustration, he slammed a hand against the steering wheel. Suddenly, his body became tense, uncomfortable in his skin. The worst scenario played out in his mind. He had to stop, just for a moment, and breath... take a break from the horror flashing before his eyes, even though it wasn't real. He took in a slow, deep breath, and then another...until, at least for the moment, he calmed himself. He pushed the ignition button and listened to the engine turn over and purr before throwing the gear in reverse to screech his way out of the driveway.

***

It was a ten-minute drive to Alexandra's house from where he lived. John's head was spinning. He remembered telling her that day, on the way back from the lake, that they lived close enough to be neighbors. Now, the distance seemed infinite. He remembered her soft lips when she kissed his cheek as they said goodbye in the driveway of her condo. He remembered the warm shower they took the first time they made passionate love. All the things about their wonderful, new relationship flashed through his mind in just a few seconds as he negotiated turn after turn, driving out of his neighborhood onto Scottsdale Road.

He hit a red light on Bell going south and, without hesitation, drove right through it. A feeling of helplessness overwhelmed him. His stomach tightened and turned. *Will I get there in time,* he thought, and then remembered Gary's words, 'Alexandra is missing.' Those words frightened him and he didn't want to believe them.

He punished himself for the things Jessica might be doing to Alexandra...if, in fact Jessica had anything to do with Alexandra's disappearance. He felt helpless, a feeling of having no control over anything at that point. As he turned onto McCormick Parkway, he thought about how headstrong Jessica was...but he never would have believed that she was capable of doing anything so evil and wicked.

"I'll call her," he said in a panic as he grabbed his cell phone and dialed Jessica's. After one ring, he began yelling her name.

"Answer the phone, Jessica! Damn it, Jessica, answer the phone!"

After listening to it ring, Jessica picked the phone up off the console. John's name appeared on the display.

"Oh, John," she said calmly, placing the phone back where she took it from, unanswered. "Why would you be calling me now, baby? I'm sorry, but I can't talk to you now. You *know* what I have to do...don't you, baby?"

Oh, shit, Alexandra thought as she listened to the one-sided conversation Jessica was having. All the while, she tugged and pulled, trying to work her hands free. *This woman has gone off the deep end, flipped out. This isn't just about her obsession with John. She's sick...sick and psychotic.*

Despite all the horror Alexandra was facing, it gave her some comfort to know that John's call to Jessica meant that he knew something was wrong and that there were people trying to find her. Although somewhat reassuring, it didn't take away from the fact that she was in the backseat of a car being driven by a maniac who planned to kill her.

Too scared to cry and too tired of fighting to free herself from the tape around her arms and legs, Alexandra decided to trust that John would somehow make his way to her. What had brought them together was more powerful than Jessica's determination to have it end, she concluded, as she closed her eyes and prayed.

She lay there remembering how strong her father was to do what he did. The danger that always confronted him in his job just gave him the strength to do more, putting his life out there for people he didn't even know just to make sure that they survived, even if he didn't. It was now her turn to display the strength inherent in her...the strength from her father. She kept repeating to herself...no fear, no fear.

***

As John sped around the corner onto the street where Alexandra lived, he cringed at what he saw in front of her house. *My God,* he thought, as he slammed on the brakes, stopping on a dime in the middle of the street. The barricade formed by the squad cars made the street look like a parking lot. Susan was sitting in her car, shaking. Frightening thoughts about what might be happening to Alexandra kept tumbling over and over in her head. She spotted John as he jumped from the Porsche to make his way through the maze of cops that were scampering around looking for clues.

"Hey, buddy!" one officer shouted. "Hold it right there. This is a crime scene. You can't come up here."

Susan jumped out of her car, calling out for him, rushing over to head him off. Just as he turned to explain why he was there, Susan grabbed him and threw her arms around him.

"Oh, John," she said sobbing, "it's terrible. Alexandra's gone."

"Susan," he said, loosening her grip. "Who do I talk to? Who's in charge here?"

She pointed in the direction of the garage. "It's him...he's the one...over there. The short stocky guy with the beard... Detective Michaels."

Gary pulled in next to the Porsche. By then, an officer was manning the perimeter and wouldn't let Gary get close. Through all the flashing lights and commotion, he spotted John and Susan standing several yards away and yelled at them. Susan turned. "You go, John," she said. "I'll stay over there, with Gary."

John rushed past one of the officers who was busy combing the shrubs with a flashlight and didn't notice him go by. When he reached the garage, the detective was on the radio with headquarters, listening to what sounded like some kind of code. Detective Michaels held his index finger up in front of John, then hung the radio down at his side.

"Would you be John Henning?" the detective asked.

"Yes, Detective. Alexandra and I have been seeing each other for a few months. Do you know where she is?"

"Not yet," he said, "but we think we know who's got her," he went on, then clipped the radio back onto his belt. "Your ex...Jessica Crawford."

"We never married, Detective," John said flatly. "We were only engaged."

"Whatever," he replied, staring up at him. "Piecing things together, we are fairly certain that, a week ago, this Jessica murdered a lady that worked for her father, Lawrence Crawford. Even though we haven't figured out the tie between the woman who was murdered and Alexandra, it could be some revenge scenario involving you."

"This is crazy," John muttered, running a hand through his hair, shaking his head from side-to-side.

"As crazy as it may sound, buddy," the detective pointed out, "I've seen stranger things. And, besides... we've found out that Jessica is a bona-fide loony-tune."

"Jesus," John said, drawing in a deep breath. His head filled up with 'what ifs.' "How do you know all this... about Jessica, I mean?"

"I've spoken to her father, who by the way, seems a little unstable himself. Your ex-finance had been seeing a psychologist over the years...considered to be bipolar of sorts."

"Jesus," John gasped. "I had no idea ."

"Being in love clouds a lot of things...if you know what I mean. The woman definitely needs help and hope it's not too late to get it for her."

"Okay, Detective, you're the expert. What's next...what do we do?"

"You don't do anything but wait for us to do our job," he replied, pulling up the back of his pant underneath his coat.

"Wait for what?" John asked in an anxious tone, swallowing hard.

"We've got every cop in the Valley looking for Jessica's Escalade," he replied, "so we *will* find her. The big question is...will we find her in time?"

John didn't like what he was hearing. His heart ached for answers. *I wish I knew where to look,* he thought.

John said, "Can I go into the house?"

"I'm afraid not, Mr. Henning. Crime scene."

John made his way over to where Gary and Susan were leaning against Gary's car. Lights were on in every house on the block. People standing on door steps and staring out windows. The police canvassed the houses in the neighborhood, hoping someone saw or heard something. Several officers were using police dogs, led by leashes, in hopes of sniffing out something.

Gary laid a sympathetic hand on John's shoulder and squeezed softly. "They'll find her, buddy."

"They have to, Gary" John said, placing a hand on top of his. "I can't lose her."

Chapter Thirty-Eight

I-10, Outside of Casa Grande

5:30 a.m.

As a black and white exited a rest stop and merged onto I-10, the officer spotted a light-colored Escalade heading south. The officer accelerated slowly in an attempt to get a make on the license plate number without being noticed. Once he was sure he had hit pay dirt, he radioed into dispatch to inform them that he had a make on the all-points vehicle. By then, Jessica had passed mile marker fifty-five with no idea the police car was in slow pursuit. The exit off the freeway where she planned to dispose of Alexandra's body was no more than ten miles down the road, five miles west of Casa Grande. The rush of adrenaline she had experienced earlier kicked back in when she reached over and touched the cold steel of the pistol laying on the seat next to her.

"It won't be much longer, sweetie," she said in a condescending tone of voice as she glanced back at Alexandra...who had given up on her attempt to break free of the tape that was binding her. Alexandra prayed that it wouldn't be much longer before help would come. Images of her father, standing strong in his uniform, and the peaceful face of her mother lying in the hospital bed after she'd passed, brought strength to her otherwise-exhausted body. In her mind, she kept picturing John holding her close, keeping her safe.

***

All at once, an officer called Detective Michaels and things started to accelerate at the scene. John thought he heard one of the officers say that the car was spotted. John, Gary and Susan rushed over to the detective to find out what the commotion was. The officer standing with Detective Michaels had his hand up to his shoulder, gripping a wireless receiver.

"Detective," he said anxiously, "dispatch has just informed me that one of our duty officers has positively ID'd the Escalade. The vehicle is now heading south on I-10, a few miles west of Casa Grande. He is currently in pursuit."

"Very good," Michaels replied, lifting the two-way portable radio from his belt clip, sprinting as fast as he was able towards his car. "Dispatch," he barked, "this is Detective Michaels. I want a 10-20 to the officer pursuing the Escalade to stay back until more units can respond... and then effect normal pursuit procedures involving a hostage. I want squad cars near and in Casa Grande to stop all traffic heading southeast on I-10 near the vicinity of the pursuit. 10-2 Southwest Ambulance and have them prepared to respond on command. I'm on my way to the pursuit team."

John, Susan and Gary, were ecstatic at what they heard. They managed to stay calm...even though they had no idea what might happen next. They watched the detective back his vehicle down the street through the maze of squad cars before speeding off, lights flashing.

***

John was lost in thought, standing there in shock. Gary and Susan stared, waiting for John to respond to what was happening.

Gary wasn't as emotional connected as John was, and rightfully so. He could think more clearly in the moment. "John...John!" Gary kept repeating, trying to snap him out of his trance, grabbing his arm to get his attention.

John looked at him and then at Susan. All he could think of was 'do...*something*', but at that point, he felt helpless to do anything. Gary chimed in,

"I knew that police scanner of mine would come in handy. See..." he went on anxiously, "and you said it was just another toy that I didn't need."

"What are you saying, Gary?" John said as he glanced at Susan.

"I'm saying we climb in my car and head towards Casa Grande. We should be able to listen to the whole thing as it goes down. We can't do any good standing around here."

"Are you sure we should get involved?" Susan said, turning to John. "We can't just interfere with the police operation."

"NO, " Gary said, grinning. "No interfering. All we do is keep tabs."

"Like Gary said, we are not doing any good standing around here doing nothing," John said, looking at Susan. "Hurry, let's move our cars down the street and then we'll head out in Gary's Cherokee."

"Good plan," Gary said. "But just so we know, we could get stopped in a police road block on the I-10 the closer we get."

"I don't care," John said, in a serious tone. "I need to be as close to Alexandra as possible. Who knows?" he continued, Jessica, might turn onto a desert road and your four-wheel drive can take us almost anywhere the pursuit leads us."

***

Jessica glanced in the rearview mirror and noticed flashing lights way off in the distance behind her. The lights were veering from lane to lane and there were headlights from another car not far behind. *This is strange*, she thought. *All of a sudden, there's only one car heading southeast with me...this is a freeway.* "Oh...I see now," she said callously. "I'd say we're being followed."

She glanced at Alexandra once more. "Do they think I'm stupid or what...? Oh...that's right," she went on, smirking, then reached for the gun on the passenger's seat. "You can't answer...can you, bitch?"

Jessica let up on the gas and slowed to fifty miles per hour to test the car behind her. The squad slowed to maintain the same distance. She was now convinced that she was being followed. She pressed down hard on the gas, accelerating to eighty. She watched through the mirror as the car behind her started gaining ground.

The officer that followed reached for the radio transmitter and relayed four words to the cops behind him. "The chase is on."

"You caused all this, you little whore!" Jessica yelled. "Did you actually think that I didn't know you were there when John had his accident? And do you think I didn't know that you brainwashed him when he was in the hospital into believing you were his guardian angel? Well I've got news for you...little angel!" she roared. "If I can't have him...you won't have him either."

She glanced in the mirror again and noticed that the one car behind her had now turned into five...all of them with rotating lights. She pushed harder on the pedal until the speedometer reached ninety-five.

Alexandra was so scared she couldn't think straight. Her body was now completely numb. Her eyes opened wide as the blood rushed through her veins and oozed through the wound caused by the blow to her head.

Finding a way out of this situation, she concluded, was impossible. The fact that she was bound with tape only made things worse. She couldn't even strap herself in the seat in the event Jessica lost control. *This can't be the end,* she thought, *not like this.* She pulled her knees up to her chest, into a fetal position.

***

The exit for Casa Grande was one mile down the road. Jessica spotted red and blue lights in the far left lane moving across to the far right lane up ahead, blocking the exit. Suddenly, the voices in her head told her to go faster…faster. The voices told her to keep going…and everything would turn out as she planned for it to be.

***

The chase was being directed via radio by Detective Michaels, who followed in his car a few miles behind. He ordered the pursuit team to maintain distance, block all exits ahead, and keep the Escalade on the freeway until it ran out of gas. Two police helicopters circled overhead, monitoring the chase activity with their spotlights directed on the Escalade. An air evacuation helicopter was positioned to set down at any moment. All possible precautions were in place.

***

As they suspected, John, Susan and Gary had been diverted off the freeway into a rest stop with several other cars. Helpless, they could only listen in on the events as they were taking place. Susan leaned against the inside of the car door, resting her head on the window and staring out. Silently, John prayed as he thought about Alexandra saving his life that rainy New Year's evening in the intersection, praying that her life would be spared from a tragic ending.

***

Sirens were now getting louder and Alexandra braced herself for what might happen. Jessica had lost complete control of her ability to reason. The evil voices in her mind had taken over. She looked hard at the two police cars positioned on the freeway near the exit about a mile up ahead and turned her nose up at them. She removed one hand from the wheel and reached for the gun again. Alexandra watched as Jessica moved the gun onto her lap this time. At that point, all sorts of dreadful endings to this nightmare flashed through her mind. *What is this demented woman going to do next? Was she going to shoot me now, shoot at the police, or shoot herself?* Alexandra was sure that any one of those situations would end in disaster.

***

Jessica lifted the gun from her lap with her finger on the trigger and pressed the barrel to the side of her face. *Oh, shit,* Alexandra thought, *she's going to kill herself while speeding down the freeway.* Alexandra braced herself for the worst. After a few tense moments, Jessica slowly turned her attention away from watching the road and looked back at Alexandra with a stony expression on her face. It now seemed to Alexandra that everything going on around her was unreal...like a bad dream that keeps repeating itself over and over. Her eyes widened and the compulsion to scream took over...but it was all she could do to make meaningless, muffled sounds.

***

The voices in Jessica's head had no physical source but she was hearing them all the same, experiencing schizophrenic intervention. Her father was yelling at her, screaming at her for losing track of her brother. *'It's all your fault, Jessica. My son would be alive today if it weren't for your greedy desire to dress up in that stupid Halloween costume. You killed your mother and you made me miserable. Your entire life has been a disaster from the minute you were born and you need to end it now'.*

Jessica's head felt like it was going to explode. The pressure between her ears was unbearable. She kept hitting the side of her head with the gun until blood trickled down her cheek. Suddenly, as if night turned to day, she relaxed her body and a wide grin spread across her face. *I'm alright now. Nothing can hurt me anymore.* Jessica moved the gun from the side of her face. Alexandra could see the blood oozing from the wound.

Sirens were wailing in the background as Jessica pointed the gun at Alexandra's head. In an instant, reacting out of immense fear, Alexandra kicked her legs forward between the two front seats towards the gun, causing Jessica's arm to recoil. The gun went off, but the bullet missed Alexandra and shattered the upper-right corner of the tailgate window. The impact from the kick loosened Jessica's grip on the steering wheel, causing the Escalade to swerve to the left and skid. In a panic, she grabbed the wheel, turned it in the opposite direction of the skid, and they headed straight for the squad car parked in the far left lane. The Escalade clipped the front end of the police car, hurling metal and glass in every direction, and went spinning out of control towards the small embankment on the right side of the freeway...hitting the embankment with such force that the right front wheel collapsed.

At that point, the pursuit team could only watch as the Escalade flipped and rolled four times, landing upside down and skidding down the side of the freeway. The cars converged in a group and were now positioned all around the scene. The fire units, rescue teams, and the police helicopter were called into action. The gas tank on the Escalade had ruptured and was leaking. Smoke was billowing out of the once-fancy grill and hood...now a wrinkled mass of metal. The driver's side door had popped open and was torn off as the car rolled and slammed to the ground. It looked like a huge hunk of bent metal and vinyl tossed in the middle of the freeway. The shattered glass shimmered like glitter sprinkled over the blacktop.

Four officers rushed to the mangled mess to assess the situation. One officer with a flashlight quickly dropped to his knees and elbows. He looked through the space where there once was a window and saw two legs bound together, protruding halfway through from the back compartment. A second officer leaned over, shining his flashlight through a ten-inch gap between the top frame of the car and the driver's door, and winced at what he saw.

Jessica's upper torso was crushed between the top frame of what had been the windshield and the dashboard. Her head extended beyond the opening of the window. The skin was peeled off the side of her face, which was pressed between the hood and the concrete.

For a moment, he moved the beam of light from Jessica's face, composed himself, and then refocused the light. Both of her eyes were open and blood was oozing from the corners of her mouth. Suddenly, her head moved and her eyes blinked once.

"Jesus!" he shouted, popping to his feet. "I've got a live one on this end, but getting her out of there will be a bitch."

"Better do something quick!" another officer standing by yelled, waving at the fire team who were getting their gear together. "This thing could blow any minute."

Down on his knees, one of the officers reached in through the rear window and moved Alexandra's legs, hoping to see her move on her own, but got no response. Meanwhile, two guys from the fire rescue crew grabbed the 'jaws of life' and other extrication tools and rushed over to the mangled Escalade. Both rear doors were jammed shut. The rear windows were shattered and sharp, knife-like shards were protruding from the window frames. They had no chance of pulling Alexandra through the windows in time without slicing up her body.

While the firemen struggled to pry open the door just enough to pull her out, another officer dropped to his knees, shining his light through the shattered hatch window. He focused the beam directly on Alexandra, who was lying on her back, motionless. The situation looked hopeless. She had been wildly thrown about as the Escalade rolled. There were multiple lacerations covering her face, and there was blood everywhere. Her arms were bound together and appeared severely disjointed. Meanwhile, the crew working the front of the vehicle needed a lift to hoist up the front end in order to have any chance of getting Jessica free.

Suddenly, flames shot up from the underbelly of the vehicle…which was facing skyward. The crew grabbed extinguishers and started smothering the fire with chemicals from several feet away. Just as they thought they had the flames under control, one member of the crew working the front of the vehicle noticed a smoldering wire drop into a small pool of gasoline that had run along the blacktop and settled to the front of the vehicle.

"Get her out of the car NOW!" he yelled to the workers tending to Alexandra, just as they pried the door open enough to get her out. "She's going to blow!"

There was no time for techniques normally used for moving injured victims. There was no time to strap

Alexandra onto a spine board to insure immobility. At this point, they couldn't even tell if she was dead or alive. They grabbed her by the legs, maneuvered her into position, and quickly dragged her through the opening. They hurried her to a safe distance just as flames ran up the side to the gas tank. The resulting explosion blew the vehicle three feet off the ground as it burst into a giant ball of fire.

***

John, Gary and Susan heard the blast and saw the flash ball of fire from the rest stop. They didn't know exactly what it meant, but they knew it had to have something to do with the chase. Suddenly, as if on cue, Gary's scanner began popping on and off every other second. The myriad voices of police, fire and rescue personnel were communicating in sequence to each other and to dispatch. John looked at Gary and Susan, then jumped out of the car. He slammed the door shut, put his hands on top of the hood of the Cherokee and buried his head. After a few seconds, he straightened, turned and walked away.

Susan began sobbing uncontrollably. Tears gushed from her eyes as Gary turned and reached into the back seat to console her. Suddenly, a voice over the scanner reported to dispatch that one of the victims had been removed before the vehicle exploded. The victim was being airlifted to Scottsdale Memorial Hospital.

"John!" Gary yelled, sticking his head out the window. "Did you hear that? They got one of them out. It could be Alexandra."

John rushed back to the car and jumped in. Gary threw it in gear and sped out of the rest stop...only to realize the freeway up ahead was still shut down.

As soon as he was able to merge onto the freeway, he noticed the cars lined up for miles back towards Phoenix.

"We can't go east and we surely can't go west on this side of the freeway," he said. "So I guess we'll have to shoot across the center."

"Do what you gotta do," John replied, looking each way. "There are cops behind us and in front of us; but they're so busy with all the traffic, they may not even see us go across the dirt median to the other side."

"And if they do and don't like it," Gary responded, squeezing his way through cars, edging onto the dirt, "...they may be in for another chase...cause I'm not stopping until we reach the hospital."

"What if it's not her?" Susan said somberly. "What if it's not Alexandra that they got out of the exploding car, John?"

"It has to be," he replied. "It has to be."

Chapter Thirty-Nine

It was six-forty-five, thirty minutes later, when Gary pulled into the emergency parking lot. The helicopter was now on the helipad, shut down and unoccupied. They jumped from the Cherokee and rushed through the lot, making their way through the sliding double doors, and headed straight to Admitting.

"John...John Henning!" echoed a voice from across the waiting area off a hallway.

John turned at the sound of his name and spotted Detective Michaels making his way through a group of people that were milling around waiting...or simply wondering where to go for assistance.

"Detective," John responded, moving over to meet him. "Alexandra...is she..??"

"She's here, John," he said, interrupting, "but she's not in good shape."

"How serious is it?" Susan broke in, stepping up beside them.

"Don't know yet. They just took her into the triage unit."

"And Jessica...what about her?" John asked, his voice dropping low.

"Gone," Michaels replied, with a strained look. "Died in the explosion, I'm afraid. They just couldn't get her out in time."

"Good!" Susan uttered without hesitation as she turned and plopped herself down in the nearest chair.

"The head of triage will be here in a moment to give a preliminary finding," Michaels said, eyeing his watch. "At least, that's what they told me when I got here ten minutes ago."

Moments later, Tucker Potts, holding a clipboard under his arm, stepped outside the double doors into the hallway and made his way over to them. He looked as though he had lost his best friend.

"We have Alexandra sedated," he said, trying to maintain a professional demeanor, not easy for him given his association with her. She was conscious upon arrival but, if we hadn't administered pain meds, she would be in a lot of pain right now." Tucker looked at John, remembering him when Alexandra brought him in. "I won't sugar coat it," he said. "Alexandra is in pretty bad shape. For now, she's stable. The woman who kidnapped her actually did her a favor. My guess is that, because her arms and legs were bound with tape," he went on, "it prevented them from flailing in every direction during the thrashing as the car flipped and rolled. She could have broken every bone in her body. According to pre-scan X-rays, the only thing broken was her left shoulder and one ankle."

John pitched his head back and took in a deep breath. Susan grabbed Gary by the arm and buried her head in his shoulder. Michaels glanced at his watch again and waited.

"The nurses are prepping Alexandra for a full body scan," Tucker said, glancing at notes on a clipboard, then turned his head and looked directly at John again. "There will be no seeing her until much, much later, you understand…maybe not even until tomorrow."

"Please, Doctor," John managed, "with all due respect, I need to be with her. You have to understand," he went on. "Alexandra…"

"I know, John," he replied, interrupting him, resting his hand on John's shoulder, compassionately. "For some inexplicable reason, it seems I recall Alexandra saying the same thing after she wheeled *you* in here on New Year's...'I need to be with him.' That is what she said. I didn't understand it then, but I think I understand it now."

"You were here when they brought me in?"

"I was," he said evenly, "...and believe me... Alexandra was just as concerned about you, and *she* didn't even know who you were before that night."

"Well, if you know how I feel, Doctor, then you know I have to be with her."

There was a pause in the conversation, they stood there locking eyes. Meanwhile, after listening to the whole confusing conversation between the two of them, the detective, Gary and Susan stared at Tucker, waiting for his response.

"I'll tell you what, John," he said flatly, "when we are through with all of the tests, I'll see if I can get authority from the attending physician to let *you* quietly...and I mean quietly...sit in the ICU with her," he went on, looking at the others, "...but only you."

By the look on Susan's face, John could tell she wanted to wage a protest. John moved between Gary and Michaels and took Susan in his arms "Go and explain to the other girls on the team what has happened," he whispered into her ear. "That's enough for you to have to deal with right now...then get some rest. Alexandra will be just fine. I'll call you if there is a change in her condition," he continued, then kissed her cheek.

"Uh...*excuse* me," interjected Michaels, who had been waiting patiently on the sidelines to get a word in. "Before anyone goes anywhere, you all need to wait right here while I take your statements. If we don't do it here and now...we'll all just mosey on down to headquarters and do it there. After all," he went on, somewhat frustrated as he jerked his pad out of his back pocket, "two people ended up dead in all this, and *I* need to try to figure out why."

It didn't take long for the detective to deduce why Alexandra was kidnapped. However, figuring out why Jessica murdered Millie was going to be another story. As close as John had been to Jessica, he couldn't provide answers about that motive to satisfy Michaels. The more Michaels pondered the tie between Millie and Jessica, the more confusing it became. *I've got to look elsewhere for the answers...and it isn't with these three,* he thought. He sat quietly, stroking his beard. *Lawrence...Lawrence is the missing piece to this puzzle,* he concluded.

***

Gary and Susan left, and John waited for the chance to see Alexandra. He thought about how ironic it was that he would soon be walking into a room in the same hospital, and more or less under the same circumstances, that sent her to him.

One of the assistants walked up holding a cup of coffee that had been freshly brewed in the staff members' break room.

"This is for you, Mr. Henning," she said, interrupting his thoughts. "Tucker asked me to bring it to you."

"Oh," said John, looking up at her with a weak smile. "...thank you."

"I took a chance and left it black."

"It's perfect," he replied, taking a sip.

"Tucker is just sick about what happened to Alexandra. You know," she said softly, nodding her head, "he really loves her."

"He loves her?" John replied, a little taken aback by the comment.

"Oh...no," she responded, somewhat embarrassed at the inference, "I didn't mean it like that. I just meant that he loves her like a sister. All of us in emergency who know her feel the same way."

"I see," John said, smiling. "I could easily understand how that would be," he went on. "Alexandra's a
wonderful girl."

The assistant went off and left him to his thoughts.
He was so exhausted, he nodded off several times in the
chair until Tucker startled him awake with a tap to his
shoulder. "OK, John," he said softly. "You can see Alexandra now. I can take you."

Chapter Forty

They made their way to the elevator and up to the third floor. The duty nurses were busy scurrying from room to room, checking patient status and administering medications. John followed a few paces behind as Tucker's long legs moved him quickly down the hall towards room three-thirteen. When he reached the room, the door was closed. He pushed it open just enough to look inside, then turned and put his hand up. "We can't go in quite yet, John," he warned. "The nurse is in there doing her work...shouldn't be but a few minutes," he went on, reaching deep into his coat pocket for his humming pager.

"Damn," Tucker said under his breath, glancing down...quite obviously irritated. "Why now?"

Responding to a page that would pull him away was not what he wanted at this moment. *Thirteen hours is enough,* he thought. Instead of running back to Emergency, he wanted to march right into that room with John and reassure himself that Alexandra was alright.

"She's a great gal, John," Tucker said, crossing his arms over the stethoscope hanging around his neck. Leaning back against the frame of the door, he glanced up at the ceiling. "But I'm sure you already know that."

"From the moment I laid eyes on her," John replied. "I have no one to blame but myself for what happened to her, you know."

"I'll tell you what, pal," Tucker said, pushing away from the wall. "Don't ever let her know you said that, or that you even thought about saying it. She's tough and has always taken responsibility for her own actions. That's why she's in there and still breathing."

"You're right," John replied, nodding. "You know her pretty well, don't you?"

"That I do."

Suddenly the door swung open and the nurse scurried out with an armful of things and hurried across the hall into another room.

"Okay, then...get on in there, John. I'll have to catch up with Alexandra a little later," he said as he smiled and turned towards the elevator.

He really does love her, John thought, as he pushed the door open. When he stepped into the room, an eerie feeling of déjà vu took hold. His mind went back to the moment he woke up from the coma without any recollection of what had happened or why he was there... having no one with him except a busy nurse he didn't know from Adam...with no one to reassure him as he lay there in the midst of strange sounds and equipment. He didn't know whether he was waking up in hell or some other unfathomable place. He walked over to Alexandra's bed and stood gazing at her as she lay motionless, surrounded by mechanical ventilators, dialysis equipment, heart monitors and thin, aluminum poles holding bags of clear fluids connected to tubes leading down to her arms.

For the moment, it was quiet and peaceful. The top of her head down to her forehead was swathed in white bandages. Her face was swollen around her eyes and another bandage covered the bridge of her nose. Her left shoulder was wrapped with some sort of padding underneath, and translucent tubes fed medication into her veins. It was painful and shocking for John to see her in this condition. In his mind's eye, he traded places with her... remembering how beautifully angelic-like she had looked when he opened his eyes and saw her standing over him. Standing there looking at her battered and bruised body, he needed to keep that image in the fore-front of his mind.

He grabbed the chair in the corner, quietly slid it over next to the bed, and sat down. He thought about how strong and sure of herself she was when she climbed out of the racing scull that Saturday morning when he took a chance and drove to the lake to find her. He remembered how their eyes met and how, even though everything around them was ordinary and mundane, they had soared off to some other world together. He leaned in and whis-pered into her ear "I love you, Alexandra," then touched his lips to hers. He felt her warm breath dust his cheek as he softly kissed her lips a second time.

***

It was five hours later, after several visits from the duty nurse who had walked in and out, taking readings from equipment and making notes on the chart that she took from the wall next to the door, that a doctor walked in. John stood up from the chair and slid it back. The doc-tor grabbed the chart that was hanging on the wall-hook and quickly introduced himself as Doctor Wallace…then went about the business of evaluating what the nurse had documented and checking for any signs of variation in Alexandra's vitals. John introduced himself as "Alexan-dra's friend" and waited for the doctor to finish his evalu-ation.

"Do you know her?" John asked, finally tired of waiting and taking it upon himself to break the silence in the room.

"No, John, I haven't had the pleasure" he replied, as he replaced the chart back on the wall-hook. "But, al-most everyone else on this side of the hospital does," he went on. "Tucker Potts tell me that she's quite the gal."

"Tucker is right, Doctor" he replied. "She's the best."

"Well, don't you worry," he said. "She is strong and will recover just fine. She was heavily medicated earlier but should wake soon. She will experience some pain for a few weeks; but the broken shoulder will heal, the ankle will mend and the contusions will disappear in no time. She is a lucky girl," he went on. "It was good to meet you, John," he said, as he swung the door open and hurried out of the room.

After listening to what the doctor had just said, John felt like celebrating. His anxiety tempered, his heart rate quickly slowed, and he felt like his life had new meaning. He slid the chair back to the bedside, sat back down, and reached over and took Alexandra's hand in his...it felt smooth and soft and warm. It was the miracle he'd hoped for...the reassurance he needed to free his mind of all the unpleasant things that had happened over the last several hours. He was able to dismiss any thought of Jessica and what she had done. She was gone and would never make a difference in his life again. His only thoughts were now focused on the woman he loved and desired infinitely. Suddenly, he felt her fingers move slightly. He moved closer, never taking his eyes off hers, and whispered her name.

"Alexandra...it's me, my darling. It's John," he said whispering close to her ear, shifting in the chair to get even closer. "I'm with you...right here, next to you. Feel my hand touching yours. Open your eyes and you'll see me."

A moment passed before her eyelids began to flutter open. She stared at the ceiling in silence. *She's awake but will she know me?* He wanted her to hear his voice, to turn her head and recognize him, and remember him and the way things were when she last saw him. He wanted her to say his name without hesitation, without any doubt that he was there for her and that he loved her.

She slowly turned her head and gazed into his eyes. Tears began to well up at the corners of her eyes and then trickled down the sides of her face. John reached for a tissue and wiped them gently away.

"I could hear you talking to me," she said, in a strained voice. "I remember things...bad things that were happening that I had no control over and..."

"Shhh, don't think about that now, my love," John said, placing his fingers gently against her lips. "Everything is fine now, and I'm right here with you."

"How bad am I hurt?" she asked, as she moved her arm, felt pain in her shoulder and winced.

"Just a few scrapes and bruises," he replied. "Oh...and I forgot," he continued with a slight grin on his face, "a broken shoulder and ankle...not bad, under the circumstances."

"Wow," she said, blinking fast, "they must have me on morphine or something. I can hardly keep my eyes open."

"Right now, I would guess that it's a good thing," he replied. "You're going to need lots of rest."

"What about Jessica? How bad was Jessica hurt?"

"Real bad...I'm afraid," he managed, swallowing hard. "She didn't make it."

"I'm sorry, John," Alexandra said, fighting to keep her eyes open. "It must be hard for you."

"You have nothing to be sorry about, Alexandra" he responded quickly. "Jessica brought all this on herself with, I believe, a lot of help from her father. The police say that she murdered her father's secretary before she came after you. Whatever sickness she had took over her mind to the extent that she was emotionally out of control. I do, however, think her father is the one to blame for the unstable behavior that drove her to do such terrible things. It started long ago when he committed her mother to a mental institution."

"I know, John," she said, garbling her words, still fighting to stay awake. "I've seen people like that and..."

"Don't think about it anymore," he said, politely interrupting and placing his fingers to her lips again. "This is not the time for you to be thinking about this. Go to sleep and I'll be here right here with you when you wake up."

Chapter Forty-One

Alexandra's Condo

Three weeks later

With the exception of a couple of days in Seattle working a land deal for Carriage Brokers, John headed straight to Alexandra's house every day after work. Ofelia was assigned to be Alexandra's caretaker until he arrived. Usually, he would bring dinner in or, on rare occasions, he would attempt to cook...which almost always ended up being a culinary disaster. Ofelia cooked Mexican food a few times...which was more than either of them needed, in John's opinion. Although John discouraged it, Alexandra loved the enchiladas and encouraged Ofelia not to listen to him.

Alexandra's shoulder and ankle were healing just as Doctor Wallace had predicted. His orders confined her to the house with the exception of follow-up visits to her primary physician. Whenever she could, between training sessions, Susan would drop by to check on Alexandra with Starbucks in hand for the both of them. They would sit around and talk about John and Gary and rowing. Even though Alexandra had promised John she wouldn't dwell on the whole ordeal with Jessica, at times, they couldn't help but bring up that subject.

There was a time after Alexandra was released from the hospital when her house seemed like Grand Central Station. Friends showed up at all hours with flowers and candy and an occasional dog biscuit for Chester. Tucker called at least once a day to 'check in,' as he described it. Ofelia had her hands full just trying to keep the house orderly and quiet. Detective Michaels also made a visit early one evening to see how Alexandra was doing, while at the same time informing both John and Alexandra that they had found out that Millie Jones was Successor Trustee to Lawrence's Trust. Although there was no real proof, it was believed that Jessica had somehow discovered that information and decided to kill Millie to assure that she inherited the bulk of her father's estate.

***

Two weeks later

The Old Caledonia struck nine. Chester barked as John got up from the divan and made his way into the kitchen to pour them a second glass of wine. They had been talking about every subject imaginable…something they did often. They talked about Gary and Susan and laughed about the relationship between the two of them…how Susan would tell Alexandra she had Gary wrapped around her little finger but Gary was telling John it was only his way of playing to her ego. They discussed lessons of life and their careers and how, in the big picture, mere human existence was full of surprises that not only couldn't be explained but could change the course of the future at any time. They played with Chester and laughed at the way he scampered around the room chasing his ball. They kissed and touched each other affectionately and shared their feelings about the kind of relationship they had always yearned for. They talked about family and their sadness of having only John's mother left alive to share in their happiness.

John came out of the kitchen carrying two glasses of Chardonnay. He placed them on the hearth next to the fireplace, kneeled down on one knee and cranked up the flame. Chester jumped onto John's spot, but was quickly scolded so he jumped back down to the floor and laid next to Alexandra's cast-encased foot.

"Would you mind doing something for me?" Alexandra said, as John grabbed the glasses of wine, walked over and sat next to her.

"Anything, my love," he replied. "But first, I have one thing to do, if you don't mind," he went on, as he handed her a glass and raised his. "I want to make a toast... a toast to our friends who have been so helpful and concerned about you over the past few weeks...and more importantly...to us and our future together."

"I'd like to second that," she said proudly. "Mostly to the more important part," she continued, smiling as she touched the tip of her glass to his, then lifted it to her lips.

"Wait," he said, reaching for her glass. "You've got the wrong one." He quickly took hers and handed her the one he had.

Alexandra was caught off-guard at John's antics, but she just smiled and took the glass with no questions asked. As she went to take a sip from the glass, she spotted it. The ring was resting in the bottom of the glass, shimmering and sparkling in the backdrop of flames from the fireplace. Her eyes widened and she stared, opened-mouthed, as John reached over, covered the hand holding the glass and, with the index finger of his other hand, reached into the glass and fished the ring out.

"Alexandra," he said, with his eyes on hers, "even though we've only known each other for a short time, in my heart, it feels like I've been in love with you forever. Will you be my wife?"

Alexandra's heart exploded with joy. Just the look on her face promised him a 'yes' answer. She had seen this happen before in movies but was totally overwhelmed that it was happening to her. He waited patiently for her response.

"In my heart, John," she replied, with her eyes on his, "I've loved you forever. If this is a dream, please don't wake me. Yes, John...I would be honored to become Mrs. John Henning," she went on, as tears trickled down her face.

They gazed into each other's eyes for what seemed an eternity. John took her glass of wine and set them both on the table in front of them. He leaned in and pressed his lips gently against hers, as he carefully took her into his arms.

Chester sat up on his hind legs with his ears perked up as if he knew exactly what was going on.

***

Over the next two hours, they talked and sipped wine and laughed together about silly things and how they couldn't wait to tell friends and make wedding plans. She wanted Hawaii. He wanted Bermuda. He said, "Let's do both," and they laughed some more. They joked about having lots of kids and tossed around different names for girls and boys and how many they would have...and giggled like children. She lay in his arms and fantasized about permanently living together. She couldn't wait to tell Susan that she would soon be a maid of honor. He watched as she lifted her hand several times to admire the ring that fit perfectly on her slim finger.

Then, suddenly, John remembered that Alexandra had wanted him to do something for her.

"What was that thing you wanted me to do?" he said.

She paused a moment, thinking hard. "I can't remember. Whatever it was, it was certainly trumped by your wonderful proposal of marriage."

"Well...I'll tell you what," he said grabbing the two empty glasses and standing, "you try to remember while I pour us more wine to celebrate."

"Wait...*I* know," she said quickly. "I was going to ask you to go into my bedroom closet and, on the top shelf, there is a small metal box with personal and private written in marker on the side of it...could you get it down for me?"

"Wine first or metal box?" John asked, twirling the glasses by the stem, glancing back over at her.

"By all means..." she grinned..."the wine."

Chester curiously followed John into the closet and, without John realizing it, got shut in. As John made his way out of the bedroom with the box, he stepped into the hallway and heard Chester yipping loudly and scratching on the inside of the closet door.

"Sorry, little fella," he said, opening the door. Chester darted out of the room with his tail wagging.

"OK," John said, making his way over to Alexandra. "Mission accomplished."

Shortly after her mother died, all of her assets, clothes, personal things and the like were either sold or disposed of...with the exception of a few Precious Moments figurines, the Old Caledonia and the metal box which Alexandra had found stashed underneath her mother's bed. The box was the one thing left from her mother that Alexandra had not been able to deal with. It was like whatever was in there would recreate the sadness and grief of losing her. The box was locked and Alexandra had never found the key.

For some strange reason, she had been reluctant to pry it open. In her mind, she felt that the recurring dreams she had about her father were in some way tied to the box. She took the box, set it on her lap, placed the palms of her hands on top of it and lowered her head.

"Well," John said, as he sat down next to her, "aren't you going to open it?"

"I can't," she replied. "No key."

"Where is it? I'll get it."

"Don't know," she replied, still gazing down at the box. "I never did find it."

"Am I imagining things or is it that you really don't want to open it?" John said curiously, taking a sip from his glass.

"No, John," she replied, looking at him, "you're not imagining things. The box was my mother's, and I know this might sound silly," she went on, reaching for her glass of wine, "but ever since she died, I have not been able to bring myself to open it."

John brushed his hand against her cheek, leaned in and kissed her. "Sounds perfectly normal to me...and as far as I'm concerned, you never have to open it."

"No, John," she replied, handing it over to him. "It's silly for me not to open it."

"OK..." he said grinning, as he took the box and set it on the table. "I'll make like a thief and go find something to pry it open."

It didn't take more than a small screwdriver and a grunt to pry the box open. He watched as Alexandra slowly went through the contents. Pictures of her father and mother on their honeymoon in Hawaii were at the top of the pile. There was a picture of her mother in a yellow prom dress standing next to a boy that Alexandra didn't know.

They laughed at images of Alexandra's baby hands and feet pressed with finger-paints. There was an emotional letter that her mother had written to her father after he died and numerous newspaper articles mentioning her father in various heroic situations.

John picked up one of the newspaper articles, stood up and slowly worked his way towards the fire-place, reading silently.

"Oh...my...God," he said, under his breath...then started pacing. "Listen to this one. This article is about your father saving two people from a burning building in San Diego.

'Frank Morgan fell to his death while saving two vacationers from the flame-engulfed ninth floor of the historic El Cortez Hotel yesterday. Morgan was a decorated and well-respected fifteen-year veteran of San Diego's Fire and Rescue Department's Station Thirty-Three. Karl Henning and his pregnant wife, Laura, stood one hundred and thirty feet up in the bucket of the fire truck ladder and watched in horror as Morgan tragically fell to his death after heroically saving their lives.'"

John sunk down next to Alexandra, not trusting his legs any longer. "Alexandra, look at this," he said, pointing to the article. "This is ironic. There's a photograph of my father and mother up on that rescue ladder here next to the one of your father."

For long moment, you could hear a pin drop. John and Alexandra just sat quietly, speechless, looking at each other in disbelief, clutching each other's hands.

"I had no idea, John," she said as a lonely tear trickled from the corner of her eye. "My mother never told me the names of the couple my father rescued that day..."

"Look, my love," John interrupted, pressing a finger to her lips, "deep inside, both of us have known all along that being together like this wasn't just by chance. I believe it was always meant to be this way," he went on, smiling. "That night in the intersection, you desperately needed me to survive that accident. *You* saved me that night. It was fate that brought us together...do you believe that?"

Alexandra looked deep into his eyes and clutched his hand. "I do."

"And...ironically," he said..."it all started with your father. He saved me first...for you."

The End

MEET OUR AUTHOR

MICHAEL LIVOLSI

MICHAEL J. LIVOLSI, A FORMER SINGER/SONGWRITER, WAS BORN IN BROOKLYN, NEW YORK, IN 1945. HE SPENT HIS EARLY YEARS IN SAN DIEGO, CALIFORNIA, AND MOONLIGHTED FOR SEVERAL YEARS AS A SINGER IN NIGHTCLUBS. FOR THE LAST THIRTY-SEVEN YEARS, HE HAS LIVED IN ARIZONA. MICHAEL EARNED CERTIFICATIONS IN HUMAN RESOURCE MANAGEMENT AND BUSINESS MANAGEMENT AT ARIZONA STATE COLLEGE OF BUSINESS WHILE WORKING FOR A MAJOR AEROSPACE CORPORATION. DURING HIS TENURE IN AEROSPACE, HE HELD VARIOUS POSITIONS INCLUDING AN EIGHTEEN YEAR STINT IN HUMAN RESOURCE MANAGEMENT AND TEN YEARS IN SALES WHICH PROVIDED HIM THE OPPORTUNITY TO TRAVEL TO SEVERAL COUNTRIES AROUND THE GLOBE. MARRIED FOR FORTY-SEVEN YEARS AND A PROUD GRANDFATHER, MICHAEL IS NOW RETIRED. HIS INTERESTS INCLUDE MUSIC, EXERCISE AND ENJOYING QUALITY TIME WITH HIS FOUR CHILDREN AND EIGHT GRANDCHILDREN. MICHAEL HAS ALWAYS LOVED TO TELL STORIES AND OTHERS HAVE LOVED TO LISTEN. BEING A WRITER OF FICTION SINCE HIS RETIREMENT HAS BROUGHT HIM GREAT JOY AND EXCITEMENT, ESPECIALLY WHEN THE LATE HOURS OF WORK WRITING ARE REWARDED WITH THE MEMORABLE ENDINGS TO HIS NOVELS. MICHAEL HAS WRITTEN THREE NOVELS. HIS FIRST NOVEL *"HIDDEN PURPOSE"* IS A CAPTIVATING THRILLER-LOVE STORY. HIS SE-

COND NOVEL A WONDERFUL ROMANTIC FANTASY OF ADVENTURE AND THE THIRD NOVEL "*THE BRAIDED LOCKET*" A ROMANTIC MYSTERY THAT SHARES SOME OF THE AUTHOR'S REAL LIFE PERSONAL EXPERIENCES HAS MOTIVATED HIM TO PRESS ON AND CONTINUE WRITING THE MANY STORIES THAT ARE STILL EVOLVING IN HIS MIND.